BOOK THREE OF THE ILLUMINATOR SAGA

By

Heather Wohl

Praise for The Illuminator Saga Series

"Wohl is a force, taking the torch from legends like Tolkien and running with it full steam ahead." - Erica Summers, author of *Vanity Kills & Writhe*

"From the very first page, this book sweeps you into another world and doesn't let you leave." - Amazon reviewer

"Fast-paced with action and mystery. You will be gripping the pages to find out what happens next." - Alexandria Williams, book reviewer

"I was captivated by this series from the start!" - Amazon reviewer

"I was waiting for it to let up and slow down but shockingly it didn't. I recommend this book over and over." - Amazon reviewer

"The world is wonderfully crafted... from the whiskey to the characters."- Amazon reviewer

The Undead Queen:
Book Three of the Illuminator Saga

By Heather Wohl

The Undead Queen: *Book Three of the Illuminator Saga*

Second edition paperback

Casper, Wyoming, United States

www.heatherwohl.com
www.rustyogrepublishing.com

Cover by Erica Summers

More by Heather Wohl

From Ashes

Desdemona in Embers

The Undead Queen

The Harbingers of Hope

Call of the Wyl

The Choice is Yours: Escape From Sugarland

The Choice is Yours: The Branson Ranch

The Choice is Yours: The Australian Outback

The Choice is Yours: An Earth Day Adventure

Writhe (As H.M. Wohl)

Maid in Heaven (As Aurora Alba)

Maid in America (As Aurora Alba)

The Ugly Sweater Party (As Aurora Alba)

Scan here for an expanded full-color map of the Isle of Destoria

NOTE: A complete creature glossary of all of the Isle of Destoria's beings is available in the back of this book.

ILLUMINATOR SAGA RECAP

Quistix Daedumal, a half-elf blacksmith in Bellaneau, lost everything the night Soren Everbleed, an Emerald Bandit sent by the new queen murdered her son, Danson, and set fire to her home looking for something mysterious called *The Illuminator*.

After living in the woods for months, the feral woman robbed an ewanian named Gregor and discovered a wounded wyl in one of the crates in the back of his wagon. She aided in Twitch's recovery and he, in return, offered to help her find the Emerald Bandit for revenge. They traveled north to Silvercrest and soon encountered a pleom named Frok and her well-read esteg caretaker, Aurora. After a battle with sentient inelm trees, they banded together as a group.

Destoria's queen, Exos Tempest, worked to legalize a potent, addictive drug called dikeeka while Vervaine (the queen's sister) and Arias (the head of the Obsidian guard) stoked the flames of a forbidden romance. Battling a mysterious illness, Exos struggled to maintain control of Destoria. In an act of desperation, Exos employed the help of a magic-wielding quichyrd named Ceosteol. Ceosteol assisted Exos, but didn't receive the pardon she was promised.

During a showdown in the Emerald Bandit's den, Quistix discovered that she had powerful magical abilities. Seeking answers, the group then headed to Apex, the floating city containing the Institute of Magic seeking answers about the elusive Illuminator.

Exos sent Omen, a cursed human banished to a life of pain in eternal flame, to find *the Illuminator.* Exos spread word through the isle that Quistix was a wanted woman.

Omen attacked Quistix, Twitch and Aurora but Quistix won.

Later, on a long journey through the frozen tundra of Evolt, the gang met Samael, a kind barbarian who offered them asylum.

As they were leaving, Twitch stole from Samael.

Exos decided to double-down with her erratic behavior, imprisoning Vervaine in the infernal caverns to be tortured by crimson soul reapers until she complied with Exos's demands. By mistake, overeager reapers took Vervaine's punishment too far, killing her in captivity. Exos demanded that Ceosteol bring her back as one of her soul-bonded undead. With a notorious past for similar experiments, Ceosteol agrees. As a result, Ceosteol now had total control of Vervaine's body and mind any time she wished to inhabit.

After hearing murmurs of a revolt, Ceosteol came up with a clever plan to force the remaining council holdouts to kill each other after ingesting a toxin in the wine. With them out of the way, she filled the council seats with new provincial leaders of her choosing.

A vote was taken and the council legalized dikeeka. Exos quickly distributed it throughout the land, taxing it to restock her dwindling treasury. Arias accepted a new position as the head of the Royal Guard. Soon after, the dikeeka supply chain was interrupted and the absence of the cure-all drug left provinces full of addicts in withdrawal.

After a ride on a sapphire-colored dragon named Veynan, Quistix and her friends finally arrived in Apex where she soon learned that her estranged father had recently passed, a professor at the Apex Institute of Magic. Due to her family connections, and finding out that the institute's headmaster, Madam Aerendyl, was her step-mother, she was granted access to the school and its courses. She learned to somewhat control and hone her abilities. Meanwhile, Aurora studied at the school's famous library. Quistix learns of a legendary set of armor that could withstand the damage of her magic.

Heading away from Apex, Quistix returns Samael's stolen goods. In return, he gives them a note he'd withheld in anger. It was her old friend Kaem's call to arms, requesting they come fight Exos alongside her.

Quistix and the gang made their way to Kaem only to find out that Omen had joined their side and had become an informant in aid of their rebellion. Arias, informed of their uprising, secretly orders the Royal Guard not to intervene, allowing them to go into battle without resistance.

During the battle at the Ruby Palace, Arias was killed. Quistix and Twitch ventured through the Crypt of Hadina to find the magical armor. After defeating a throng of undead beings, they made their way back to Frok, Aurora, and their newest pleom recruit, Dally.

During the battle, Exos, Frok, and Dally were slain and Ceosteol disappeared. The Ruby Palace went up in flames.

The crew mourned the loss of the pleoms and they disappeared in the wilderness to regroup.

Ceosteol returned, resurrecting Arias and forcing him to wed the new undead queen, Vervaine. With Exos out of the way and the king and queen soul-bonded and under her full control, the mad quichyrd, Ceosteol, had become more powerful than ever...

1

Knight Harbor Pier
Desdemona, Willowdale

Storm clouds threatened to douse the city with a frigid fall rain. Despite the impending storm and ominous, overcast sky, the sea was eerily calm. Quistix's metal boots thudded hard against the salt-worn boards. Twitch suspiciously eyed the gaggle of filthy sailors and rugged pirates from the rear of their single-file line. The noise of his stealthy wyl feet was drowned out completely by the clatter of Aurora's hooves. Careful not to attract any attention, the trio made their way to the furthest vessel, a massive ferry endowed with a bustling crew bobbing at the end of the Radiant Pier.

Squat merchant stalls lined the edges of Knight Harbor in neat rows, each housing shouting peddlers. Soot-streaked shoppers cinched their cloaks tighter, warding off the chilly autumn breeze.

Quistix pulled the hood of her black cloak tight around her face, grateful that Twitch had stolen from the back of someone's cart on the way to the pier. It was infused with the stench of body odor and wet fur, but it disguised her bright red hair and uniquely citrine eyes just enough.

After their treasonous takedown of the tyrannical Queen Exos, the three had managed to stay hidden. They'd made a temporary home in the bowels of the forest surrounding Oakenmeadow, bathing occasionally in the frigid Promise River. They'd scrounged for food and sheltered in a lean-to made of chopped donik wood and debris, both of which were in short supply after the Willowdale fires displaced the area's wildlife into smaller patches of forested land. Tired and malnourished, the three had lain low for months, hoping the isle's hunt for them might die down enough that they could slip onto a boat and trek to Asera, where they'd be safe from punishment for the murder of the psychotic queen and the devastation they'd caused to the capital city of Desdemona.

The newest and most threatening storm, the one looming over Willowdale, was what finally forced them out into the public. The last autumnal storm had flooded their campsite, demolishing their shelter in seconds. Aurora was nearly lost in the raging waters of it, swept beneath the swift-rising, murky tide for several minutes. Just in the nick of time, Quistix and Twitch were able to pull her by the horns onto a high-enough bough with the help of a sympathetic inelm. Aurora had nearly died that day.

This new storm, however, felt even bigger, far more dangerous in scope, size, and pressure. Quistix could sense it in her bones. They couldn't chance trying to survive something like that in the wilds again.

The sight of the Aseran ferry was a relief to them all. Twitch nervously fondled the sparse circles of metal in his coin purse, hoping they'd have enough currency for the transport of all three. For a moment, he toyed with the idea of lifting coin off a nearby sailor, one of the ones too busy tying their watercraft to the docks with soaked ropes to notice how vulnerable their back pockets were. It would be so easy...

But Twitch knew that in the event of a rare failure, that sort of attention could mean the end for all three of them. He thought it best not to chance it.

Quistix angled her way through the narrow, overcrowded pier with her signature masculine gait until they stood in the back of the long ferry line, avoiding eye contact with those around her as if all of their lives depended on it.

The sugary scent of fresh-baked goods mingled with the pungent stench of all the freshly-caught fish showcased on jute stringers along the cove. Sailors hefted heavy crates of herbs and spices past them, adding to the overwhelming aromatic mixture.

"This place smells like a brothel I went to once," Twitch mumbled just loud enough for the other two to hear.

Quistix glared at him, her lemon-yellow eyes begging him to shut his maw.

"*What?* It was an observation."

"But was it a necessary one to say aloud?" Aurora growled between gritted herbivore molars.

Twitch scoffed and tugged the sides of this hat down. "I miss Dally. *He* would have thought that was hilarious. It was nice to have another man around. Now I'm but a lone male awash in this... *sea* of femininity."

Quistix scoffed. "Hardly."

"Dally was simple. He wouldn't have understood the joke," Aurora said. "Frok wouldn't have *either*."

At the mention of Frok, the group fell silent and soon found themselves peering in the direction of her grave, one that overlooked the Glitter Gulf they were about to sail away on. Their pink pleom companion had been laid to rest, and none of them had ever quite been the same.

Aurora's head hung low. Tears welled in her eyes.

"She's in a better place. I'm sure she's tossing leaves around the Ethereal Sanctum right now." Quistix stroked the fur of Aurora's neck before quickly pulling her hand away. "Sorry. I forgot you don't like touching."

Aurora lifted her head and offered a weak smile. "It's alright. I'm getting used to it. It's almost... nice."

The line started to crawl forward, people boarding the vessel slowly after giving their names to the ewanian captain and his furiously scribbling eaflic first mate. The captain eyed every patron, often glancing back to the weathered announcement board behind him. The notices pinned on it were shriveled, warped, and damaged from the recent, vicious rainstorms.

Quistix froze as she saw her own face on the board. The wanted posters had been redone by someone with skill this time. It seems someone had seen her and described her down to her eye color. She straightened, a bolt of fear pulsing through her as she looked at the hand-drawn faces beside hers, all surprising likenesses of Aurora, Twitch, Kaem, and Ralmeath.

The line continued forward again.

Quistix was visibly rattled. "Guys, we need to leave now."

"What?! No. We're fine." Twitch's eyes darted around, paranoia evident in his fur-covered face.

"*Look at the wanted posters,*" Quistix whispered, gesturing her head toward the images.

"*By the Gods,*" Twitch said quietly.

They were mere *feet* from freedom.

The ewanian glanced their direction and narrowed his eyes.

Aurora stiffened. "I think the captain recognizes us."

Twitch flexed his fist, wishing he could punch something, but knowing to do so would draw a massive amount of unwanted attention.

The captain signaled to one of the barbarian guards on the ferry. The guard approached quickly, the thud of his massive feet echoing over the water. He craned down toward the captain, and the entire ferry bobbled precariously onto its side, nearly capsizing at the sudden shift in weight.

The ewanian whispered something into the guard's huge ear and gestured toward the trio. Then, with a bulbous, green finger, he pointed at the bounty posters on the notice board.

Quistix reached over her shoulder to grab *Swordbreaker*, but then, she thought about Rowland. She remembered how she had wished she could have gutted the bastard who had slain her husband for simply doing his job.

Perhaps these men had families, too. Wives. Children...

Quistix looked down at her hands, feeling the burn of her anger flare through her irises. She pulled back with all of her mental might against the force. The pier was too crowded for destructive magic, too flammable for fire. There were innocent civilians all around. She would end up hurting bystanders if she cast a spell in such a crowded area.

"*Aurora, run,*" Quistix whispered.

"What? Why?" Aurora asked calmly, masking her emotions far better than her comrades.

Quistix shook her head. "They're onto us. The pier is too narrow and the dock is too crowded for us all to evade them at once, but you gallop much faster than either of us can run. *You've* got a shot at rushing past them. Go, now."

"Run *where*? To *what*? Without you both, I'll be butchered and turned into steaks before sundown. No! I'm staying."

Brushing past the people in line, the barbarian guard made his way toward them.

Quistix looked back at the other end of the pier to plot a last-second escape, but a wall of unwashed people now formed a living barrier between the three wanted fugitives and the end of the dock.

Quistix took a step toward them, heavily debating a risky dive into the frigid waters, if needed.

Suddenly, a brawny hand clasped onto her shoulder, with fingers as long as her face. As it clamped down hard, the metal plates of her shoulder pauldrons bent inward from the forceful pressure. He'd crushed the metal with ease. She only imagined what he could do to measly bone...

"Going somewhere?"

The man's other mitt latched roughly onto the meat beneath Aurora's mane. She mewed in distress, her unmistakable esteg bugle ripping through the now-quiet port.

Quistix turned and snarled. "Hands off the esteg!"

The guard barked out a laugh that shook the rotting boards beneath their feet. "You're all wanted. The reward is much higher if you're alive, but make no mistake. If you don't come peacefully, I will *end you* right here and now."

His threat was chilling, his low voice promising violence.

The once-bustling crowd stood frozen in place, riveted by the commotion. The guards placed their hands on the hilts of their swords and waited for her response.

The captain hobbled over toward them all, his slit pupils wide, his expression euphoric as he thought about the bounty he'd soon be the recipient of.

Twitch grasped Quistix's hand and gave it a reassuring squeeze. Then, he addressed the men. "Thank the *Gods* you found us. This *is* the ferry to the prison, is it not? We were on our way to the stockades to turn ourselves over to the authorities. Thank the Ethereal Sanctum we found you! Please, gentlemen, do lead the way."

Quistix flashed Twitch an angry glance, one he'd long grown an immunity to. Aurora swallowed hard, her feet clumsily stumbling as the barbarian yanked her away from the boat.

"Make way!" The captain shouted with the dramatic flourish of his amphibious hand, his kind known across the isle for having a penchant for theatrics. He smiled at the gaping swarm of townspeople, relieved that his fate as a lowly ferry captain had surely just changed forever.

Unwashed people in drab frocks hugged the sides of the narrow pier, staring as the fugitives were shoved back down the dock. The only noise was the sound of boot heels and hooves marching across the damp donik planks. Their vessel to freedom gently faded back into the low fog.

They stepped begrudgingly onto the pebbled beach of Knight Harbor, and the harsh weight of their new reality bore down. The arduous half-mile trudge and three-mile carriage ride to the newly rebuilt dungeon stockade in the bowels of the somewhat restored Ruby Palace allowed plentiful time for their daunting new reality to set in.

As the captain and barbarian marched them to the palace gates, Quistix savored the crunch of gravel beneath her boots and the threatening crack of thunder as it roared overhead in the humid gray sky.

It would likely be the last time she'd ever experience any of it again.

2

Dungeon of the Ruby Palace
Desdemona, Willowdale

"I'm not built for the dungeons!" Twitch shrieked, his furry arms chained up to the cell wall.

"Twitch, breathe," Quistix said, lifting her face until her lemon-yellow eyes appeared through her disheveled tufts of red hair. She'd been shackled to the adjoining wall, directly across from Aurora.

"I'm small and I have a face chiseled by the Gods, Q! It is a face that has made a *lot* of enemies."

"Oh, trust me. I *know*." She scoffed.

"There's no air down here!" The panic in Twitch's voice reverberated off the stone walls. His eyes ricocheted around the room.

"Twitch!" Aurora shouted. It was the first time the esteg had seemingly ever raised her voice at him. The sound of it startled the wyl. "Please, silence yourself. We must think about this logically. Panicking will not help anything right now."

Quistix just flashed Aurora a half-smile that said, *I didn't think you had it in you*.

The dank dungeon cell grew deathly silent save for the wyl's worried panting. The chill from the stone walls seeped into their bones. The stench of bodily waste filled the air. Wet hay littered the floor. Dried blood decorated the walls. Sobs and muffled screams oozed down the windowless hallway and through the bars of their cell.

Aurora clenched her eyes shut. So much pain around her made her feel physically ill from the empathy. "Quistix, I know you have shown much magical restraint up to this point today. I'm not sure why, exactly, but I think that the *old you* needs to make a re-appearance."

Quistix clenched her hands into fists, hoping the movement would ease the numbness. She stared at the floor.

Aurora murmured, "Can you... melt your shackles? Or maybe freeze and break them?"

Quistix shook her head. "No. I've been trying."

"Why didn't you do something with your magic when we were on the *pier*?!" Twitch growled between his sharp, gritted teeth.

Quistix's lips pressed into a line. "I couldn't! There were innocent people all around us. Women and children. What was I supposed to do? Endanger them all?!"

"Yes!" Twitch howled.

"Be serious, you selfish twit! Those guards were just doing their jobs, doing what they swore an oath to do. I slayed the queen who ordered the murder of my son and the festering boil-of-a-man who held the knife. And, in doing so, what have I become?" She kicked a loose rock angrily in Twitch's direction. "I never set out to be some ruthless monster! I have taken too many lives already. By the Gods, even growing up, I was an *assassin*! I deserve to be locked in the dungeons. I've hurt enough people and, frankly, I'm done running."

"So, you're just gonna let us *rot* in here because you've developed a *conscience*?" Twitch asked incredulously. "Exos Tempest, Soren Everbleed, and those Emerald Bandits... those people *deserved* everything they had coming, Q! Your vengeance was just! You did the world a favor. Killing Exos saved more Destorian lives than you could *ever* take. *And lest ye forget, madam*, that you are not *alone* any more! *We* depend on you! If we find a way out of here before they cut off our heads, I *know* you can do even more good in the world to outweigh some of the bad. You will have *time* to right those wrongs. But only if you *live*. Only if you're free."

Quistix stared down at her lap, her pale, malnourished legs covered in a tattered prisoner's uniform. It was a nearly-identical match to the one that Twitch had on, right down to the filth and urine stains.

"Twitch, you have no *idea* how much damage I've truly done."

"Well," he rested the back of his head against the stone wall and sighed dramatically, "I've got nothing but time. *Enlighten me.*"

After an uncomfortably long pause, Quistix finally spoke. "I was a member of the Assassin's Guild when I was young. I'm ashamed to admit that I... ended a lot of lives at their behest." The words tumbled from her mouth, burbling out as if she were vomiting a vile wad of darkness from the depths of her soul. "My grandfather wasn't happy to be stuck raising me. I was sent away to live with him after my grandmother passed. He was a *miserable* old bastard.

Drank way too much. His floundering smithy couldn't support us both."

Aurora turned her head to look at Quistix, the chains wrapped around the base of her wide throat, clinking softly.

"The Assassin's Guild approached us one day after one of their members, Weaver, watched us test out a new blade. They were in awe of the way I wielded a knife, especially for being such a young, innocent-looking girl. One day, when my grandfather was drunk, they returned. They said they wanted me to join the guild and, in return, they'd pay him handsomely every month that I stayed and did their bidding. My grandfather gave me up. Just like that. Like I was livestock. Despite my protests, I was whisked away to their fortress, where they spent weeks training me in stealth and various weaponry. Eventually, I was sent out into the wilds of the Donik Forest to kill. After all, who'd suspect a filthy red-haired half-elf to be a bloodthirsty mercenary?"

Twitch's eyes grew large. "As a *child*?"

"Yes."

"Did you... *like* it?"

Quistix glared at him, eyes flashing a dangerously-pale hue. "No! I was *killing* people. But I didn't want my grandfather to lose his home or his smithy. He was all I had left!"

Aurora's mind swirled with questions. "How many?"

"What?" Quistix snapped.

"How many *people* did you kill?"

Quistix answered without hesitation. "Thirty-two."

"By the *Gods,*" Twitch mumbled. "You didn't even have to think about it."

"I could name every one of them, too. Contrary to what you might think, I don't take murder lightly."

"Does that number include Exos and all the Emerald Bandits?" Aurora asked.

"No." Quistix shook her head solemnly, voice dripping with shame.

Twitch thought back to long ago when he had first heard her prayers and all of the names she'd mumbled. He remembered recognizing one of them at the time.

"Gohra."

Quistix looked up, her eyes pulsing platinum at the mention of the name.

"I heard you say her name once during your nightly prayers. She was a fellow crook back in my days in the Thieves Guild. I always thought she died in her sleep." He narrowed his eyes. "Gohra... that was *you*, wasn't it?"

Quistix's head drooped again, and she nodded solemnly. "Poisoned the rim of her goblet."

They all sat in silence for a long time.

"You know I would never do anything to you, right, Twitch? You've danced on my nerves, but have I ever hurt you?"

"Intentionally?" he joked. "No."

"Aurora?" Quistix asked, swinging her gaze to the four-legged esteg tethered to the wall with heavy chains.

"Never." Aurora swallowed hard and trotted in place.

Quistix sighed. "See, that look right there, that look of distrust and fear, that's why I never tell anyone. I could sit here all night and tell you I would never hurt you, but there is always that little piece inside of you that'll wonder."

"I've wondered what you were capable of since I saw you scare Gregor so bad he evacuated his bowels." He snickered. "By the *Gods*, what a waste of a fine pair of Obsidian cotton pants."

Aurora looked from one of them to the other. "You made *who*... do *what*?"

"You're missing the point," Quistix protested.

Twitch leaned forward uncomfortably, his furry arms being tugged even further above his head by the chain contraption on the wall. "I used to be a thief. Screwed up so bad they didn't even want me anymore. I've lied, cheated, and stolen. Plus, I've killed right alongside you. So I'm even worse, I guess."

Quistix fought a smile, not wanting to be cheered up.

Aurora spoke. "I gored a hunter who had me trapped once."

Quistix and Twitch sat, stunned.

"I mean, he healed immediately because of my horns, and he was fine. But, the point is, I tried."

Quistix shut her eyes tightly to try to stifle a laugh.

Twitch snickered along with her. "That counts, sort of. *Almost.*" Twitch recomposed himself. "The point is, Quistix, we *all* do messed-up things. Sometimes it's for self-preservation. Sometimes it's for revenge. Let's face it, you are no dainty lass."

"Gee, thanks."

"No, I mean, a woman like you isn't made for long dresses and formal courtship. You are a slayer of men."

"And women," Aurora chimed in.

Twitch side-eyed her. Then he glanced back at Quistix. "You, my darling, are a revolutionary. You fight for what is right. The trail toward progress is always carved through blood-soaked soil."

Quistix scoffed.

"Wallowing in self-pity benefits no one. Yes, you have done horrible things. What'll make you feel better is *fighting* again, fighting for what is right and what is *just* and *good*. Without you, Aurora would never have gotten to visit the library in Apex. I never would have made it out of that crate. And surely none of us would have ever ridden a dragon! And Frok..."

The room went silent, the single word bringing everything to a grinding halt. The room's upbeat, electric energy changed to one of somber reverence.

"Frok is a perfect example of why I belong here. I got her involved in that whole mess to begin with. She'd still be here right now."

"Statistically," Aurora mumbled, "she was already nearing the end of her life cycle. Pleoms typically only live for three—"

"She never would have died if it wasn't for me!" The words came out of Quistix's mouth like a bark. Tears flooded her dazzling eyes.

"No." Aurora sniffled and shook her head, chains jingling. Trails of her own tears streaked the gray-brown fur around the sides of her snout. She stared at Quistix and spoke firmly. "If it wasn't for you, she never would have *lived*."

3

Dungeon of the Ruby Palace
Desdemona, Willowdale

The first two nights in the dungeons were loud and sleepless. A man's moans carried through the stone halls. His cries, screams, and fits of thrashing had sudden onsets that always woke the trio from their slumbers.

On the third day, two guards in black, noubald leather masks breezed past their cell with axes. Moments later, following the crack of metal on bone and flesh on stone, the sobbing man was silenced in an instant.

That night, Twitch had nightmares about the bloodied flour sack that one of the guards had left the man's cell with. He couldn't get the image of the long stringy hair poking through one of its rodent-chewed holes out of his worried mind.

He imagined soon the guards would be carrying his head in the crook of one of their arms with the effortless ease of bringing a watermelon home from the market square.

This night, however, was silent, save for the scurrying mice who had made homes in the soiled hay of their cell. Twitch snored softly on his side, arms tingling above him.

Aurora slept on buckled knees, her head tucked awkwardly against the wall in an attempt to conserve her warmth despite her chains being so short.

For Quistix, however, sleep still had not come. She quietly mustered her rage to try to melt the shackles on her wrists. All she needed was to heat the metal enough to make it slightly malleable. She feared setting the straw beneath her ablaze again, just as she had the first night.

She tried over and over, each attempt weakening her a little more. It was no use. A losing battle. Every time she heated them, the cuffs flared with a swirling amber hue. They were imbued with a form of magic that combated her own. They made her feel weaker as the days went on, draining her energy.

Suddenly, a door squealed open and shut with care in the pitch-black hallway beyond their dungeon cell. Footsteps clattered down stairs, heels on stone, each step growing louder as the mysterious person approached.

Quistix kicked hay at Twitch and Aurora to wake them quietly. They looked around, groggy. She motioned to the hall violently with her head. She could hear the woof of a blazing torch and the jingle of metal.

A guard walked past their cell and halted abruptly just beyond. From the darkness, Quistix saw a fire-lit face emerge from the shadows, face half-burned, her hair combed over to obscure the gnarled flesh. She wore a silken robe over a thin nightgown.

"Quistix, Twitch... Aurora," she murmured. "I wish we were meeting under better circumstances."

Twitch scoffed. "I don't believe we've had the pleasure. You would be...?"

"My name is Vervaine."

Aurora gasped. "As in... Vervaine Tempest of Obsidia?"

"A lifetime ago, perhaps. It is Queen Vervaine Brius now."

Twitch stared at the massive jewels in the queen's loose-fitting ring as they twinkled in the fire's light. If he were a free wyl, the gaudy monstrosity would have already been swiped off her finger and tucked safely in his coin purse without her ever having felt a thing.

"Your majesty," Quistix said, her throat parched, lips cracked. "I wish I could say that it's an honor." She tried to laugh, but it hurt too much. Her mouth was as dry as the deserts of Obsidia.

Twitch spoke. "To what do we owe the pleasure of this late-night visit to our humble cell? I mean, I'm assuming it's night. It's impossible to tell, really. You might've noticed there aren't actually any windows that lead to the outsi—"

"Please." Vervaine held up a hand to silence the wyl's train of thought. She turned and nodded at one of the guards. He promptly unlocked the gate and tugged it open for her.

"I was wondering how long it would take for you to come," Quistix said, shaking her head.

But Vervaine didn't approach the filthy half-elf. Instead, she cautiously walked through the soiled straw and kneeled beside the esteg.

"It is you that I seek, Aurora."

Twitch's eyes widened, and he whipped his furry head over to look at Quistix. She shrugged.

"Aurora, it is no secret that your kind are hunted for the healing properties of their horns."

Aurora stared at the queen.

Vervaine tugged the hood of her robe down, pulled her curtain of dark hair back, and exposed the scarred half of her face and bare scalp. "Can you heal this?"

Aurora winced and pulled away. "Those wounds are old, your majesty. The wounds must be fresh for me to heal them. Scars are already healed tissue."

"I see." Vervaine nodded. "What if the skin were to become damaged again?"

"Then, yes. I suppose I could heal the fresh wounds, but—"

"Not so fast," Twitch interjected. "What's in it for *us*? Surely such a life-changing restoration would be, say, three pardons, perhaps?" The sharp teeth of his sly, toothy smile glinted in the flickering light of the guard's torch.

"You are in no position to bargain, wyl," Vervaine snapped. Then, she turned her attention back to Aurora, her voice softening again. "I can only imagine how you must see me, a queen pleading for your help while you're imprisoned. It's pathetic, I know. I know what the three of you have done, and I assure you that we fight on the same side of justice. All of us in this room want something better for the isle. Exos was spinning out of control. You helped stop my sister, and, for that, I am grateful."

"Yes," Twitch adjusted himself, jingling his chains, "shackles and a dank dungeon cell. Your show of gratitude is truly *overwhelming*."

The queen turned to Twitch. "I am the reason you weren't hung, disemboweled, and buried in a marker-less grave."

"Oh, sweetheart, I hate to break it to you, but I'd have been hung either way." He winked and then glanced down at his lap.

Quistix rolled her eyes.

"Watch your tone," Vervaine growled. "I may be grateful, but I will not tolerate disrespect." She turned back to the esteg. "Aurora, I'm not a saint, but I am not a monster, either. A monster is someone who gets an entire isle addicted to a sedative to maintain control and fill her gold reserves. A monster leads with terror and revenge, leaving the blood of innocent people in her wake. A monster is someone who could do *this* to a child." She pointed to the scars on her face and stared into Aurora's fearful eyes. The esteg's ears folded back in fear as Vervaine stroked the fur of her head, inspecting the green nubs atop Aurora's head. "I see you only have spikes. Did you shed your rack?"

"Yes. In the wilderness a few weeks ago. Females shed every two years, your majesty. During a hormone shift, they weaken at the base and—"

Vervaine cut her off, quietly asking, "Would your spikes be enough to heal all of this?"

"Hey, you can't just take away our freedom and waltz in here and start to use us like tools, okay." Twitch narrowed his eyes at her. "We may be prisoners, but we saved this isle. We're being treated like treasonous vermin instead of heroes. We helped *make* you queen."

"So you admit to your crimes, do you? Creating a fire that claimed half of the castle in our isle's capital? Murdering the previous queen?"

Twitch's smug smile disintegrated.

"Twitch, stop before your tongue gets us all gutted. Aurora can speak for herself. Her freedom is not ours to barter with." Quistix's eyes glided back to Aurora's face. "It's your choice."

Aurora nodded at Vervaine. "Yes. They could heal something small, but at this size, it will exhaust me."

Vervaine placed a hand on Aurora's quivering back. "Will you heal me?"

Aurora nodded, almost imperceptibly.

A tear rolled from Vervaine's eye, down the wrinkles and ridges in her scarred cheek. "Thank you, Aurora. In exchange, I will grant you a pardon."

"What about *us*?" Twitch asked. "We're kind of a package deal here!"

Vervaine whipped her head and glared at Twitch. "You were an active participant in the murder of a queen. As Aurora can neither wield a sword nor a shield, she could be considered an accomplice at worst."

Aurora spoke up. "If you release us all, I'll heal you to the best of my abilities."

Vervaine clenched her teeth. "I have tried to be more than reasonable with all of you, but clearly you do not fully comprehend your current situation. Things could be much worse for you all. I may not be the kind of monster my sister was, but I am no timid tulip either."

Aurora stared at Vervaine's scarred skin.

"If I have to have the guards hold you down, I will. Please allow me to touch you, and this will all be over soon."

Aurora closed her eyes and nodded. Twitch let out an exasperated sigh.

Vervaine motioned for one of the guards. "Come."

One of the guards stepped inside the cell. "Yes, your majesty."

"Give me your sword."

The guard hesitantly unsheathed his sword and handed it to her. Resting the hilt on the ground, Vervaine dug the razor-sharp tip of the blade into her cheek, dragging her head down with a pained hiss. She whimpered as it cut her from her chin to her temple, and she groaned as she made another long cut beside it, removing a wide sliver of flesh.

Quistix winced as she watched it fall against the straw. A rodent stirred beneath it.

Twitch stared in horror, unable to avert his eyes from the scene.

Blood dribbled as Vervaine carved, staining the blade of the guard's sword with wavy crimson tendrils.

Once she had finished, Vervaine tossed the sword onto the dirty straw near the man's boots. Then, she unlooped the chains from Aurora's neck and freed the esteg. Aurora begrudgingly tipped her head, and the desperate queen nestled her bloodied cheek against the esteg's glowing spikes.

Warm tendrils of light coiled through the glowing, calcified nubs and dispersed through the fresh wound. Slowly, the gaping sliver of flesh closed, and the pink seam flattened and paled. The once-gory wound in Vervaine's face had been re-molded into pristine flesh. New sprigs of hair sprouted from the bare spots on her temples.

Aurora's legs buckled, and she slammed against the hay-covered floor, scattering fearful rats in every direction. Her neck cranked at an angle, and Vervaine struggled to adjust her massive body against the wall. Aurora was drained of all of her energy, barely able to open her eyes.

"*Did it work*?" Vervaine whispered, turning to face the guard behind her.

"Yes, your majesty."

Vervaine couldn't contain her grin. She traced the blood-soaked scars on the side of her throat and smiled at the drained esteg.

"We can save the rest for next time. Now, you must rest. This has obviously taken a toll on you."

Aurora's eyelids drooped. "Yes, my queen."

Vervaine stroked the short fur on Aurora's head again. "Thank you. We'll discuss your freedom soon. For now, rest."

Vervaine rose to her feet and exited. One of the guards locked the cell door.

The guard with the torch led the way down the long, winding dungeon hall. As he unlocked the door to the stairs, Vervaine extended her hand out to the other guard.

"Let me see your blade once more."

The guard hesitantly handed her his blood-smeared sword.

She rubbed a section of it clean with the sleeve of her robe and held it up. In the flickering light of the torch, Vervaine caught a glimpse of her partially-restored face in the blade's shiny surface.

Tears of joy filled her eyes.

4

The Ruby Palace,
Desdemona, Willowdale

Night had fallen over the scorched city of Desdemona. Once-white columns were now stained gray from soot. Homes were dilapidated. Memorials were nothing but ash. The buildings closest to the palace were smoke-damaged. The port city now had a dark, horrific stain on its history from the day the reign of Queen Exos Tempest abruptly ended.

Inside the newly renovated castle, Vervaine stared at the new wooden throne that had been created and installed just for her. Its crest had a deep rinceau design hand-carved into the burgundy-colored wood. The intricate relief in the center was a tree with seven limbs, each major branch representing one of the provinces. It was symbolic of the Isle of Desdemona. The arms of the seat were carved into two owls, representing wisdom. The legs were all different. A human. A ewanian. An eaflic. And a wyl. All had their arms stretched upward toward the Gods, making it appear as though the seated person was being held high by the people, the true foundation of the isle.

Vervaine ran her arms along the avian armrests and took a seat in it. This was new. All hers. None of the mad Tempest family had sullied the new throne with their deceit or destruction. This would be a new era that she would be able to finally call her own. No more lying to the people. No more drugs. Destoria could finally return from being a chaotic, second-rate civilization to a smooth-sailing ship with a sane captain. The people of Destoria needed a real leader this time. After living under the rule of her crazed father and, later, her unhinged sister, Vervaine understood the people's coldness and hesitancy to show support. Despite assuring them that her intentions were pure, she knew she would have to win the people back.

But how?

After two murderous monsters, how could she convince them that she genuinely cared about their health and well-being?

She had already set to work on her first task: to rebuild Desdemona. She no longer wanted the stigma of being the *Queen of Ashes*.

Instead, she vowed to be the *Queen of Rebirth*.

Her mind whirled with anxious thoughts. Images of bloodied Willowdale streets and the sounds of wailing children flooded her mind. She cupped her head in her hands and pinched her eyes closed, forcing away the images in her brain.

A hand suddenly gripped her shoulder. "I thought I might find you here."

Vervaine jumped reflexively, calming only when she saw it was her husband. "By the *Gods*, Arias!"

He chuckled as he sat in an identical throne to her left. "Didn't mean to spook you. What's the matter? Can't sleep again?"

"No. And, frankly, I'm not sure how *you* can."

Though their soul bond to the quichyrd remained, they had not felt Ceosteol's presence in weeks. Vervaine and Arias had both come to recognize that their individual lives had ended, and a new, *borrowed* life had merely begun.

Arias's smile faded, and his eyes widened. "What...? How...?" He rose and approached, grasping her chin delicately. He studied the side of her face, where scars once dominated her pretty face. They were nearly gone now. As if he had only ever dreamed them. “What did you do?”

“I forced the esteg in the dungeons to heal me as much as her small spikes would allow,” she said with joyous tears in her eyes. “I didn’t want to wake you. You were sleeping so peacefully.”

“My love, you’re... absolutely stunning.”

Vervaine blushed. “I feel... different.”

“In a good way?”

“Yes.” She nodded, and her smile faded a little. “Ceosteol is overjoyed as well. I can sense her chastening herself for not thinking of it first.”

Arias pressed a kiss to her surprisingly smooth temple.

Vervaine shivered. The deepest depth of her soul felt as if it were on display for the whole world. “I never know what thoughts are my own and what are hers these days. Every nasty thought, every bit of concern, Ceosteol knows it the second I feel it.”

"Cherish the small victories, my love. You mustn't let the dismal parts of life eat you alive, especially after a victory such as this." He kissed her mended flesh again. "Now you are as beautiful on the outside as you are inside. I'll have to start sending men off to battle every time I catch them flirting with you."

Vervaine bashfully giggled, tears of joy dribbling down her now-smooth, alabaster cheeks. "I am yours, Arias. And only yours. Beyond death. Beyond time."

There, encompassed in her husband's muscular arms, all seemed right in the world.

He leaned down and kissed her. It was just a peck, but it was enough to set Vervaine on fire. No matter how many times they had kissed, his touch sent her body into a tingling state of excitement.

He pulled her out of the chair and pushed her several feet backward until she was pressed up against the nearby stone wall. Vervaine pressed a passionate kiss to his lips, hands gripping his neck and shirt, tugging his body flush against hers.

Gripping her face, their forms evolved into a mass of melded lips and hot skin. He pulled her close, his hands expressing that he needed her *desperately*.

Arias watched her eyes start to glow green. Her lips curled into a mischievous grin. The voice that emerged from her lips was not her own.

"Oh, Arias," the quichyrd's voice said.

Arias pulled away from his beloved wife, clearly overtaken by Ceosteol. Furious, he shouted. "Stay out of my wife, you mad, twisted bitch!"

Suddenly, Vervaine's eyes morphed back to normal from their toxic coloring. She erupted in tears at the betrayal of her own body. She crumpled to the stone floor, sobbing, beating the sides of her skull with balled fists. "Get out of me! I never wanted this! Just leave us alone!"

Arias dropped to his knees and grasped his heartbroken wife in his arms. As he held her sobbing body, they both came to the devastating realization that they'd never truly be alone with each other ever again.

5

Irenas Parnix's Underwater Dome
The Radiant Sea

The wizard's plush robe tickled his bare legs as he swished his hips. The teal fabric made his pale, human skin seem almost sickly. His gravelly voice croaked out the lyrics to an old song:

> *Kings and Queens in the making,*
> *They're the same as you and me.*
> *But there is one big difference.*
> *Someone holds it while they pee.*

Violet snatched up the dirty goblets strewn around her grandfather's desk. Her hazel eyes scanned the room, glancing around at the remains of what looked like a raging party. There were spilled bottles of wine and tomes piled on the floor in disarray, with pages ripped from their bindings. There were wads of clothing heaped around the sandy floor. She placed the dishes in the full wash basin, the weight of it all straining its driftwood stand. Her shoulders sank at the thought of so many hours of cleaning ahead of her.

Had living underwater for so long made her grandfather go mad?

Now that she was down there, how long would it take for her to go crazy, too?

Violet looked through the circular window carved out of the wall above the basin. A dim light streaming through the waves high above wove delicate shapes on the ocean's floor. A storm raged above the water's surface, but from the deep ocean floor, the white-capped waters and lightning weren't worrisome in the slightest. The seaweed outside the window danced with the current like thousands of green and red tickling fingers.

Violet stared out at the serenity of the underwater landscape and the silent appearance of a school of fish. She toyed with a gold band on the thin strap of leather around her neck, tracing the metal circle absentmindedly with her finger.

Her grandfather's portal had opened at an inopportune time. It was rush hour at the bakery. Her boss surely burst a blood vessel in her brain once she'd learned that Violet had abandoned her at the busiest time of day.

But one could not simply *ignore* the call of a portal.

Violet had only seen the swirling void a handful of times in her life. She knew her grandfather was prone to closing them hastily if they were ignored. Patience was never one of his strengths.

She remembered the stories her mother had told her about him. She said that Irenas was quick to correct and slow to congratulate. Her mother could recall both times she'd ever seen Irenas smile genuinely, with teeth.

Once was the day that Violet was born. The other was on her mother's wedding day.

Violet's childhood memories of Irenas were hazy. It had been more than a decade since she had seen him, and he seemed nothing like she remembered. His furrowed brows had relaxed. The wrinkles on his forehead had smoothed. His face seemed more youthful, despite the passage of many years. If there wasn't more salt than pepper in his beard now, she'd have thought she'd teleported backward through time, too.

Irenas Parnix spun around, waving his hands beside his face, in some strange game of hide and seek. His robe flew open, exposing the saggy skin of his chest. Dingy white bloomers hugged his hips and thighs.

Reflexively, Violet averted her eyes in revulsion. She gestured to his bare chest and watched his eyes dart down to his bare skin. Grandfather, your robe!"

Irenas laughed, carefree. "Oh! We are all but mere skin and bones, my darling, comprised of the same materials, you and I. The same as every other living creature in this world, I might add. It's beautiful, isn't it?"

"What's beautiful?" Violet started scrubbing some of the goblets in the basin.

"That we are made of the same materials! The same materials as the three moons above... and the rocks on the Bramolt Mountains... and the plants in Apex... and the mollusks in these waters! We are all one, don't you see? All brush strokes of one beautiful piece of art that make up the most intricate masterpiece one can imagine!"

Violet's eyes widened. "Okay. That's... fine. But I don't need to see your, um...

masterpiece. Just tie your robe closed. Not every painting deserves to be on display."

Parnix belted out a hearty laugh, the sound of it like a boom of thunder vibrating the air between them, filling their dry bubble-like dome beneath the Radiant Sea with an uneasy energy. She felt unnerved by his random, uncharacteristic display of levity and joy.

"Right you are!" He chuckled, tying his robe closed. "Now," Parnix seated himself at the dinner table near her, nearly toppling clumsily onto the bench. He crossed his legs and folded his scrawny arms across them. "What brings you down to my little sub-surface oasis, my dear?"

Violet dropped one of the goblets and turned to face Irenas. "Grandfather, you sent for me."

"What?"

"You sent me a portal!"

"A portal?" His brows furrowed in confusion. "That's absurd! I did no such thing. I'd remember casting a portal to you, my darling. You must be mistaken."

She quirked a brow. "How did I get here, then? Did you think I shape-shifted into a shark and swam to the bottom of these waters to find you?"

"Perhaps." Irenas narrowed his eyes at her, trying to decide if she was being serious or not.

"You sent a portal to my work. I thought something was wrong, or that you needed me, so I came."

His dilated pupils ricocheted around the underwater room. "I suppose... I must have. I thought that was a dream. I was thinking about you and your mother and how your laugh brightened up the whole world when you were a child. That was before she died." He swallowed hard. "Before she was swallowed up by Kackaroth."

Tears fell from his eyes, carving their way through the wrinkles of his face, burying themselves in his long beard.

Violet stared blankly for a moment and then approached him. She spoke again, this time, with some compassion. “Grandfather, I assure you, my mother is still very much alive.”

“You’ve seen her?” He asked. Then he gasped, his light eyes suddenly full of hope.

“Yes.” Violet thought back to the last time she had gone to visit her at the Lagdaloon Saloon in Silvercrest.

She had last seen her mother two years ago. The woman’s skin had lost some of its luster and elasticity. The hollows of her cheeks were more pronounced and there were dark circles beneath her eyes. Still, the woman was hauntingly beautiful, draped across a filthy farmer’s lap, breasts heaving out the top of her corset, her skirt shorter than Violet’s patience. Her mother had been a harlot for decades. Had Violet not struck out on her own, she would’ve surely been wrangled into the trade at an early age.

Violet’s mother slurped black liquid from a vial, never blinking. Despite her thick, leather cloak, Violet felt the chill from her mother's stare seep into her bones. Then, her drugged mother giggled as the farmer lifted her up and whisked her off into one of the inn rooms available by the hour.

Now Violet was here in a secluded underwater dome, staring into another family member's eyes that looked equally as lost as her mother's.

Was Irenas losing his mind? Could the walls of water come crashing down at any moment if Parnix somehow bungled the spell he'd once cast? Surely, she'd drown before she could ever swim back to the surface.

Violet shivered, looking out the window at the schools of shimmering fish, grouped as though they were all interconnected. Suddenly, their bio-luminescent bodies darted, scattering in every direction at the presence of a nearby predator. The water behind them darkened, choking out the last of the light as something massive cruised by overhead.

Violet gasped. "Grandfather?" She pointed out the window. "What in the Nether is *that*?"

The wiry wizard rose and hobbled toward her, peering out the hole.

His eyes grew wide, and he grabbed the wall, thrusting his wrinkled face hard against the see-through magical barrier. Violet could see his pulse racing through the thin skin of his neck.

"By the Gods..."

"What?!"

He looked like he'd seen a ghost. "Kackaroth... has been freed! The only way that could *possibly* be... is if..."

He pulled away from the barrier and blinked his watery eyes at Violet. A look of horror spread across his face.

"Is if *what*?!"

"Is if... *I let him out.*"

6

Dungeon of the Ruby Palace
Desdemona, Willowdale

As the frigid nights wore on, Quistix's ankles had grown bloody around her shackles from all of the squirming during her attempts to escape. Twitch had worn off the fur of his wrists.

Aurora, however, had done nothing but sleep for days, only waking to reposition. The only words she mumbled in response to Twitch's questions had been laced with despair. She had resigned herself to her new fate as the queen's healer, despite the energy it drained. Despite barely being able to keep her eyes open, the esteg was certain it was only a matter of hours or days before Vervaine returned for another treatment.

Unable to sleep, Quistix stared at Aurora, hoping to use the love for her found-family to dig deep and find the fury to break through the shackles' magical bond.

Still, nothing happened. Her inner fire and fury dwindled in tandem with her vanishing energy levels. She was a campfire with no wood. A kite with no wind. Over and over, she had tried to heat and weaken her magically-bound steel shackles to no avail. After more than a week, after thousands of attempts, it was all so utterly hopeless.

Exos was dead, but things did not feel peaceful in Destoria. Her mind drifted back to the crazed quichyrd with the toxic-green eyes that fought beside Exos on the night the trio sealed their fates as treasonous fugitives, the night the very building they were chained in the bowels of went up in flames.

What exactly did the old crone want?

Suddenly, the clatter of keys sounded in the hall, and a hooded figure approached their door.

Quistix hoped it was a dream, or delirium from the near-deadly dehydration.

"Damn," a woman's voice whispered as the keys jiggled clumsily in the lock.

Aurora peeled her eyes open as much as she could muster and readied herself for another session of exhaustive healing.

Quistix wrenched her neck toward the door and spied a familiar face in the darkness. She smiled, splitting her chapped lips. She tasted blood, but she didn't care.

Twitch squinted through the darkness, trying to make out the face beyond the bars.

"I never in a million years thought I'd see you here," Quistix managed.

"In the flesh," the woman said.

"You sound familiar. Who goes there?" Twitch grumbled.

The woman lowered her hood and stared at the wyl. He gasped.

Aurora lifted her head and perked up a little. “Madam Aerendyl? Is that you?”

Emma Aerendyl nodded.

Quistix tugged at her chains, “What are you doing here?”

“Surely you are not that simple, darling. I have come to spring you from this Gods-forsaken pit.”

“Emma, this is treason,” Quistix whispered.

“Q! Stop trying to talk her out of it!” Twitch rattled his wrist shackles. “Please, Aerendyl, help us!”

Finally, she got the jammed lock to budge, and she swung the barred door wide open. She crept into the dank cell and grabbed Quistix’s cuffs. She mumbled a long spell under her breath, and the shackles glowed bright blue and then fell open, freeing the half-elf’s bloodied wrists.

Madam Aerendyl grabbed her step-daughter by the bony shoulder and shook.

"Hurry, Quistix. We have to go. Come with me. There is little time!"

"Wait!" Quistix rose onto her weak, unsteady legs, as wobbly as a newborn landigo. "I can't just leave. Not without them."

Madam Aerendyl looked around nervously and finally sighed and handed over the set of keys. Quistix riffled through them quickly, desperately trying to find the one that would free Twitch.

Meanwhile, Aerendyl un-looped the chains from Aurora's neck and helped her up. Quistix handed back the key ring, and Madam Aerendyl cast another spell. The ring of keys floated inches above her open palms and promptly vanished into thin air. Then, she chanted again, and a scroll materialized in her hands.

"*Whoa*," Twitch said quietly, amazed by the headmaster's abilities.

Emma unfurled the scroll, one drenched, dripping from the edges, stinking of ocean brine. The filigreed metal ends were encrusted with salt and fine bits of seaweed as if it had just been plucked from the depths of the sea.

"Bear with me. This is in an old tongue. I can barely read this."

Quistix stared, hope and curiosity in her yellow eyes.

Down the hall, two male voices chatted, followed by the *clank* of metal.

One said, "Once all these prisoners is free, I guess we'll be out of a job. Willowdale gon' have all this-here riffraff out ins the streets again."

"It's not *my* fault," the second voice said. "Things happen. We've gots five skilled thieves in this dungeon alone. Any 'a them coulda taken them! Theys all gots sticky fingers and fast feets!"

"Yous better hope we find 'em. If this mangled freak is anything like her sister, she'll hang you just as soon as look at you!"

The guards neared their cell.

"Read this," Madam Aerendyl growled.

"Why do we all need to read it?" Twitch asked.

"*Shhhh!*"

"*I can't read that language, Emma!*" Quistix whispered.

Aurora shouldered in to get a closer look at the scroll and whispered, "*I can. Repeat after me.*"

Aurora read aloud. Twitch and Quistix repeated the words after her.

Together they chanted:

"*Lamellae sicut pisces, ambulans in area oceani, sicut aliquis vellet in terra.*"

"Now, take a deep breath!" Madam Aerendyl flashed a wicked smile and stepped back. "I'll come for you all soon. Until then, stay out of trouble and out of sight!"

"Where are we—"

Quistix couldn't even get the last of the words out. The squirming hay on the floor began to spin, and the ground beneath them opened up. A gaping portal widened until all three dropped down through it, each screaming at the sudden weightlessness.

They tumbled down and spun as if being engulfed by a powerful tornado into blackness.

Their fall slid them straight into a seemingly endless expanse of water, submerging them without warning. Their tired, shackle-burned arms found new life and scrambled to latch on to anything beneath the surface. Their lungs begged for air. They were rocketed further, faster, straight toward the ocean's bottom, feeling as though they would soon be crushed by the pressure.

They slowed, bobbling in the saltwater, discombobulated, not knowing which way was up. Everything around them was the same rich shade of aquamarine. The trio looked around, trying to right themselves.

Unable to hold her breath any longer, Quistix opened her mouth and sucked in a panicked lungful. But instead of water, in came *air*, as if by pure magic. Quistix took another deep breath and smiled.

She could breathe!

Something touched her neck. She felt around, slipping her fingers along the edges of what felt like gills in her flesh.

She swam to Twitch and felt his throat. The same gills were on his neck, only his were swishing, furry flaps.

She pointed to her gills. They fluttered open and closed. She illustrated taking a deep breath, trying to get him to do the same.

He shook his head, terrified.

"Take a breath!" she yelled, frustrated. The sound of her own voice, as clear as a bell in the water, stunned her.

Twitch gave in and finally took a breath. To his surprise, he, too, got a lungful of air.

"We can breathe!" Quistix yelled, grabbing him by the fur-covered shoulders and shaking him.

"How in the world can I understand you?" Twitch beamed, thrilled that he'd been spared a watery grave.

"It was the scroll," Aurora said, spinning awkwardly through the current, unable to right herself with thin, angular limbs. "We chanted the *Spell of Waterbreathing*."

"How do we get up to the surface?" Twitch asked.

Quistix pointed in the direction of the aqua-tinged light above them.

"That's down," Aurora said.

"What? No, it isn't. That's the glow of the moons through the surface," Twitch said.

Aurora motioned to something beside them. "Then why is that school of glitter guppies swimming upside down?"

Quistix watched. The fish were, in fact, upside down.

Twitch pointed to the glowing light. "Then what in the world is that?!"

Quistix shrugged and swam toward it. "Only one way to find out!"

They swam for what felt like a mile through inky darkness, slipping down toward the aqua-tinted lights glowing on the ocean's floor.

As they neared the lights, an underwater city emerged. Sunken ships littered the sandy floor, some busted into splintered pieces. Toward the crest of a sandy hill in the distance sat a towering castle, with orbs of glowing light hovering above each of the four corner spires. Winding paths wove through a submerged city lined with buildings, columns, and statues, all covered in a fine layer of deep green algae.

The city's inhabitants swam from building to building, each with a tail instead of legs. Their upper bodies resembled a human's, only covered in reflective scales of varied hues. Their faces were smooth and scaleless, each with a set of gills.

"Merfolk? Did I hit my head when I fell through that hole? Is this real?" Twitch asked, mouth agape, full of saltwater.

"I see them, too," Quistix said quietly.

"I have only ever read about them. Fascinating." Aurora's eyes were wide with wonder.

"They're... real?" Twitch sounded incredulous.

"I'm learning that *anything* is possible." Quistix swam closer to get a better look.

As they paddled over to a building along what looked to be a main thoroughfare, they ducked into the murky shadows, inspecting the townsfolk from a distance.

"What do we do?" Aurora asked. "We have legs. The merpeople will notice us immediately."

Quistix nodded and trained her eyes on the gravelly path of white seashells, each one seemingly chosen from elsewhere in the waters and placed with intention.

"We look extremely out of place with these additional extremities."

"Who'd have thought having all these legs could make us such outcasts," Quistix said with a hint of sarcasm so the esteg might realize how ridiculous it sounded aloud.

Aurora missed the humor in it. “Very little is known about these people. I have no clue if they’re an amiable species. I don’t even know what dialect they speak to attempt communication. I’m afraid I won’t be much help here.”

“Alright,” Quistix looked around. “I’m just going to try my native tongue. If it all goes south, I’m going to try to make it to that reef in the distance and hide beneath some coral.”

“Ah, the ol’ *straightforward* approach. I love it when you have a plan. I find it stimulating when you take charge.” He smirked.

“Keep it in your trousers, Twitch,” Quistix snapped and then swam out from the alleyway behind the building.

Quistix, Twitch, and Aurora slowly paddled through the underwater city, watching for merfolk. The city looked like an underwater version of many of those above sea level. There was a market with signs advertising nets of shrimp and minnows. There were neighborhoods full of makeshift homes fashioned from jetsam, each with lawns made of sand divided by tidy seashell borders and walkways. Each apparent property contained tree-shaped hunks of coral in various sizes.

Colorful seashell pathways cut through the city, speckled with the occasional scuttling spider crab or swaying exposed half of a partially-buried sea worm. Schools of smooth-gliding glitterfish passed through the streets, their wild array of reflective scale colors blending into vibrant blurs against the aquamarine glow of their surroundings, each grouping a work of art.

Aurora smiled, her soulful eyes reflecting the radiant mass of swirling bodies. “Frok always wanted to see those. Now they are so close… I can almost touch them.”

Looping back through, the school of glitterfish spotted them and dispersed instantly like a small explosion, each launching itself in a different direction in an act of self-preservation.

Aurora's eyelids drooped. "I am afraid I cannot continue this trek much longer. I'm exhausted."

Twitch nodded, small bubbles rising from the fur around his gills. "I may not be as tired as you because of what the queen did, but I am exhausted as well. There were far too many mice in that dungeon for my liking. I loathe having tiny claws skittering across me." He shivered involuntarily. "Such filthy little things."

Quistix stopped paddling and rested her feet on the shell path. She looked around. "We need food and somewhere safe to sleep. Keep your eyes peeled for anything that looks edible. Clams, Oysters, shrimp..."

"Stop. We get it. I'm already starving. I don't need a full menu to make things worse," Twitch said, looking around at his potential options. "I'm only worried that if we start eating living things in an underwater city, we could get off on the wrong foot… or *fin*… with these merpeople."

"True," Quistix chewed her lip, tasting nothing but salt.

"Sorry, we ate your pet, madam. We didn't know spider crabs were like rakaabys to you down here," Twitch said to the trunk of a coral tree, as if it were a mermaid. Then, he spotted a ball of sand-colored spikes. "I wonder what the *rats* of the sea are."

The wyl bent down and reached out to touch the spike. It rapidly flexed, reeling away from his finger and puffing out to twice its original size.

"Good. I'm not the *only* thing repulsed by your touch," Quistix mumbled.

Dark figures oozed through the darkness and into the light, weaving through the buildings, around coral trees, heading straight toward them.

Quistix felt her stomach flip. She was without *Swordbreaker*, surrounded by shadows that were now circling them from all sides. Quistix swatted at a tuft of unruly red hair as it gracefully drifted in front of her field of vision, now seeming brown in the blue-green illumination of the city orbs.

Twitch instinctively reached over his shoulder for his quiver to ready an arrow and his bow, and then cursed quietly as he remembered it was probably in some chest in the Desdemona dungeon.

They stood tall at the mercy of the beings that surrounded them.

"If these things attack," Twitch whispered, "It has been a real honor knowing you both." His ears flicked nervously. He extended his claws and readied himself to swipe.

Knowing Aurora didn't have the energy to defend herself, Quistix stepped in front of her, a half-elf barrier between the esteg and the creatures.

From out of the darkness, a floating orb of light, a paler hue than those posted on spires around the city, drifted toward them and hovered above the throng of creatures, casting a subtle glow that illuminated the beings just enough. The light was attached to a thin forehead tentacle, bowing out in front of a fierce-looking fish with a vicious under-bite full of razor-sharp teeth and foggy eyes.

In the cast light of the evil-looking fish bobbled an array of other aquatic beasts. Some were eight-tentacled, octopus-like beings that circled them, like a predator sizing up prey. Small butterfly-shaped fish flapped their fins, leaving a trail of bright blue, glimmering bioluminescence in their wake. A shark loomed like an ominous cloud, watching them from above with wide, black eyes.

Just then, something far larger passed over them, its shadow blotting out all the orb light above the entire underwater road.

Twitch swallowed hard and grabbed Quistix's hand. Terrified, for a moment, she allowed him to hold it, squeezing back with reassurance that they would somehow survive.

“Alright!” She bellowed with every ounce of ferocity she could muster. “If you want to fight, you had better break every bone in my body, because the ones you don’t, I’m coming back with to kick your ass. Now... who’s first?”

7

The Ruby Palace,
Desdemona, Willowdale

It had been the longest of days. Vervaine Brius was fatigued. Her eyes burned, aching to rest. For sitting on a cushioned throne all day, she never thought ruling a nation could be this tiring. Exos and her father had made it look so... *exciting*. But, so far, she had only experienced day after day of Destorian bureaucracy, constant complaints from commoners, humoring tirades from provincial leaders, and engaging in the most boring minutiae.

Arias wove his callused fingers through hers and gave her a gentle squeeze. The pads of his palms and the coarse skin of his fingertips had softened over the last few months. The grip she knew of the man she loved had slowly transformed into something delicate and foreign. His warmth was the only thing about him that had remained truly familiar.

The graze of his hand used to light her body up like a torch, flooding her with a rush of heat, setting every inch of her body ablaze. The mere sight of him made her heart pound like a war drum. His whispers readied her body in moments for the sensual ravaging that often ensued.

Their marriage had come swiftly after the death of her sister and the devastation of the capital city. What Vervaine dreamed would be the happiest moment of her life was overshadowed by having to lead Willowdale's exhaustive campaign of rebirth and restoration. She would have preferred her wedding to instead, have been a quiet affair with sweet traditions like being swept off her feet and carried off to some cabin in the woods. It was a formal affair, a political show, a necessary step before the coronation of a new king.

Alas, no elderberries had been tossed on her white gown as she'd imagined as a girl, a tradition said to bless the new couple with all of the sweetness life had to offer. Not one tear was shed. No father was present to grace Arias with a dowry or to walk her down a carpet of fragrant red thyme to symbolize the end of her old life. There had been no mother to kiss their cheeks or to recite the traditional prayer for a happy home. In fact, there was no family at all, as she was the only Tempest left in existence.

The lonely feeling ate a hole in her stomach, cauterized only by an anger that seethed inside her undead form with nowhere to go. Exos had robbed her of nearly everything, and then Ceosteol ruined what remained of her life. The quichyrd had created a monster in her, a hollow puppet, a mouthpiece for her spreading disease.

Vervaine's soul was bound to a body that no longer desired to host it. She shouldn't still exist. Yet, here she was, warily seated in a new throne in one of the reconstructed domes of the Ruby Castle.

She looked up at the roof. The old arched ceilings had been decorated in exquisite hand-painted scenery bearing depictions of her lineage and the crown, reminders of lives that existed before this one.

Above her now, sprawled out on bowed scaffolding, was an overweight orc. Inside of her meaty hands sat a small horsehair brush dancing along stone, slathering on paint the color of snow at dusk, swirling the bristles in an artful path to depict ethereal smoke. Beyond the orc was a nearly-finished ceiling fresco bearing a mural of Willowdale's history from its start as a wheat field, through its early days full of ratty hovels, and ending in an image of the bustling capital city that it had become.

At the bottom were the portraits of Vervaine's predecessors, each wearing their custom crowns. The first was her great-great-grandfather in his modest golden band. Then there were two more relatives she'd never met, each wearing a circlet that was slightly more ornate than the last. Then, there was her father's scowling face wearing a stately onyx crown that was just as bold as he was. Next was Exos, her face forever locked in that smug, signature smirk. Her eyes were hauntingly realistic. Atop her head of black hair sat a painstakingly-painted obsidian-and-ruby headpiece with wicked spikes that were nearly as sharp as her tongue had been. Inside her slender right hand was a bottle of dikeeka. On her left, a ball of fire. As Vervaine stared at it, she wondered how much coin it would take for the orc to scar her sister's face in the image.

She'd lived with a marred face for nearly two decades before the imprisoned esteg finally healed her. It felt fitting that Exos might be cursed with similar scars forever.

Even if it was just paint.

Arias waltzed into the vast space and stopped in the middle. He followed his wife's line of sight up to the image of her sister, to painted eyes that seemed to stare at him like a ravenous kleax would at a slab of esteg steak. He could still remember Exos's cold, bony fingers grasping his forearm or the desperate amount of cleavage she always displayed like she had done it only yesterday.

He shivered and looked away from the mural on the dome, lying politely. "Looks nice."

Vervaine's eyes didn't budge. Arias waved, trying to pull her attention from the fresco above.

“What is going on in that brain of yours? I can practically hear those cogs grinding.”

“Hmm?” Vervaine finally snapped her eyes away from her sister's depiction. Arias approached, and she rose from her throne, brushing a stray hair from one of his ram horns.

He slid his hands along the small of her back and caressed her silken gown with his thumb. “Do you ever miss her?”

Vervaine answered, eyes returning to the haunting image. “Not even a little.” She sighed. “But, I suppose she is a part of the history of this isle now, isn’t she? Her charred remains are buried in the cracks and crevices of all that is broken in Destoria. She and my father have stained our legacy, tainted anything I could ever hope to achieve, soiling this nation with bloodshed and division. I will always be the Tempest who fought to right the wrongs of my father and my sister. Never the queen who succeeded in making better lives for her people. I am doomed to simply control damage for my entire reign. I'm a bandage expected to pull together a bleeding civilization and then be discarded like trash."

Arias stilled his thumb and grinned. "Do you feel better now that you've rained pity down upon yourself?"

"It's not pity, Arias. It's reality."

"These are the ramblings of a woman deprived of restful sleep. You barely close your eyes anymore at night. Every morning, when I wake up, you are already at your desk, writing down new plans, rewording speeches. You need some rest, my love. It will give you a new perspective."

"Arias, are you serious?! Rest?!" Vervaine shouted, turning to face him. Her words reverberated off the stone walls, filling the massive room with an echoing cacophony of frustration. The orc jerked, swaying the scaffolding.

"Arias, how can you sleep so peacefully after the last year of our lives? Does the blood and soot and turmoil around you mean nothing?"

"Vervaine—"

"How about us turning into," she looked at the orc and quieted herself, "into *this*... this undead *monstrosity*?" She gestured to her eyes, now the color of polished jade stones. "This new life has not disturbed your slumber?"

She threw her hands into the air and whispered, "*What am I even saying? Life?* Life? *Arias, we died! We aren't even living*!"

The orc above them peered over the edge of the wood slats, clearly trying to eavesdrop.

Arias snatched Vervaine's wrist and dragged her into an unoccupied side corridor.

Once they stopped, Vervaine snarled and yanked back her arm. "Arias Brius, if you *ever* lay another hand on me again in anger, I will—"

"What?" His tone was flirtatious. He pressed her into a shadowy patch between the sconces and pinned her against the stone wall with his body. "Hmm? *What'll you do to me*?"

"I'll make you beg for mercy," she growled. Then, she inhaled deeply. He smelled faintly of donik wood shavings and fresh rain, a combination that made her feel alive, feral. She felt her fury slowly replaced with lust.

Arias toyed with lace draped across her cleavage. His burgundy eyes seared into her, melting away the world around them. "Will you now?"

Down the hall, someone cleared their throat, offering a polite reminder that they were not alone. Arias and Vervaine peeled apart, turning in unison toward the sound.

From the shadows, Alvanak made his way into a tangerine patch of everburn torchlight.

"Pardon me, your majesties, but the other council members await your arrival in the meeting room. I'm afraid we have much to discuss." He blinked his slit eyes, throat sack puffing in and out rapidly. His slick green cheeks were dusted in a rosy hue.

“Very well,” Arias said, straightening his royal attire.

Alvanak turned and strode back toward the council’s chambers. The split tail of his formal cotton jacket fluttered behind him as he retreated.

“I forgot that was tonight,” Vervaine mumbled, thoroughly embarrassed. She straightened her gown and turned to follow the ewanian.

Arias grabbed her by the waist and yanked her back against his thudding chest. He used a hand to brush away a chestnut-brown chunk of hair from the once-scarred side of her face. He found it endearing that she hadn’t styled her hair any differently since she’d been healed. Hiding her alabaster skin seemed to be an old habit that proved hard to break.

He leaned down, lips grazing the shell of her slightly pointed ear. His breathy whisper made her knees weaken. Heat spread down through her abdomen.

"You are becoming more unruly by the day. Perhaps I should teach you a lesson in not making idle threats."

Vervaine softly laughed and turned her face. "Who said the threat was idle? I will make you beg for mercy." She pulled away from his grasp and turned. "That's not a threat. It's a promise, my dear."

Arias chuckled and followed his wife into the meeting chambers. Vervaine smiled at the fresh faces of her new council.

An elderly orc waved politely. His skin had faded with time, giving him a frosted olive pallor. His yellow irises darted between them as Vervaine strolled by, chin high, cheeks blushing.

She recalled the morbid tales of the previous council's massacre, feeling almost as if she had been there, almost as if she had not been locked in an Obsidian dungeon, enduring the torture of crimson soul reapers.

She'd heard all of the gory details about the night of the council's implosion and the bloody rampage that claimed the lives of Dacus and Duke Grayson. It was said that there had been neat streams of blood between the brick seams of the polished stone floor, the life force of several species coagulating together in the muddy grout. Bits of tissue had been wiped from the walls., bone fragments swept up with wet brooms.

As she made her way to the chair at the end of the donik wood table, she glanced at a crater marring it where a stubborn brown stain remained.

Had it been from the collision of a skull, she wondered, studying its peculiar shape.

A fist, perhaps?

She stood next to her seat, striding graceful and even, just as she'd seen her father and sister do so many times throughout the years.

A young landigo darted toward her heavy chair. The spotted leopard fur along his arms did nothing to hide the obvious lack of muscle definition beneath. He struggled, trying to get a solid grip on the wooden backrest, but the chair was too heavy. He dragged the legs awkwardly along the floor. His youthful face contorted with strain, eyes apologetic as he fought against the heft.

Several nearby councilmen rose in unison to assist, but Vervaine held up her pale palm to halt them. "He can do it. I believe in him."

The landigo boy smiled graciously and pulled the seat the rest of the way out, panting so hard that his rough tongue could be seen by all.

She took a seat, and the landigo used all of his might to shove the chair toward the table.

Once he was finished, he bowed reverently and retreated to another room.

Arias took his seat at the opposite end of the table and smiled as he watched Vervaine nestle into the chair's silk cushion.

So regal. So beautiful. So pure. His chest swelled with pride.

She was meant to sit there.

She was born to be queen.

The men and women of the council stared at Vervaine's face, some unable to keep their mouths closed from the shock of her transformation.

"M-My queen, your *face...*" Nynal, the snow-white wyl representative from Wyl Isle, stammered from her assigned seat. "Has Hezrus blessed you with her gift of beauty on this day?"

Vervaine smiled, touching the flesh of her face, once marked with patchy divots and ridges, now as smooth as tumbled sea glass. She felt her response catch in her throat. She wondered if she would ever get used to all the attention.

"Such is the healing power of an esteg." Varvaine motioned to her face.

"Ah, but true beauty lies not in the skin, but in the soul, does it not?" asked a voice she recognized instantly. The corners of Kleego's beak turned upward as he leaned forward in his seat, jutting his teal, feathered face out beyond the others at the table.

The familiar face from her past made Vervaine feel at ease. Once a loyal underling in Obsidia, Kleego had rightfully moved up in the ranks to become part of the formal Destorian council. "Well put," she said sweetly.

"Sayin' it all pretty like 'at don't make it so," grumbled Helga, a beefy barbarian woman, across the table from the frumlan. She swung her large head with attitude, accidentally whipping the human beside her in the face with her long braid. "Childbearing has marred my body and stretched skin of every mother's belly since the dawn of time. It's too bad that those who gave others *life* can't be graced with such a gift."

"Excuse me? And what of *us* warriors, Helga?" asked the human beside her. It was *Ives the Unbreakable*, the formerly demoted head of the royal guard, the chiseled

Willowdale heartthrob who had half the capital city smitten. "Should men who feel the sting of the blade risking our lives in battle not be *just* as entitled to such miraculous healing, if not more so?"

Helga balked. "Ives, you have *got* to be kidding me."

"I'm not! We soldiers put our lives on the line knowing full well that we might *die,* and you don't think *that* is more noble than simply... *incubating a child*?"

"No! I do not, as a matter of fact!"

"You can carry a baby lying on that giant straw mattress of yours! Can you say the same about the battle at Swiftwater?! I nearly lost my life there, fighting for this very province!" He looked around the table. "I have scarred, too. I have shattered my bones protecting this very castle while it was engulfed in flames!"

"Maybe if you were a better *fighter*, you wouldn't need any healing," Helga spat.

Ives gasped. "Madam, brawn and strategy win the wars that beauty brings about!" He eyed her up and down and sneered. "Well, maybe not *yours*..."

"Enough, Ives! You don't sound like a soldier. You sound like a petulant child. Come off it already," Arias's angry voice boomed through the meeting room.

Everyone quieted. Helga scowled and crossed her arms.

"Now that my *appearance* has been addressed in depth, shall we move on to actual *pressing* matters?" Vervaine growled.

Helga stiffly readjusted in her seat. "Queen Brius, before we get started, I wish to thank you for the continued aid you've provided to us in Adum, the scorched city in eastern Bellaneau."

Vervaine nodded. "It was one of the first cities ravaged by the Emerald Bandits during my sister's foolish hunt for *The Illuminator* and that fugitive, Quistix Daedumal."

"She's been captured and is now imprisoned in the Ruby Castle dungeon here, has she not?" Guarin, the Silvercrest representative, asked, his throat sack puffing as he inquired.

"No." Vervaine forced a chuckle and glanced at Arias. "I would know if the most wanted woman in Destoria resided in this very building."

Guarin and the other council members turned to one another, confused. "But, your majesty... a red-haired female, a male wyl, and an esteg were marched from the harbor to the palace several weeks ago. Many can attest to seeing their apprehension firsthand."

"That was, unfortunately, a misunderstanding, I assure you." Vervaine mustered an insincere smile. "It is true that three such people were marched here, but, after interrogation, it was discovered that it was merely a coincidence."

"A *coincidence*?" a quichyrd beside Arias chirped. Sabet was cloaked in a white silk robe, mindlessly preening her feathers as she listened. She clacked a talon against her canary-yellow beak before speaking again.

"Hmmm. Highly unlikely. Perhaps even less likely than a red-haired elf with Apexian training in the ways of magic, say, escaping a poorly-guarded dungeon."

"What?" Vervaine tried to hide the panic in her voice.

Sabet shook her feathery head. "Your majesty, lying to the people of Destoria is one thing. Lying to your royal council is another entirely. If you're going to do so, at least make the story believable. Don't insult our intelligence."

Hadox, a kleax, stood, slapping his clawed palm-pads against the table hard enough to send several goblets leaping. His mane whipped as he swiveled his head to face Sabet. "Enough of this squawking and pettiness. You are in the presence of royalty. Respect your queen. Show her that you are to be trusted with the truth before you try to *pry* a confession from her lips."

The quichyrd swallowed so hard that a lump in her throat bobbed with uneasiness.

“Thank you, Hadox,” Vervaine said with a nod. Then, she looked around. “May we continue?”

“Your majesty,” Ives said, his smoldering brown eyes flashing her a knowing gaze. “Secrets of the throne have a way of clawing their way out of the grave and walking among the living, so I wish to ask outright... Have the sorceress, Quistix, and her accomplices somehow escaped? Were the guards not paying enough attention?”

“The guards aren’t to be blamed. She was bound in magic-infused shackles, Ives. They were *guaranteed* to work by those damned *wizards* of Apex.” Vervaine motioned to the empty seat in the middle of the table in front of the place-setting labeled *Apex*, where Madam Aerendyl should have been sitting.

The others erupted into a buzz of whispers and muffled gasps.

“Quiet down,” Arias bleated, stunning the council members. “We are not to blame for the elusive nature of those practicing that disgusting dark magic. The traitorous half-elf has the support of many others, perhaps even an underground network of people, to help aid in an escape. Our men are searching. Once she's apprehended—"

"She'll be conveniently released again, I'm sure," Sabet cawed loud enough for all to hear.

Arias gritted his teeth and shoved his chair away from the table. He walked over and snatched the lapels of Sabet's robe and jerked her onto her avian feet.

No one rose to her defense.

"Does all of this amuse you? Does interrupting me offer you some illusion of power? I assure you, your position holds no promise of security or protection for when you run off at the beak, spewing your discontent. We do not need a bunch of insidious halfwits infecting this council meeting with such utter disrespect. Sabet, consider yourself relieved of your position as Taernsby's representative."

"But, your majesty," she chirped.

"Guards!" Arias shouted, jerking Sabet around like a weightless doll, shoving her toward the two sentries flanking the doorway. "Escort her off the grounds. Do not allow her back on site."

Arias jerked as a hand firmly gripped his shoulder from behind. He softened when he caught a waft of the floral scent of Vervaine's perfume.

Her voice was low, a gentle purr. "Steady, my love. There has been too much escalation in the isle these last few years. Your days as a guard have passed. Destoria needs unity and stability, *not* more division."

Arias spun and kissed her fingers gently, peering into her eyes. "Right you are, my queen." He looked out at the others. "My apologies to all for the outburst."

"What is a king if not the protector of his queen, first and foremost?" Hadox laughed nervously and raised his wine chalice. He hoisted it in the air toward the akiah. "That is something of which we can all agree, I'm sure."

Arias returned to his seat. "Quistix Daedumal has already been the focus of far too much of this council's time. Thousands of Destorians depend on us to make life-altering decisions. We cannot make the same mistakes that Exos did and be so focused on the singular tick burrowing behind our ear that we ignore the malnourished hands reaching out for aid in front of our eyes. After all, children are starving to death in Taernsby. Isn't that right, Sabet?"

She responded with a solemn nod, still embarrassed by his earlier outburst.

"Illness and rage from dikeeka withdrawal are sweeping through the isle, and a harsh winter will surely only complicate these maladies further," Arias continued.

"Where is the representative for the floating city?" Helga pointed to the empty chair.

Arias shrugged and played with the rim of his goblet. "We do not know what is happening in Apex right now, seeing as though the assigned representative has not even bothered to grace us with her presence tonight."

"She had better have a good excuse," Ives said, stabbing at his steak.

"Worry not, your majesties. We shall appoint a replacement right away since these matters seem to be of no importance to Madam Aerendyl anymore. Apex has been isolating itself more than usual from the isle these last few months. I assure you, we will get to the bottom of whatever is causing this provincial rift," Alvanak said, smoothing his parchment against the wood of the table.

Vervaine leaned forward. "We must work together to mend this broken land. There will be many challenges. But, perhaps, if we work together, Destoria can become something better than it has ever been."

"Cheers to that," Arias raised his goblet.

Vervaine smiled and continued, "The Ravoltians of Asera allegedly have a method of melting down precious metals and using the liquid to bind broken pottery back together. Those marbled pieces are sold at the market for exponentially more than if they'd never been broken. It is an art form that takes something useless and fractured and makes it whole again with an end result far more valuable than before. They call the process *iugo*. Today, *we* are the craftsmen molding a new Destoria. Let us iugo. Let us bind together in our brokenness and make this land more valuable and prosperous than anyone ever dreamed."

The council members murmured, the room now buzzing with slight optimism.

Arias smiled across the table at Vervaine, beaming at her gentle approach. He slapped the ewanian next to him on the back. "Alvanak, why don't you go ahead and read us the first item on tonight's agenda?"

Alvanak's slit eyes blinked a few times, and he lifted his parchment with a trembling hand. His sack pulsed quickly, and he reached into his pocket, tugging out a vial of pearlescent black-and-gold liquid.

Beneath the table, Arias grabbed his hand and held it tightly. He leaned toward the ewanian's ear holes and whispered, "Your path diverges here, my friend. Will you strafe left and keep falling down that burrow? Or will you take the harder path, the one that is right?" With his red eyes, he motioned to the dikeeka bottle in Alvanak's shiny fingers.

"While that vile, hallucinogenic sludge is still legal... *for now*... you, sir, are a representative of Destoria and of this palace, which has been embarrassed enough by those that have come before us, has it not?"

Alvanak nodded with reluctance. With a tremoring hand, he tucked the vial away and slapped a slick finger against the first artfully scrawled sentence on his list. He stared at the onyx ink and felt the unpleasant shakes from detoxification ripple through him. "Item... one... We must... discuss whether or not further aid is required for the scorched city of Adum."

Helga stood, using her mighty calf muscles to shove her chair back with ease. Her breasts poured out of the top of her leather cuirass. "Adum of Bellaneau is in great need of aid, your majesties. This humble town, ravaged by fires we now know were set by the Emerald Bandits at Exos's command, is in the process of being restored to its former glory. As you know, it is the oldest city in the isle, and the population is slowly returning from being displaced along the outskirts, where they've been living in temporary huts and hovels. We humbly ask for lumberjacks to help us chop and for some of the royal wagon masters to deliver the shorn trunks from the Donik Forest back to town so that the locals can continue to rebuild the homes there."

"Done," Arias said firmly.

"There is a skilled family who could assemble a shipment of axes in bulk in Wannik if you'd like to use some money for the treasury for a bulk purchase of implements. For six hundred gold, I could ensure a hundred of them are on a wagon to Odeta in a week," Sabet volunteered.

"Yes," Vervaine said quickly. "Deal. And Helga, we will send you with enough gold to assemble a team of cutters in Odeta."

"Thank you, your majesty," Helga said.

"Alvanak, make sure you take note," Arias said, nudging the ewanian's quill.

"Yes, your majesty." Alvanak scribbled it all down and then read the next item. "Silvercrest wants to discuss manpower in regards to defending against the scourge."

Guarin rose to address the akiah king. "Your majesty, I humbly ask on behalf of Silvercrest that you allow an extension so that the enforcers you so *generously* sent two months ago can remain in place to ensure this menace remains at bay. At least... until we have some sort of assurance that the last of the Emerald Bandits the former queen dispatched have been incarcerated. We don't wish to see a repeat of the devastation that our friends to the south are dealing with." He pointed to Helga.

Arias nodded. "That is wise. The twelve guards we sent already may remain in place. I will dispatch another six to join them this week to assist with shift duties and patrols."

"Thank you, your majesty." Guarin sat, relieved.

Alvanak let out an involuntary croak, "Our next order of business... Taernsby is formally requesting immediate and substantial aid in the form of more food rations and noubald milk."

"Aid granted," Vervaine said. "Seven hundred gold from the treasury to import bananas, nuts, pineapple, and coffee exports from Wyl Isle."

"Of course, m'lady," Nynal said with a nod.

"Take one thousand for various bulk vegetables to the farmers in Bellaneau. Whatever's in season. Whatever they have in reserves. Potatoes and such."

"Of course. We had an exceptional wheat harvest this year," Helga bragged, "so perhaps some flour and bread as well?"

"Yes," Vervaine said. She turned to Kleego. "We will give eight hundred gold to Obsidian ranchers. Have them load up some noubalds in crates for harpy transport. They can milk them once they arrive and then butcher them fresh after they've dispersed through Taernsby."

"Yes, Queen Brius," Kleego said with a respectful nod.

"Thank you, merciful queen!" Sabet exclaimed.

Arias pointed to the quichyrd, "This isle is tired of bailing Taernsby out time after time, though. Get it together, Sabet. We will not keep pouring money into your causes. You are a wound on this isle that won't stop bleeding."

"Next on the agenda is another request from Silvercrest regarding the Emerald Bandits as well." Alvanak stuck his slick palms together and pulled them apart repeatedly, waiting a while in silence for someone to speak.

Guarin cleared his throat, terribly nervous. "There has been a resurgence of criminal bandit activity as of late."

"These damned bandits are the bane of my existence..." Arias stared at Vervaine. "The bandits are one of the last tethers this isle has to Exos. They have raped, pillaged, and slaughtered innocent Destorians. The people of Silvercrest must be protected. What do you need from us, Guarin?"

"Guards and patrolmen. I'm afraid we don't have nearly enough. Robberies are becoming frequent, both in homes and on the main thoroughfares."

"How many men do you need?"

"One hundred royal guards, ideally."

"We don't have a hundred. After the ones we are assigning to Adum, we have roughly fifty left. You can have those."

"No, he can't, Arias." Vervaine clenched her fists under the table at the unilateral decision. "We don't have enough people to send royal guards to both provinces and still protect Willowdale."

"Yes, what about Willowdale? You'll leave us exposed and vulnerable," Ives said.

Helga scrunched her large, barbarian face. "That's not fair! You gave us *six,* and you're giving them *fifty*?"

"No, we gave you six *more*... for a single *town* with little in it in need of protection," Arias hollered. "Silvercrest is *vast*. Fifty men are surely only a dent with how widespread everything is!"

"Arias!" Vervaine snapped. "Our militia will be too dispersed to be effective here in Desdemona if a large threat arises. We must keep some men on reserve here in Willowdale."

"We don't need them *here*, Vervaine," Arias said.

"Yes, we do! This palace was already attacked once? Or do you not *remember*?" Her eyes flashed something deeper, something *angrier*, in hopes that he'd recall that he gave the ultimate sacrifice -- his life -- and forever forfeited his freedom during the siege.

"Perhaps," Kleego began, his voice uneasy, trying to cut through the tension, "you could use some of the treasury money from the dikeeka distribution to incentivise more of the younger or poorer Destorian citizens to join your royal ranks."

Arias sighed. "That wouldn't be wise."

"Why?" Vervaine asked, a hint of obsolescence in her tone. "It sounds like a perfectly reasonable solution to me."

Arias gripped his goblet and gulped down the remaining wine inside. He returned it to the table with an emphatic *thud*. "Soldiers have to be able to depend on each other. They have to be trained. Shaped.

So that when one man sleeps, the other knows instinctively to keep a watchful eye. It's what keeps good, hard-working men *safe*. If you start a conscription that floods the ranks with a bunch of ill-trained fools, our army weakens. They are stronger as a small, skilled unit."

Vervaine looked up at the ceiling.

Arias shot a glance her way. "I take it you disagree?"

"I think we might be at an impasse for now on this matter."

"For what it's worth, Arias, I agree with you," Nynal said.

"Oh, what do you know of the ways of war. You're a woman. You'll never see combat." Guarin scoffed and looked around. "*This* is why I petitioned that the Wyl Isle's representative should not have a seat at this table! It's not even a providence! You're a pathetic, lonely little island. A tropical vacation destination where you pick the tourists' pockets all damned day! Meanwhile, my opinion somehow holds the same weight as *yours,* even though my province makes up a quarter of the isle!"

"You men always think everything of yours is bigger than it really is," the snow-white wyl said slyly. "I have just as much a right to be here as *you*, a concept that is somehow still *foreign* to an amphibious *prick* like yourself."

"You know what *isn't* foreign to me?"

"What?"

"How good a *wyl* pelt feels as a stool-removal tool when cleaning one's *backside* in the latrine!"

Several people at the table erupted into argumentative chatter, jabbing fingers in the direction of one another.

Vervaine and Arias remained silent, their gaze locked through the chaos, daring the other to cave on their decision first.

As the meeting unraveled, Alvanak looked down at the list of remaining items on the parchment in his vibrating hands. It was likely none of the rest would see any resolution today.

8

The Lost City of Elathia
The Radiant Sea

The small aquatic army dragged Quistix, Twitch, and Aurora through the current to the far outskirts of the merfolk's city. Twitch tugged his arms and growled, feeling the resistance of the octopus's tentacles wrapped around each wrist. Several more suction-cupped arms constricted his chest.

"Are these restraints really *necessary*?"

As if to shut him up, the thick barb of a sea urchin thrust up through the tattered fabric of Twitch's pants, piercing the fur-covered meat of his butt. The wyl yowled, bubbled screams making their miles-long trek to the white-capped surface above.

"Hey! Watch it, you little spiky bastard," he yelled, looking over his shoulder. "You were an *inch away* from the two of us being *far* more intimate than you might have intended, you little degenerate."

"Twitch, *shut up*," Quistix grumbled. "I'm trying to think. I know that's not something *you* commonly do..."

"What?! That thing almost just went up *inside* me!"

Quistix glared at him from the clutches of another tentacle, her gills flapping angrily. She craned her neck until the muscles burned. A large gray shark circled inches behind her, its eerie teeth forming a haunting smile that made her blood run cold.

Aurora spoke now, her neck encircled by the extremities of a translucent squid, the body of which dragged lazily through the sand in resignation, unable to hold the esteg still. “We might be the only thing that speaks any sort of language down here. Strangely, these creatures seem far more intelligent than texts have implied. Although shockingly little has been written about sea life.”

Twitch wriggled and the octopus twisted, driving the wyl’s snout down into the sand. As a cloud of particles settled slowly around him, he wheezed to regain the air that had been forced from his lungs. “What... was that for?”

The squid dragged the esteg with all of its might into the murky darkness. The octopus whipped its tentacles playfully like an organic carousel, spinning Quistix and Twitch in circle after circle.

“I’m going to be sick,” Twitch burbled.

The glowing fish with the underbite and the school of glitter guppies retreated, darkening the ocean’s depths once again.

The squid released its hold on Aurora and squirted a cloud of jet-black ink. Aurora squinted in the darkness.

Then, seemingly out of nowhere, the octopus's tentacles detached from them with a series of wet pops and slipped away, sending Twitch and Quistix shooting through the water like loosed arrows.

Almost as if they were a singular jellied mass, the aquatic creatures jetted backwards toward the city orbs of the merfolk town in the distance.

Quistix and Twitch felt their surroundings change. The water became a huge pocket of open air. All-over pressure turned into lightness and gravity. Aurora followed through the almost imperceptible barrier.

The group gasped for air and choked as their newfound gills sealed closed again, leaving jagged parallel seams of pink flesh along their necks. Twitch recuperated first, stumbling onto the pads of his clawed feet in the sandy darkness, no longer swimming.

"Where are we?" Twitch sputtered.

"I can barely see a thing!" Aurora sounded panicked.

Twitch dusted the sand from his soaked pants and helped Quistix up from the pebble-laden ground. They scanned the area.

They were in some kind of underwater dome, from the looks of it. Water was suspended, flowing around the translucent, rounded ceiling-like barrier far above them. They watched a school of confused glitterfish bump into the see-through boundary and glance off, unperturbed.

"Hello?" Twitch shouted into the center as they trekked. From the sound of his voice echoing, the space was far more vast than he'd realized.

Aurora whispered, eyes wide with wonderment. "*By the Gods... I think... we're in... Flathia*!"

"What exactly is Elathia?" Twitch studied Aurora's dumbstruck expression through the dim blue.

"Quistix. You've heard of it, right?" Aurora's tone was almost pleading, tinged with a hint of desperation for a spark of recognition. "The dilapidated underwater city?"

Quistix shook her head. "Never heard of it."

Aurora stomped her hoof, shattering the thin layer of fragile sand dollar shells beneath. "The lost city of Elathia!" Her ears flicked with frustration. "You know, the city cast down into the watery depths from the fringes of Hope Harbor?"

"No, I just said I've never heard of it," Quistix stared, a look of irritation on her face. Her citrine eyes lit up in the muddy blue air.

"For years, it is said that quakes shook the coast, causing fissures in the land. One day, decades back, one of the wizards from the Institution of Magic in Apex began to feud with a band of amateur experimental magic weavers."

"Ohhh!" Twitch glanced at Quistix and nodded, his eyes telling her to play along. "Elathia. And the wizard weaver things. Of course. Surely *everyone* has heard of that little tiff."

"You're mocking me."

"I would never do such a thing." Twitch couldn't hide his smile.

Aurora narrowed her eyes and turned away. She trotted slowly toward the worn stone buildings of the small city inside the bubble.

"I'm sorry we don't stay buried in books, like you." Twitch hopped up onto a bench made out of driftwood and playfully landed down in the sand again, sending a plume of blue-tinted particles all around him.

"I would wager a bet that you can't even read," Aurora sassed, never looking back at him.

"I'm more of a numbers guy. If you need the contents of a coin purse counted while running from authorities, I'm your wyl."

"This city was only a fable, according to the books in the Apex library. A made-up bedtime story to tell young wizards. Now, I see that it exists."

Aurora gazed at it. Bone-white stone pillars propped up decaying flotsam roofs. Patchy strips of degraded seaweed adhered to the outer walls of some of the structures, drooping like lace streamers. Shriveled coral chairs looked so delicate and fragile that a gust of wind might cause them to fracture into pieces.

"*This place looks abandoned,*" Aurora whispered to herself as she wove between crumbling homes of the underwater wasteland. "If no one is here, how is this bubble dome being maintained?"

Twitch clicked his tongue on the roof of his mouth. "We should see if—"

"*Shhh*!" Quistix held her hand up to shut the wyl up again, a motion almost reflexive after travelling with him for so many weeks.

Twitch put his fists on his hips. "Rude."

Quistix stared out, her yellow eyes fluttering from one worn building to the next. Shifting his ears, Twitch listened, finally hearing the noise that had captured Quistix's attention. It was the faint sound of a squawking bird in distress. Quistix led the way, waving for the others to follow. Slightly crouched, she walked silently toward the sound, her old assassin ways ingrained. She avoided the brittle seashells and dried seaweed on the path. She crept closer to a somewhat-preserved stone building.

The sharp sound of breaking glass and mad giggles rang out, making her flinch.

"Wait! Stop!" yelled a fearful, feminine voice.

Quistix approached a window, one with the warm amber of flickering light oozing out into the sapphire-blue atmosphere of the dry dome around them.

Twitch rose onto the tips of his hind toes and peered inside the stone house. Through the glowing haze, he saw a room that looked like it was being ravaged by a tornado. Swirls of torn paper and knick-knacks swirled in a cyclone in the air. Small flames waggled and waved against the scorch-marked walls.

In the corner, a petite woman with strawberry-blonde hair was hunched down, protecting her face with dainty human hands.

In the center of the stone room, a fire raged, the cyclonic winds whipping it into a tall, frenzied spike of glowing heat and light. Behind it, an old man with a long white beard cackled like mad, his arms raised as if to heighten the flames.

"Get some water to put out that fire. I'm going in!"

"Why?!"

"To save the girl!" Quistix barked, her irises flashing white with panic and fury.

Twitch looked around at the coral furniture and shelled streets around them. "Right! Of course. Any idea where I might find some?"

Quistix's alarmed expression turned annoyed. "Right now? You wanna make this joke *right now*?" She groaned and stormed off before he could reply. She climbed onto a cluttered pile of wood and crab traps and made her way in through the window furthest from the flames.

Twitch shrugged at Aurora and started looking for a container in the jetsam littering the building's lawn. "Humor is how I handle stress!"

Finally, he found a worn wooden bucket sitting half-submerged in the sand. Snatching its rope handle, he yanked it out and dumped the contents. It reeked with a noxious odor that made Twitch's eyes water. "Ugh! Smells like a latrine." He covered his snout with the crook of an arm. "This'll do, I think."

As Aurora rooted through the pile looking for another container, Twitch raced over to the bubble's perimeter on the outer edges of the city.

He shoved the bucket through the barrier. Tiny bubbles and frigid water tickled the pads of his hands. Once the bucket was full, he pulled it back through the boundary only to watch the water slink sideways over the top of the bucket and back out of the bubble into the ocean outside until it was empty again.

"What the...?" Twitch tried again.

And again.

Each time, the water seeped back out of the bucket, through the wall of the bubble, flowing back into the ocean outside. Frustrated, Twitch threw down the bucket and sprinted back to the house.

From the sizzling stone floor near the window, Quistix watched the saggy-skinned wizard swirling his arms over his head to music no one seemed to hear but him. His white, curly hair puffed wild in every direction with static. His unkempt beard swished across the chest of his robe. Between them, a whirlwind of flaming paper raged toward the vaulted ceiling.

"What sort of magic should we use for this?" Aurora asked through the window. "Ice to freeze him? A spell to slow time, perhaps? Oh, no, you don't know that one yet." She shook her horned head. Then, she gasped. "Oh! What about the summoned wave spell?"

"Yes! That one you taught me. Let's see if I can remember how to do it." Quistix held her hands up, eyes flashing platinum as she attempted to produce the swell of a wave from the ground.

"*Vocare fluctus*!" she chanted.

A fireball whizzed past her face, and she ducked. No water appeared.

She held her hands out again, training her eyes on her own hands. "*Vocare fluctus*!"

Nothing.

The tingling vibration she felt when summoning elements never came.

"Occasional magical dysfunction is perfectly normal," Aurora said reassuringly. "It's nothing to be ashamed about."

Quistix pressed two fingers to her mouth and let out an eardrum-piercing whistle to get the old man's attention off the towering flame.

The wizard spun toward her, robe opening wide as he swiveled.

"How about you take a rest, old man?" Quistix pointed to the fire.

"Ah, a direct approach. Sure. Let's try asking politely over performing magic," Aurora said sarcastically. "That'll work." The esteg rolled her eyes and pulled her head out of the window.

The wizard stared at Quistix blankly. "Was that... an esteg? You brought an esteg here? How?!"

The flying papers and odd knick-knacks fell to the floor in an instant. Glass shattered, wood clattered, and scorched books thudded to the ground.

The giant flame lowered to the height of a fading campfire. The woman huddling in the corner slowly stood.

"What do you mean, *how did I bring her here*? We were *sent* here by Madam Aerendyl. Isn't she your friend? Or is there another wizard down here that we should know about?"

Quistix glanced down at the gleaming, wrinkled skin exposed through the center of his open robe and grimaced.

"Friend? I suppose you could say that. I mean, as much as *any* person can truly call another such an abstract thing. Where does the true bond lie in friendship? Is it in loyalty? Trust? Companionship?"

The huddled woman studied Quistix from across the room as the wizard rambled on, picking up items off the floor and examining their scorch marks with fascination and curiosity.

"Emma is more than a mere friendly acquaintance. I consider her family as much as one of my own daughters." He said, dazed, wobbling on his feet. He held up a burned book. "Who did this? Hmmm? This tome is ancient and very valuable. Someone has some explaining to do!"

"*You* did it, Grandfather," the woman in the corner said.

"What? That's preposterous! I would never!"

Quistix scrunched her dirty, salt-encrusted eyebrows. "We just watched you."

The wizard scoffed and set the book down on a pile of others with a thud. "What were we talking about again?"

"Madam Aerendyl," an all too familiar pair of voices bellowed from the doorway. Brilliant blue flames painted the bricks in the blackened hallway at head height.

Recognizing the sinister voice immediately, Quistix reached over her shoulder for *Swordbreaker*, feeling its absence like a heavy loss. She'd forgotten that the guards had stripped her of it.

"I swear to the Gods if that is *you*, Omen..." She clenched her fists, body stiffening.

Omen's voices chuckled as his eternally-youthful face appeared out of the darkness, his features illuminated by the perpetual blue flames that danced on its surface.

"Omen!" The blonde in the corner raced to him, wrapping his leather-clad torso in a tight hug. He squeezed her back, careful not to set her blonde curls ablaze with his flaming chin.

He smiled at Quistix as the petite woman pulled away. "Good evening, Ms. Daedumal. I figured you would have gone running to step-mommy the first time you were in a pinch. Still, it's a pleasure to see you, especially this far below the surface."

"I never forget a face, but in your case, I wish I could make an exception," she spat, disgust oozing through her tone.

Omen snickered. "Aren't you the *least* bit curious how I knew she was your kin?"

"I would, but I wouldn't be able to understand you. Both of your voices seem to spew nothing but nonsense."

"How rude." He took a step toward her. "I risked a lot to help you defeat the queen. How soon we forget!"

"Exos is dead and buried. What is not forgotten, however, is everything else you've done, you treacherous bastard."

"Pfft. Feels like eons ago."

Twitch climbed through the window and sat on the sill. He threw his head back the moment he recognized Omen. "Oh, by-the-freaking-Gods. Not *you* again!"

Twitch turned his head, his furry ears flattening as he saw the wizard's open robe. "Sir, cinch your robe! *Ladies* are present." His eyes locked on the attractive strawberry-blonde behind Omen. He flashed his most charming smile and waved.

She smiled and blushed a little. Her blue eyes rivaled the beauty of the ocean surrounding them. Her freckles were like speckled constellations. Her reddened cheeks were streaked with tears that seemed to stop at a set of full lips.

The wizard looked down at his exposed privates and grumbled, “Gah! This damn thing won’t stay tied!” He staggered through a door leading to a long hallway. “Come, come.” He waved for them to follow. “I’m parched. Time for tea.”

As Quistix unlocked the front door to allow Aurora entry, Twitch approached the mysterious beauty, feeling like he was walking on clouds to get to her. “My dear, are you alright? Are you hurt?”

“I’m... fine.” She flashed a brilliant smile. “What is it with magic wielders throwing such destructive tantrums?”

He snickered and motioned to Quistix. “I know what you mean. I’ve been dealing with this temperamental sorceress for months. It certainly keeps life... *exciting*.”

Twitch held a crooked arm out to escort her. She slipped her hand around it, and Twitch felt a zing of energy in her touch. He searched her sapphire eyes for the answer to the question burning in his mind. “I know you, don’t I?”

Her delicate, freckled cheeks rose over another arresting smile. "I don't believe so. I'm Violet."

"Twitch."

"Peculiar moniker."

"I suppose."

Omen forced a hip and shoulder between the two, rudely pushing their bodies apart. "Violet is my sister."

Twitch didn't respond. He just followed Violet and Omen down the hall, quietly fuming.

"Seems grandfather cast a portal to summon us both, Omen said to Violet. "Maybe the old fart is getting lonely."

"Did Aerendyl send you to help my grandfather?" Violet asked Twitch over her shoulder, voice hopeful.

Quistix spoke for him. "She did."

Her eyes lowered to a piece of sea glass on the ground. It glinted blue, reflecting the flames of Omen's face.

"I'm not surprised she came to us, either. Practically begging. I know we are well-known, but the neediness never seems to stop when you're as legendary as we are," Twitch boasted, glaring at the back of Omen's leather cuirass. "Nope. No problem too big or too small. Need someone evil slain? We are the ones to summon, whether it be a bandit or a queen."

"*Twitch*," Quistix warned.

Twitch continued, trying to agitate Omen and impress Violet simultaneously. "Need order restored to an entire isle? We've got you covered. We're the... harbingers of hope, the... legends of the land, the... four knights of justice."

"*Three*," Aurora said solemnly.

They walked the rest of the hallway in silence.

Frok's absence left a deep well of pain in them all.

Quistix leaned over Violet's shoulder and spoke lowly near her ear. "Your grandfather. Is he *always* like this?"

Violet shook her head, worried. "No. Something is wrong with him. He's normally a humble, brilliant man. Sharp as a tack. Not… whatever this is."

"Is he drunk?"

"I can't say for certain, but I don't think so. Although, to be honest, I've never seen him imbibe anything beyond water or tea. He usually likes to keep his wits about him."

The wizard stepped out from behind a dressing curtain, twisting the toggles on his tunic into place. The pale color of it exacerbated his gaunt complexion and the stormy circles beneath his dazed eyes.

Violet gasped and buried her face in Omen's chest. "Grandfather!"

"Yes, my love?"

"The tunic is… is lovely, but how about some pants now?"

As though he was completely unaware he had been naked from the waist down, he glanced down at his bare legs. "Huh! Would you look at that!" Diving back behind the privacy curtain again, he grumbled, "You know, for years I was able to walk around naked as the day I was born!"

Violet turned to Aurora. "Estegs can heal, right?"

Aurora nodded.

"Can you heal my eyes? They'll never be the same after seeing that."

Twitch barked out a laugh and slapped his knee. "Oh, I like *her*."

Quistix looked at Aurora, no trace of a smile on her face. "Any idea what's wrong with him?"

Aurora watched the wizard wobble clumsily out from the curtain, this time with billowy pants on. He struggled to tie them at the waist. Aurora watched him botch the simple task repeatedly. "Not yet. I'll watch and try to assess what is ailing him, but estegs cannot read minds." She turned her head toward Violet and took two steps. The sound of her hooves echoed off the cavernous space. "Has your grandfather recently received a violent blow to the head?"

"Hey, I'm old, not *deaf*." Swaying, the wizard still continued to struggle with a simple bow tie. "You could talk right to me. I'm right here," he said, shaking the ties in frustration.

"Screw it." He tied the strings into a double knot. He shuffled off into a space that resembled a kitchen. "Great. I'll have to cut these off later."

"Are you feeling alright?" Violet asked, approaching him cautiously. "You gave me a scare back there."

"Yes! Of course! In fact, I've never felt better," he slurred. "I'm *free*! *Pain*-free, *terror*-free... For the first time in decades, I feel at peace! Perhaps I have simply transformed into a being of higher intelligence, my mind ascending to a new plane of reality. After all, we are merely fluctuating tangles of thoughts in walking, talking *meat bags*." He wobbled over to Quistix, looked her up and down, and stuck out his hand. "Irenas Parnix. Former

Professor at the Institute of Magic there in… in… in…”

“Apex,” Aurora volunteered.

He smiled. “What’s in Apex?”

“The… Institute,” Aurora said, confused.

“Institute of what?”

“Of… magic.” Aurora looked at Quistix.

“It’s a pleasure,” the half-elf said as she shook his hand. “I’m Quistix. The esteg is Aurora. And the mouth that doesn’t ever stop running over there is Twitch.”

“This is my granddaughter, Violet.”

“Yes, we met already.”

“And this is sort of my honorary grandson, Omen.”

“We are *well* acquainted, sir.” She couldn’t help but growl a little when she said it, her eyes flashing white as she looked at Omen’s flaming face.

“So you two aren’t really related?” Twitch pointed at Violet and Omen.

She laughed. “No, but we’re basically family. He’s been like a brother to me since I was born.”

“I was going to say, there’s no resemblance. You’re a stunning goddess, and he looks like a tundra goblin that has been perpetually lit on fire,” Twitch said, flashing Omen a cocky smile.

Irenas Parnix continued on as if he hadn’t heard the insult. “Omen and I have worked for decades down here, trying to lift that blasted curse of his. Obviously, my efforts have been unsuccessful. But at least the water down here can offer him a reprieve from the pain.”

Eyes slightly squinting in sympathy, Quistix looked away from Omen. “Maybe we can help, Irenas. Maybe we can get to the bottom of what is making you... like *this*.”

“Like *what*?” He chuckles. “I’m fantastic! Stupendous. Never better. A person can change, can’t they? ‘*Where the waves drift, my soul shall follow. Ever drifting, ever changing, transcending beyond comprehension.'* So, Violet, what makes you believe anything is *wrong* with me?"

Violet let out an exasperated sigh. "Well, for starters, your pants are on backwards and inside out."

He glanced down and plucked at the fabric. Then, he erupted in another cackle followed by a fit of giggles. "Ah! So they are."

Violet turned to Quistix. "I think you've come just in time. He was well a month ago when I last visited. This can not simply be from the ravages of time on his mind, but, instead, from something else."

Behind her, a crash sounded. The wizard took a tumble, stumbling into a pile of pots and pans and crashing down on the floor. Violet gasped. Parnix flopped onto his back and lay motionless. He stared at the ceiling as if its worn surface contained the most beautiful piece of artwork the world had ever seen.

Omen had stepped closer. "I'm afraid I must ask for your help, too. Seeing him like this..." He looked away, emotional. "Violet and him... they are all I have left in this world. They may not be my own flesh and blood, but Irenas Parnix took me in when no one else would. Whatever you can do to *fix* this... I promise, you have my full support and gratitude."

Quistix chewed her lip and looked down at the floor. "I know all too well what it's like to watch your family slip away. I wouldn't wish it on anyone. Even a monster like *you*."

Omen turned to her. "Perhaps we can start fresh, on level footing this time. Deal?"

He stuck out his flaming blue hand. She took it, feeling the heat seep into her. Her irises lightened and she tugged him close to threaten him quietly. "Rest assured, I forget nothing."

"Fair enough," he said with a smile, looking down at their clasped hands, lingering in the heat of each other's grasp for a little too long.

She finally slipped her hand from his and straightened her posture. She glanced down at the old man on the floor, who now had a mobile of pots floating in a circle a few feet above his head. "Let's see if we can find the source of this nonsense before we all end up as mad as a rabid raakaby."

9

Dungeon of the Ruby Palace
Desdemona, Willowdale

Werner's spotted landigo fur glistened in the firelight that found its way into the metal bars of his cell. He tossed and turned, his subconscious tainted with the unshakable image of Duke Grayson's small thumbs puncturing the eyes of Dacus, a human he considered a close friend after years of faithful service together on the Destorian Royal Council. The memory of the man's screams haunted his dreams and made him shoot up from the wet hay panting, just like he did every night. He sobbed and licked his teeth, teeth that claimed lives the night he fell from grace. He swore he could still taste the metallic tang of blood.

Through tear-filled eyes, he balled his trembling paws into fists and pummeled the lumpy hay in a fit of fury. As his knuckles made contact with the cold stone beneath, he barely registered the pain. He punched until his hands bled, the skin beneath the fur splitting wide.

Something strange was in the air tonight, something beyond the normal self-pity and rage. He held his busted fist up and watched, stunned. As if by magic, his wounds closed, the skin slipping back into place, the fluids seeping back into the cracks and seams. His tired feline eyes darted around until he spotted a tall shadow, something even darker than the nearly opaque blackness in the corner of the cell.

"Who's there?!"

The shadow shifted, and a beak slid out of the patch of dark and into the dim firelight. Her green eyes illuminated the black feathers surrounding it. "I would lose my mind in these four walls."

Werner scoffed and wiped his tears on the short fur of his forearm.

"I have been imprisoned myself," she said. "I have been confined to cells and underground lairs, forced to skulk about for decades as one of Desdemona's best-kept secrets. Rarely feeling the warmth of the sun or the mercy of a cool breeze. No one to talk to. Just stone, dirt, straw, and misery."

More tears dribbled down the landigo's wide snout, cheekbones more pronounced from malnutrition, eyes hollow and sunken in his once-regal leopard-like face. "If you are here to gloat, you can save it. The guards do a fine enough job of breaking my spirit. There is nothing left in me to be broken. Now please, whoever you are, leave me to die in peace. "

"Ah," she cawed, moving closer. "Horrible people can do good deeds. Good people are capable of vicious ones, too. Where does the line lie, hmmm? What is the difference between the martyr and the monster?"

The quichyrd stepped out of the shadows a little more, her green eyes brightening.

"What makes you so deserving of a barbaric punishment such as this, hmm?"

Werner wasn't sure what answer she was fishing for, but he wasn't about to give her a graphic recap of the violent slaughter that landed him in the dungeon for life. The mere thought of that fateful night made his stomach roil. "My punishment fits the crime, unfortunately."

Ceosteol shook her feathered head. "Just like beauty, right and wrong are in the eye of the beholder. Murder is wrong to some, unless it is on the battlefield. Giving money to the homeless is seen as kind by some. That is, unless it's the coin he needs to get him the dose of dikeeka that finally kills him. They say all lives end, Werner. But what if I told you," her knobby knees creaked as she tightened her plum robe and lowered down onto the hay in front of him, "*they don't have to*?"

"Get away with your nonsense. I have no patience for games of the mind. If you wish to have a battle of wits and speak in riddles, I urge you to go down the hall to the professor around the corner who never stops talking and, just... leave me be."

Ceosteol placed a hand on the torn fabric of his knee, squeezing slightly, fighting the urge to sink her claws into his fur-covered flesh. "No, none of that. I'm here because I want to offer you a chance to redeem yourself, to be free of these chains."

"If this is a prank, it is a sick one, you old bird." Werner narrowed his eyes.

"It's true."

"How? Can you take me back in time to the night before I took lives in anger? Before Due Greyson gouged out Dacus's eyeballs with his thumbs? I am a *murderer*. I am not meant to be free. If I am to believe in a just world worthy of being a part of, then this is where someone like *me* belongs."

She tilted her head, her green glowing eyes somehow seeming closer to him with every passing second. "You do not believe in redemption?"

"A heart for a heart. A life for a life. When order is lost, all that is left is *chaos*."

The room seemed to pitch, throwing him off balance.

"Then let us restore order. You see, Werner, I could use someone like you by my side."

"Why?"

"Because you know the politics of Destoria. You know all the little secrets of the people who run this isle. I need this information."

"I don't understand."

"I see a different future for this isle, one where things are accepted that aren't right now."

"Like what? Exos already made dikeeka legal, if that's what you're talking about."

"Exos was greedy. She did that to fill the treasury to fund her ridiculous whims. I'm talking about something that hasn't been allowed in ages."

Werner thought for a moment. Then it dawned on him. "Dark magic." He said it as a statement, not a question. A revelation.

"At my age, I am wise in ways you can't even imagine, but I know your loyalty in this could lead to your redemption."

"I have nothing to offer you. I have no desire to add being a traitor to my list of sins. At least if I die here, I can salvage a modicum of dignity."

Ceosteol stood abruptly, the skirt of her robe grazing his soiled legs. She laughed. "Gnomes, barbarians, ewanians, landigos... you're all the same. It's always about *dignity*. Your whole identity hinges on an illusion of your morals and legacy." She snickered. "Legacy. That's a funny thing. Sometimes it's a reputation or an accomplishment. Other times it's a wife and kids."

She started to walk back into the shadowed corner.

Werner's chains jingled as he rose to his feet. "Wait! If I were to... help you. Would I... ever get to see my family again?"

She turned and doubled over with laughter. When she stood, she wiped a tear from her eye with the sleeve of her purple robe. "Of course. I'm not a *monster*."

10

The Ruby Palace
Desdemona, Willowdale

"Why do I feel as if a chasm has formed between us? And why does it feel like it is widening?" Arias whispered, rocketing from the council chambers after his wife. They were growling their way through another disagreement, this time over tariffs.

Vervaine flung open the door to the chef's kitchen, a place rarely frequented by royalty, so they'd be far less likely to be followed. "I'm surprised a brute like you has a word like *chasm* in your vocabulary, you *oaf*."

Arias slammed the door shut behind them, the wood booming against the jamb. Turning around, half a dozen commoners in the kitchen gawked at the altercation, dusted with flour, glistening with sweat. One even had what Arias *hoped* was a tomato sauce and not noubald blood across his apron.

"Please, everyone, leave us!" Arias demanded.

The stunned scullions darted out of the room, leaving one small boy standing on an upturned bucket beside the stone washbasin.

A wyl spun around, nodded at the akiah king, snatched the boy up, and carried him out. "My apologies, your majesties. Take as long as you need."

Once they were alone, Arias clasped Vervaine's hand in his. "Darling, I may be a brute, but I am your brute. I am here to protect you and our people. It has been my duty since I signed up for the royal guard as a mere *squire*. I have not changed since the day you laid eyes on me. Why, suddenly, has all of this become an issue?"

Vervaine took a step back and touched the lapel of his jacket. "I love you today just as much as I did when I was that little girl hopelessly smitten with this noble akiah soldier. But you are no longer the head of the guard. You are a *king*. Diplomacy and common sense must prevail over brawn and military might."

He seethed with sarcasm. "Ah, yes, *many* a vicious battle has been won by the kings and queens sitting on cushioned thrones talking about *taxation* all day."

Vervaine peered up into her husband's burgundy eyes for what felt like the first time in days. "Is... that... what you *think* of me? That I'm just some spoiled heiress? That I'm pretentious and lazy? Do you think that I've been locked in some ivory tower all of my life, away from the plight of the commoner, oblivious to the scourge around me?"

"Of course not," he said, softening his tone.

"When I was growing up, you saw every split lip, every skinned knee, my burns... You did nothing."

"Vervaine, I had a *job* to do. A royal guard is not there to bandage a child's skinned knee."

"You saw me dragged away and you did nothing." Her voice was full of ire. "You stopped *none* of it. Now you're acting like you're some protector all of the sudden." She jabbed her finger at the door. "You act like you care more about them than you ever did about me. How am I to trust you can keep *anyone* safe when every scar on my body was seen by your eyes first?" She shoved his chest, but his toned legs never budged, unaffected by her show of force.

His jaw tightened. He listened, letting her voice erode his resolve like caustic acid. Hearing this from her perfect lips made him feel weak and small. He leaned against a stone block island covered in flour and rolled dough. "You're right. Of all the blood I have shed, not enough of it was for you. I should have protected you. I should have done something. I know that I failed you. Over and over and over. I'm responsible for so much death. I deserve to burn in the Nether for eternity for all of it. But for some reason, you love me despite it all. I don't know what I did to deserve you. Frankly, I *don't* deserve you. But I am yours. If I could go back and absorb every one of Master Tempest's beatings myself, I would. Your father had my loyalty. He saved my life when the mobs wanted to disembowel people like me. But the first time I saw him raise a hand, I should've killed him then, like I had wanted to in my very *soul*. I could have stopped decades of pain and destruction for many with such a sacrifice. But I didn't. I was a fool. I was weak. I did *nothing*. I *had* nothing. I belonged *nowhere*. I followed orders with spineless obedience. I vow to you, Vervaine, that as long as I draw breath, I will not stop trying to right that wrong."

He cupped her cheek in his hand. "We have a voice now. And if we stay a strong, unified front, we can stop Ceosteol from doing to others what that mad quichyrd did to us. Together, we can rescue innocent people, people who should never have to see the dark side of life, as *we* have. We can make this isle a place of harmony and peace." He snickered. "Listen to me, a warrior speaking of peace."

Vervaine smiled at him for the first time in days as the fight left her body, draining from her like an uncorked cask of resentment and anger. Her shoulders lowered.

"The tallest-reaching trees still need strong roots to ground them. While you reach for the Sanctum, I can anchor you. I vow to give you everything I have to give. From this day on, I vow to make things right with how I failed you in the past."

He extended his hand toward her, his hand waiting in the air between them. She took it. Arias pulled her in close.

"I'll tell the cooks to return and, then, in a bit, we can go for a long walk in the garden, just like we used to in Obsidia. You, bookworm, should grab one of those hardcovers in the tower and read to me like the old days."

She nodded. "I'd like that. I'll choose one with a lot of battles and bloodshed for you."

He groaned and grabbed her, speaking lowly into her now-healed ear. "I'll meet you at the courtyard entrance in half an hour. I'll assign some guards to keep watch. Nothing says *romance* quite like being surrounded by a bunch of sweaty, voyeuristic men in armor." He rolled his eyes.

She grinned and trailed a finger up the exposed hair between his lapels. "You know I've *always* had a thing for soldiers. I can't resist a man in uniform."

"Oh, darling, I *know*."

Vervaine jogged toward her old bedchambers, running through a mental catalogue of books she used to keep by her bedside. Gathering her skirt, she took the stone stairs two at a time to the second floor, her breath hitching when she realized the door to the room was wide open. That was strange. She used to leave it closed and locked.

Who could be inside?

The chambermaids? The laundress?

Uneasy, she looked around. No guards. Arias had sent so many of them south to help with the other provinces.

She tiptoed to the door and heard the ruffling of papers and the loud slam of books slapping against the stone floor. When she finally gathered the courage to enter, she saw a face she'd not seen in ages.

It was the widow Haldrin, Exos's seamstress, who had narrowly managed to stay in the royal family's employ. She was snooping, toppling stacks of books, shifting torch sconces, and tugging open bedside drawers, rummaging through the contents.

Vervaine cleared her throat.

Nina Haldrin froze, slowly turning around to face the queen. "Your majesty! I... I can explain."

"Please, do. In fact, I *insist* upon it."

Vervaine's bemused smile fell.

Nina's face was rife with fresh scars, one across her cheek, another over an eye that had become foggy and blind. The woman's hair was a tangled mess. Her face was sunken, eyes rimmed with dark circles. Her jittery fingers rubbed against each other nervously at her sides. Her forehead glistened with dripping beads of sweat. Her blue ankle-length gown hung from her spindly frame, caked in grime. The apron at her waist was wrinkled and streaked with mud and blood.

"Are you alright?" Vervaine asked quietly. "Maybe you should take a seat. You look unwell."

"I'm fine. I just need to find some, and I'll be out of your hair." Nina returned to rifling through the contents of Vervaine's old bedside table, mumbling to herself.

Vervaine cautiously approached, her voice even despite the anxiety. "Find some of *what*, Nina?"

"Where is it? *Where is it*?!" Nina shrieked, tugging another drawer all the way out, dumping its contents onto the rug. She scanned the items on the floor and then hurled the polished hunk of donik wood across the room. It splintered into pieces against the stone wall.

Vervaine stepped back. "I'm going to go find you some help."

"No!" Nina's chest heaved, her wild gaze darting around the room to other possible hiding places. She rushed over to Vervaine, grabbing the queen by the shoulders. "You can help me look! It'll be faster."

"What are we looking for?!"

"Don't play coy, your majesty. Exos drank loads of it. Surely, you did, too, for the abuse and the burns." Nina tucked a chunk of disheveled gray hair behind her ear and nervously laughed. "I took some for my back. Just a little. You know, for the pain. Crawling around on your hands and knees to hem gowns for decades takes a toll. After one of Exos's violent tantrums, I couldn't get out of bed. The lashings..."

Nina was panting now, eyes juddering frantically in their sockets with a look of sheer desperation.

"One of the chambermaids gave some to me. She said Exos had just made it legal."

"Dikeeka?" Vervaine's eyes widened. "You think there would be dikeeka in my room?"

"Of course."

"Nina, I never *touched* that garbage."

"Well," Nina chuckled, wringing her apron with filthy hands. "There must be some left from Exos, right? Your father created it, right? That's what I'd heard through the grapevine. If you could just let me have a vial or two, just until I can get my own again."

"Absolutely not. Nina, you can't take that stuff. It's poison. And from the looks of it, you are in the throes of addiction already. You must cut it out of your life."

"I can't!" Nina screamed. Then, she laughed maniacally. "It feels like the supply has dried up. No one has been able to get it like they used to. And the pain is back, Vervaine. Please, you've got to help me."

Vervaine stepped back and shook her head in disbelief. "I had no hand in legalizing that vile poison. I have no vials, and Arias and I are already laying the groundwork to make it illegal again. Take this as an opportunity to quit."

The old woman's chest heaved with anxiety. "No! No. You're lying!"

"We need to get you to a physician. Perhaps they can find something else for your back. A poultice or a steam treatment, maybe."

"A poultice?!" Nina shrieked. "I am in *pain*! Have you no empathy?" She shoved Vervaine hard against the back of the chamber door. The force slammed it closed. Nina whispered, as tears welled up in her eyes, "*Have you ever felt a pain so acute that you prayed for the release of death*?"

"Nina..."

The seamstress cried, her words almost gibberish through the heavy sobs. "Only one thing makes it all go away." Her eyes seemed to pierce through Vervaine. "I know you're lying. You've been sent by the Gods to make me suffer."

She dug into her corset and produced a small dagger that had been hidden between her breasts,

Vervaine stiffened at the sight of the metal's sheen. Nina grabbed the blade and offered Vervaine the hilt.

"If you will not help me. Then, at least give me the courtesy of ending my pain. I can't do it myself. I've tried. I'm a *coward*.

But *you* can. After generations with your family, you are all ruthless."

"Nina, you know me! You know I'm not ruthless!"

"You have your father's icy blood in you," she sobbed. "Do it. *End my suffering.*"

Vervaine shook her head. "I'll get you help. I'll seek out the finest physician the isle has to offer. I will have one come by ship from Asera for you!"

"Please, Vervaine," Nina begged. "We don't have much time."

"I have *enough* blood on my hands. I will *not* have yours!"

Metal boots clanked against the stone stairs outside the room.

"Help!" Vervaine cried out. "Guards!"

Nina's voice was nearly drowned out by the hurried stomps outside the door. "Fine. If you won't... *they* will."

Nina snatched the front of Vervaine's gown and swung her into the middle of the room. She turned the dagger's blade toward the queen just as the door burst open. Nina lunged forward with the knife, sinking the blade into the hollow of Vervaine's throat so deep that the tip burst through the other side.

Vervaine blinked in disbelief, her windpipe obscured by metal, blood trickling down her breasts. The guards drew their swords and fanned out, barking orders at Nina that she no longer could register through the bloodlust.

Nina removed the blade only to stab it into Vervaine's heart next. Blood gurgled from the slit in the queen's throat. She tried to cry out.

In a flurry of stabs, Nina jabbed the weapon into Vervaine's stomach, her lung, her ribs. Nina didn't even seem fazed by the long swords of the guards as they buried in her flesh.

Vervaine's bleeding body dropped like a rock onto the rug, and she writhed on the floor, joined soon after by the mangled seamstress. For good measure, two guards pierced the widow Haldrin through the chest at once.

On the cold stone floor, Vervaine choked on blood, wheezing through a slit throat with shallow gasps. Nina Haldrin's haunting smile was the last thing she saw before Vervaine's eyelids fluttered shut and her punctured heart ceased to beat altogether.

11

Outside the Lost City of Elathia
The Radiant Sea

The water bubbled and percolated, boiling where it met Omen's flesh. He stood in solitude just outside the air barrier, cheeks puffed, breath held, hands swishing in the near-silent waters as if he were composing a symphony.

He relished the tranquil silence and the temporary respite from the agony his body experienced since the curse. In the watery depths of the ocean, his limbs didn't feel scorched. The web of blue veins beneath his skin cooled more with every passing second.

Lungs aching, heart pounding, he took one large step back inside the bubble, the depression falling back over him like a veil. The briny air engulfed him, fueling his combustible skin.

He breathed deep, listening to the water on his body sizzle, evaporating into steamy vapor until his flames roared back to life.

His body went rigid as a voice spoke from behind him. "Does it... ease the pain?" He spun to face her, his face morphing into an expression of discomfort. Quistix stood atop the broken remains of a toppled pillar.

"Momentarily, yes." He stared out through the barrier, the ocean teeming with a harmonious array of organisms. "If this place had whiskey and sunsets, I imagine I'd stay forever."

"Well, that makes *one* of us." She guffawed.

He grinned, the dried sand shifting beneath his boots as he made his way toward her. "I take it the sea does not call to you?"

"Nope." She gazed upward, watching the water undulate serenely above the barrier. Schools of glitterfish darted overhead like a meteor shower, bright and blazing. The light from the three moons was suddenly blotted out by a massive moving shadow. "It feels suffocating down here. Feels like I'll be crushed by the weight of the world at any moment when this dome crashes down. And drowning is the last means of death I'd ever wish to experience."

"I can think of worse ways to die." He chuckled before taking a seat on the collapsed column remains beside her feet. "It would be relatively painless."

"I'd prefer something more epic. Like being slain in battle while trying to save the world."

"So humble. No grandiose ideas for you," he said sarcastically.

"I just know what I am capable of." She managed a sly smile.

Omen felt a pang of guilt knowing his lost love might be watching his disloyal gaze from the Ethereal Sanctum, though he knew he would never make it beyond their gates to see her in any afterlife. His nefarious deeds had damned him to the Nether decades ago. In death, just as in life, the fates had decided they were to remain eternally apart.

"I saw what remained of the Ruby Castle... and of Exos. I believe you're a force of change... or destruction. I can't decide what is more accurate."

"I'd say both." She flashed a tight grin before looking away.

An awkward silence spanned between them before Omen spoke again. "I had *orders* to kill you, you know. It wasn't as if it was personal."

Quistix turned toward him and laughed. "Really? Because it felt incredibly personal to *me*."

"Well, it wasn't." He straightened his posture. "If it finally meant the end of my suffering, I'd level every living thing in Destoria. Thankfully, I might've found a solution. I think you can help me."

"After you tried to kill me? That's rich. You're lucky you're still standing."

"No, I'm not. Quite the contrary," he said somberly. "I'll tell you what..." Omen rose and plucked the emerald dagger from his belt and offered her the hilt. "Get your revenge. Then, when you feel like we are even, you might finally hear me out. If you want blood, take it. Let our feud end here."

Quistix snatched the dagger from his hand and smiled. "You don't have to ask twice."

Stabbing the dagger's blade deep into Omen's chest, she watched his blue eyes pinch closed, his body rocking from the force. Pulling out the blade, she watched flames dribble from the metal along with molten, cobalt-blue blood. The flesh sealed back together almost in an instant.

In quick jabs, she stabbed several more times. Each time, the wound healing in a moment or two.

She smiled a little. “Are you immortal? Or do you just have remarkably-fast healing capabilities?”

“Immortal, unfortunately.” He looked down and shook his head at the sliced noubald leather. “Damn. This curiass cost me a small fortune.”

She snickered.

He smiled up at her. “I don’t suppose you mend?”

“Not on your life.” Quistix handed him back his knife.

“Now it’s my turn. Hold still.”

Her eyes widened, and she took a reflexive step back.

“Relax. It was a joke.” He tucked the blade back into its leather sheath at his hip. “Do you feel better?”

Quistix nodded. She ran a finger delicately against his healed skin through one of the gashes in his cuirass. "Is this some sort of fire-resistant magical armor?"

He smiled and nodded. "I got tired of walking around naked after burning up all of my clothes. I asked Master Tempest for a custom set of armor. Took me forever to work off the debt."

His muscles tensed beneath her fingertip. She realized she was still touching him and quickly stepped away. "Sorry. It's nice. Good craftsmanship. Reminds me of some of the fire-resistant robes I saw in Apex."

"Pfft. They're a bunch of pretentious twits in Apex." He snorted. "I bet you stuck out there like a wyl in the desert."

Quistix laughed. "Something like that." Her yellow eyes raised to meet his gaze. "So I take it you've been?"

"Yes. Before the *Ward of Protection* cut off all travel back and forth."

"So you've been to the institute? You didn't happen to meet any fae there, by chance?"

"Yes, they weren't quite the majestic creatures I'd expected."

Stretching her legs, Quistix shook her head. "The females were on par with what I expected. But the males..."

"Foul."

"Yes!" she shouted, eyes wide. "They had the voice of someone who has inhaled dragon smoke all of their life. Pudgy little things. Like pleoms but less adorable."

Omen snorted. "That's a very accurate description."

"And flirtatious! They wouldn't stop propositioning me."

"By the Gods." Omen chuckled. "Brazen little beasts, I'll give them that." he looked her up and down for a moment. "Can't say I *blame* them, though..."

The sound of a cleared throat cut their private moment short.

"*Ahem*. What is *this*?" Twitch asked suspiciously as he circled them, finally standing like a soldier at attention, body erect, heels snapping together.

"What, *this*?" Quistix motioned to her and Omen. "Just a cursed immortal and a late-developing sorceress commiserating about the horny fae of Apex in a crumbling underwater realm."

Twitch squinted at her. "Fae are the worst."

"Agreed." Omen nodded.

"Especially the males. Absolutely *foul*."

Quistix barked a laugh. Violet and Aurora approached, stopping behind Twitch.

"There you are, Omen. What's that stupid look all about?" Violet tilted her head like a curious mutt. "Oh, never mind. That's just your face."

"You know, I could kill you right here and not a court in the land would convict me. I'd probably get a damned parade."

Violet looked at Quistix. "You might want to keep your distance from this fool," she teased. "His stupidity is contagious."

Omen snickered. "Says the shape-shifter who spends her time around the simpletons in Taernsby."

Violet stuck her tongue out. "If you'll excuse me, I need to borrow this beautiful little thing before you bore her to death." She pointed behind her. "Quistix, we could use some help with Irenas. He's been rambling, going on these nonsensical tangents."

"What am I supposed to do about it?"

"Well, Aurora and I were observing him. We want a fresh set of eyes. I think maybe somewhere in all of his gibberish is a clue to what is happening to him."

"I hate to point out the obvious," Twitch said. "What if this is just the cruelty of years of isolation taking a toll on his mind? It's not unheard of for a human of such an advanced age to become... confused."

Aurora nodded, her gaze uneasy as she scanned the others. "I thought the same thing at first, but now, I believe there might be more to it. His pupils are enlarged, like he'd consumed a toxic substance. He's unsteady. His mood swings abruptly, and his bodily odor is... unusual, like something I've smelled before. Like rancid, potent berries and something acidic. Maybe it's a plant he is ingesting, or toxic tea leaves, or some sort of mold from all of the humidity."

"What about a spell that old coot cast that's gone all cuckoo?" Twitch asked.

"Possibly. We must assess before we dismiss it as some cruel act of time. He is behaving like he has over-imbibed, but there wasn't a drop of spirits in sight when we examined the contents of his pantry."

Omen rose from the pillar. "Well, Ambrosia..."

"Aurora," she corrected.

"Sorry. Aurora." Omen bowed apologetically. "Let us all go. The sooner we figure this out, the sooner you can all be on your way to wherever you're going next. I'm sure you'd all rather be anywhere but here."

"Actually, I enjoy it here in Elathia." Aurora's proclamation stunned Quistix and Twitch.

Quistix stepped closer. "Really?"

"Affirmative. Much of this underwater realm is uncharted territory. I've never heard of Destorians having the opportunity to explore a place like this. To my knowledge, Elathia and that merfolk village aren't places that even the scholars of Apex have written about. No one seems to have documented the world under the Radiant Sea in any book I've ever read."

"That's exactly why grandfather came here in the first place," Violet added, "He took his retirement early and coordinated this residency with the institute in Apex in order to document it all for the library. It was a perfect mission for a hermit like him."

Aurora smirked, her lips turning up in a smile.

Quistix turned back. "Let's get this over with." She paused for a moment and turner toward Omen. "Parnix is a wizard skilled enough to have been a professor in Apex, yet he was never able to help you break your curse?"

He shook his fiery head. "A curse of blood and oath can only be stopped by death or rescinded by its caster. And since I've been curse to immortality…"

"…You're stuck until the caster removes it."

He nodded. "Who was it?"

He cracked a sad smile. "Your favorite quichyrd."

Quistix sighed. Then she looked at Aurora. "Have you ever found any information that might contradict that?"

"No. Dark magic is not talked about in most of the texts I've read about. It is one of the subjects that was restricted. What little I've gleaned only seems to confirm Omen's claim." Then, she turned toward him. "What if the curse's caster were to perish? Theoretically, your dark magic link would be broken, could it not?"

Omen shrugged. "She and I are bound. If she dies, I might die, too. And if somehow I didn't die when she did, would the curse of immortality disappear with the eternal flame? Or would only one of the curses be broken?"

"I truly don't know enough about dark magic to answer that," Aurora said.

Quistix turned to Violet. "We could speculate all day. But, frankly, I'd rather tend to Irenas Parnix before he casts a spell that drops this air dome and sends us all to our watery graves." Then, she smiled and shook her head. She flashed a glance at Omen, his fiery figure evoking a pang of sympathy in her. "Well... those of us who are lucky enough to be able to die."

12

The Ruby Palace
Desdemona, Willowdale

"In my oath to the throne, nowhere did I agree to forfeit my freedom," Arias stated firmly to the head of the guards. The man, though nearly a decade older, made Arias feel childlike, dwarfed by the massive barbarian's size.

"M'lord, I'm sorry, but I'm afraid we request schedule changes a day in advance so we can adjust our men's duty requirements as needed. We don't want your soldiers to tarnish their reputation any more than they already have. The death of Exos Tempest exposed severe flaws. We are fighting to rectify them for your safety. Please understand, if we cannot accommodate last-minute changes, it is because your safety and protection are our ultimate priority."

Arias smirked. "You *are* aware that I occupied your position before you did, correct?"

The barbarian covered in gleaming armor shifted his weight uncomfortably. "Yes, sir. I didn't say it as any sort of sleight against your abilities to successfully protect Queen Tempest."

"I'm not that thin-skinned. I took no offense. I mean to say that I understand the challenges of your station. It is your responsibility to keep us alive. But I cannot always assure you that I can submit all changes days in advance. I need a little more fluidity. I may be king, but I still have a marriage to maintain. Ours is not one of convenience or political alliance. It is one born out of passion, and it requires effort. I'd like you to prepare a few designated locations beyond the throne room and our quarters where she and I can go from time to time. I won't live in a gilded cage."

The head of the guard plucked at a hair caught in the ridges of his pristine armor. "We all live in a gilded cage, your majesty. We erect the bars ourselves."

Shooting him a warning glance, Arias spoke quietly. "Be that as it may, we desire a larger cage, then. For decades, I roamed this isle. I flew through these skies via harpy. Now I can't even take a piss without three guards watching me. It just feels like a slight over-correction."

"The evening shift is set to begin soon. Once we give the men their assignments, I will shift things around to accommodate your request."

"Thank you, I-"

Arias's burgundy eyes suddenly flashed vibrant green. His legs seemed to develop a mind of their own, twisting uneasily as if something were inhabiting him like an unfamiliar vessel.

Arias stumbled and took off sprinting. Unsure where his hoofed feet were taking him, he watched like a spectator in his own body. Thoughts that were not his own rang through his head.

Blood. Vervaine. Run!

His thoughts intertwined with Ceosteol's in his mind, the urgency behind his jerking movements finally making sense to him.

Fleeing the soldier's barracks with haste, he raced across the courtyard in a panic.

Blood. Vervaine. Run!

Arias burst through the wooden doors and plowed straight into two guards who were heading out. The men staggered, nearly toppling over before grabbing the frantic king, glancing around wildly.

"Your majesty, is everything alright?" asked one.

Blood. Vervaine. Run!

"Ver-vaine!" he panted. "Where is she?"

The other guard spoke, confused. "I saw her heading upstairs, m'lord. Why? Is there danger?"

Without answering, Arias darted toward the kitchen, up the stairwell, and down the hall where frantic whispers could be heard. He couldn't understand them over his whirling thoughts and Ceosteol's mental chanting.

Blood. Vervaine. Get them away!

Arias halted in the doorway. His knees buckled, but he held himself upright.

The scene was a nightmare.

Too many people.

Too much blood.

"*Vervaine?*" His voice came out hushed, engulfed by the frenzied whispers of the guards around him.

"Vervaine!" he snarled, bolting forward and hovering over two stilled forms.

The seamstress, he'd seen in passing. He vaguely recalled seeing her around the castle through the years. Now, she was unforgettable, eyes wide and accusatory, large sword wounds gouged through her drooping breasts.

Beside her, Vervaine's twisted body lay in a large puddle of black-garnet blood. The same white dress he'd seen her in less than an hour before was now dyed, the odd shade spreading like a spilled well of red-black ink blooming outwardly through dry parchment.

Holes in his wife's skin dribbled strange, onyx-colored fluid. Thick tendrils of tar-like muck dribbled from her open mouth. Her eyes were peacefully closed, like the times he'd watched her sleep, like any moment she might awaken to admonish him for staring.

What was missing was the rise and fall of her chest, the soft whoosh of her exhalations.

There was no movement at all. No life left in her.

She was dead. And Arias hated himself for failing to protect her, yet again, when she'd needed him the most.

He slammed down knees, eyes welling with tears. He placed his hand on her, hoping his touch would awaken them both from a horrific nightmare.

But it didn't.

Men shouted his name, tugging at his arms to remove him from the room. He thrashed and yanked free, counting her visible wounds, unable to focus on anything else.

One... two... three... four... five...

Five wounds.

Get them away from her, Ceosteol screamed in Arias's mind. *I must get to her quickly! They can't witness what I need to do!*

"Get out of my head!" Arias screamed into the air.

"Your majesty!"

"Leave us be!" His words came out as a sob, face red from a sudden rush of fury and pain. He shoved the guards out the door. "Go!"

Something in his green-swirled eyes was wild, his snarl beastly. The men trampled each other to get out. Before they could protest, the king slammed the wooden door and barred it, sealing himself inside the room with both corpses.

A portal of darkness materialized near the bed, and Ceosteol appeared in it, hastily stepping through the void before it vanished. Her talons tenderly gripped the akiah's shoulder.

"We haven't much time. Move the other woman away."

Arias nodded but didn't move.

Ceosteol stepped between him and Vervainc and hissed, "If I wait any longer, there will be no bringing her back! I can't heal her if she shares blood with a tethered body. Move her away from the widow Haldrin!"

Arias nodded, the urgency granting him a burst of unparalleled strength. He lifted the seamstress's body, feeling his rage roll to a blistering boil. The dagger tumbled from between the folds of her dress and clattered on the floor.

It took every ounce of restraint he had to not eject the woman's corpse from the window in anger. Forcing away the thought, he flopped her onto the floor beside the bed and kneeled by his wife. His white robe, decorated with gold embellishments, soaked up the pooled blood like a wash rag, but his eyes remained fixed on his wife as he prayed to every God above that she would once again open her eyes.

Ceosteol dug a sharp claw into her forearm, tearing through skin until black blood oozed from her wound. A sentient tangle of electric green strands slithered out through the gash like curious snakes. She reached out with her wounded arm and swiped a claw, severing them over Vervaine's body like cut worms. She stuffed the squirming green tendrils into the holes in the queen's chest.

Stifling the urge to vomit, Arias shut his eyes and listened to the vulgar squish of the quichyrd's talons moving in his beloved's flesh. After a moment, Arias turned toward the hearth and pictured himself setting the murderess on fire inside it.

As if reading his thoughts, Ceosteol whipped toward him. "Arias! Forget the widow and help me."

He gritted his teeth, popping the muscles in his jaw as he forced himself to return to Ceosteol's side.

"Hold her hand. Talk to her. You must pull her back from the other side!"

Lowering beside Vervaine, Arias grasped her pale hand and rested her cold fingertips against his bottom lip. His breath was ragged, tears dribbling down her blood-streaked wrists, trailing a path of pink toward her shoulder.

"Vervaine... you are the love of my life." He sniffled and clutched her hand harder. "There was no *before,* and there is no *after* you. You are everything I've ever wanted. I need you here with me. We have only just begun our journey."

Ceosteol waved her hands over Vervaine's chest and chanted quietly. "*Revertimini ad me. Ego ero dux vester. Multum hic relictus es.*"

Arias blinked away his tears only to have new ones spring forth. He looked at the ring on Vervaine's finger and twisted the metal, the hideous ruby stone dwarfing her hand. "I hate this gaudy thing. I know it's the traditional queen's ring, but I vow to have the finest jeweler in the isle create something new, something without a dark past, something that symbolizes a new beginning. Please, my love, I beg of you... wake up."

Still, she lay silently, unmoving. Beneath her, the pools of blood grew smaller, almost as if her body was reabsorbing its spilled life essence.

"Keep going," Ceosteol encouraged with a gentle nod. "She can hear you."

Arias nodded, shedding more tears as he looked back down at his wife in his arms. “I always thought you’d be a wonderful mother.”

Ceosteol paused, her green eyes darting down to the floor for a moment before resuming her quiet chanting.

“You’re a pure soul, Vervaine. People are drawn to you. Your soft touch, your kind voice, your endlessly open ear... I don’t know what favor I must’ve curried for you to be mine, but I will forever be grateful for you. The world needs more souls like you. I need you, Vervaine. You have a duty, my love, an unfinished duty to unite this fractured isle. You are the only one who can truly heal the wounds your family created. These people are scared. There are rumblings of an underground revolution on the horizon. Everything you have fought to protect, everything you have worked for, would mean nothing if you don’t come back and see this through. You *can’t* leave things like this!”

Hope drained from him, fogging his mind with grief and disbelief.

A moment later, Ceosteol's chants grew louder, and the pool of blood beneath Vervaine shrank more, the red liquid sucking back into her limp frame.

Arias swore he could see her lungs rise subtly. Was it a trick of the mind or a genuine sign of life?

"You are my anchor in the storm, Vervaine. I need you. Please, don't leave me."

Arias stared at the bloody gouges in her dress as the shredded skin beneath miraculously healed before him. His burgundy irises darted back and forth over her, anxiously awaiting any sign of life. His expectant gaze shot up to Ceosteol. "Her wounds are healed. Why isn't it working? Why isn't she waking up?"

Ceosteol stopped chanting and sat back on her rough, calloused avian heels. Several moments of deafening silence passed before her shoulders sagged. "It would appear she doesn't wish to return. She's gone."

"What?" Arias croaked, his face flushing red. "What do you mean? She's healed! She can't just leave me!" His voice wavered. Their love was not one of convenience, obligation, or duty. It was something that never grew old, a feeling he wished would never end. There is no way she would have left him here. *Alone*. Not if she'd had a choice.

"Vervaine?" He propped her body up against his chest and tightly embraced her.

"Please, Vervaine." He begged, stroking wet strands of chestnut hair out of her blood-smudged face. "None of this means anything without you beside me. Come back. I'll do *anything*. Just... open your eyes for me."

No response came.

His chest shook, his body wracked with heavy sobs. He placed a jittery kiss on her chilled lips and then rested his forehead against hers, careful not to jab her with his horns.

"We must move the body," Ceosteol said callously. "If anyone should see her wounds healed, there will be questions. We must get going."

"Just... give me a damned *minute*!" He shouted, the fury from his bleary eyes sending a shiver up her arthritic spine.

She nodded and took a cautious step back.

Vervaine's eyes peeled open slowly, fluttered for a moment, and then peered up at Arias.

The noise that came from his lips sounded foreign, an emotional yelp that echoed through the bed chamber.

Watching her soul child reawaken, Ceosteol felt impossibly light. She clasped a taloned hand to her chest, the staccato beat of her heart hammering away in her chest.

She had been close to losing it all, all that she had been working towards for decades.

"Get changed and burn the dress," Ceosteol hissed. "People cannot know of the dark magic that took place here."

Arias nodded and rose, helping Vervaine to her feet.

He led her to a bedpost scrawled in etchings of ivy. She grabbed it, and Arias helped her out of her gown. The corset was sliced, perforated with stab wounds. Eager to shed her of the past, Arias stripped off the last of her clothes.

Ceosteol stood beside the pillows, kneading and groping the feathers and straw inside until she finally found what she was looking for.

Arias loosened the last bit of string from the grommets and retrieved a sky-blue robe, wrapping the queen in it before planting a soft kiss on her cheek.

Arias turned to Ceosteol, still rummaging in the shams, and cleared his throat. "Excuse me, but what is it you're looking for in there?"

Ceosteol tucked something into the pocket of her robe. “Nothing. Nothing at all.” Then, to deflect from her obvious lie, she pointed to Arias’s bloody clothes. “You must burn your garments, too. You’re covered.”

Glancing down, he was startled at the sight of so much blood. He stripped down, ripped a noubald pelt from the foot of the bed, and draped it around his waist to maintain at least a shred of modesty.

He tossed his clothes in the fireplace and glared at the quichyrd. “You know that this soul bond you’ve cursed us with flows *both* ways. I can sense your fear. What are you scavenging for? Show me.”

Ceosteol patted the pillow, fluffing it without looking at him. “Just trying to make Vervaine comfortable. She will need rest. She’s been through a lot.”

Shoving his hand in the pocket of her robe, Arias snatched what felt like a furry wad of beans and pulled them out.

Ceosteol swiped, trying to snatch them from his hand before he could see. In his palm, he rolled around black spores, furry oblong lumps.

He shook his head and laughed. "Spore hysteria? Really, Ceosteol?"

Snatching them back from his hand, she shoved the spores back in her pocket. "Undead or not, you shouldn't be handling such a thing!"

"You put that in Exos's pillow." Vervaine snapped, her jaw clenched. "That's how you knew it was there!"

"Don't worry. Such a thing was never intended for you. You have always been more reasonable than your predecessors. Spores," Ceosteol pointed to her pocket, "were necessary for a time, but not anymore."

Vervaine gasped, a look of sheer horror befalling her face. "You! It was you! You were behind my father's madness!"

"Well, I—"

"You were the one who made my sister insane!"

"To be fair, she was already a bit mad before the spores."

"All this time, you knew they were being poisoned because *you* were the one who was driving them mad! You... calculating monster!"

Ceosteol glared at Vervaine. "Rest. Heal. And *remember who you are talking to.*"

Ceosteol stopped at the door and looked at them over a frail shoulder. "Desperation is a catalyst for innovation. I will never apologize for ensuring my survival. Nor should you."

She pointed a talon toward the hearth, and flames roared to life inside it. The wad of blood-soaked clothing erupted with a *whoosh*. They watched in silence as the evidence was consumed by the flames.

Ceosteol pointed to the body of the seamstress, lying in a disfigured heap on the floor. "Wrap her in a blanket and bring her down to my lair."

“What are you going to do with her?” Arias asked quietly.

Ceosteol just smiled. “Don’t concern yourself with the details. Just bring her down to me.” Her eyes glowed a little greener. “The sooner the better, Arias.”

13

Outside the Lost City of Elathia
The Radiant Sea

The bricks tied to Twitch's ankles made his muscles burn as he and Violet ventured away from the safety of Elathia into the unknown depths, working his way through patches of snarled roots on the gritty ocean floor. He approached a tower of swaying seaweed and leaned down, using a dagger made from a busted seashell to shear the plant fibers off at the crown. He handed the bundle to Violet, and she quietly stuffed the swaying greenery into a potato sack along with the others.

They continued onward to another clump, their bodies in slow motion as the water gently tugged them in various directions. Violet waved him over as she diverged from the clearing toward a mound of stone.

"Check this out," Violet said, pointing to a hole that glowed with warm, tangerine-colored light. She handed Twitch the bag of seaweed and kneeled, shoving her hand deep into the hole.

"Wait! You don't know what's in there! What if there's an eel or a sea snake or something in there?" Twitch shouted, his ears pinned back, his gills flapping with panicked breaths.

"I do know what's in here. I've done this a hundred times," she mumbled with a grunt, tugging loose something that looked like a feathery mushroom. Its top waggled in the tide. Thin strips bloomed out, unfurling like petals in wavy parallel lines away from the glowing base.

"*Whoa*," Twitch whispered, eyes wide with wonderment. "C-can I touch it?"

With an irresistible smile, Violet handed it to Twitch.

He grasped it delicately, as if one false move would cause it to shatter. "It's incredible. So soft. The buttery texture of silk... only firm."

"Huh. To me, it just feels like a breast."

Twitch nearly dropped the squishy creature. "Pardon?"

Violet offered a sly smile. "You know. A breast. Bosom." She pointed to her chest.

"How would you know?"

"Twitch, I've touched a breast before." She chuckled.

Twitch squeezed the mushroom-like creature lightly in his hand before handing it back to her. "I'm afraid you're spot on. What is it?"

"I can't remember the name. Grandfather uses them for lots of different things, though. Potions, poultices, spell-casting."

"Interesting."

"They're edible, too. Put one in a warm cup of goat's milk and you'll be out like a light. A bugle horn sounding in your ear couldn't wake you."

"Sounds versatile."

Violet scanned the ocean floor around them. "Let me know if you see any more of those little mounds, would you?"

Squinting, Twitch spotted another lumped mound of rock several yards in the distance. He walked toward it.

"Where are you going?"

"There's one over here. I'll get it."

"Be careful. Look for the colorful glow. Otherwise, anything could be lurking down there."

"Right." A school of glitterfish darted in the distance, followed by a shadowy figure that looked like a grindylow youngling, gnashing at the slowest fish.

High above was the ocean's surface, glimmering brilliantly in the midday sun. Slivers of bright light slid across the sand, giving the rippled floor the illusion of movement.

Twitch's ears fluttered in the water, sending tiny bubbles rising toward the surface.

"You alright?" Violet asked.

Twitch nodded nervously as he fished another squishy creature out of a glowing hole. "Yeah. Just trying not to focus on how I'm one grindylow attack away from meeting a watery demise. Perhaps... you could distract me."

"How?"

"I don't know." He reached into another hole, trying his best to put on a brave face when all he wanted to do was wince. "Maybe... I don't know... maybe tell me something about you."

"About me?"

"Yes. I want to know about the brains behind the beauty." He thrust another mushroom-like creature into her burlap sack.

"Me? Hmmm. I suppose, if I had to describe myself, I'd say I live out loud. I'm honest. I keep no secrets, unless, of course, someone asks me to, specifically."

Something about the way she smiled at him made him feel as though he had downed a bottle of elderberry wine.

"I don't really keep secrets either. Not since I left the Thieves Guild. No need."

He walked over to another mound with a hole. The flickering sunlight cast amber fingers down upon the rocks. Paying more attention to the strawberry-blonde beauty beside him, Twitch lowered to his knees and fished around inside another dark hole. "I want more. Tell me more."

She wavered in the ocean's current. "Hmmm. Let's see, my middle name is Petra. I adore the smell of wet dirt. I can out-drink a barbarian. I've dated as many men as I have women. I—"

"Wait," Twitch jerked back his hand, slicing his fingers on the razor-like spines of the slender fish in the hole. He yowled into the water, snarling as his blood floated upward in front of his face like red smoke.

Violet grimaced, eyes wide. "Oh no. We have to go. *Now*!"

She pulled him up by his bicep.

"Why? What's the rush? It's just a small cut."

"Your blood is like a steak dinner to a whole bunch of things that live in these waters. Things with teeth. Things with ravenous appetites. We have to go!"

Twitch clasped his hand over the wound. "I'm taking these bricks off, then. We should swim for it."

"Wait!" Violet protested as he poised to slit the ropes tethering the bricks to his ankles. "It's better to go slow. If you panic, you'll draw way too much attention to us. Here, wrap this around your wound." She tore a chunk of seaweed out of the bag. "Wrap it tight. The water's pressure will help."

Twitch hissed as he applied his makeshift bandage. They walked back toward the bubble of air that Parnix had cast. A large shadow loomed overhead, blocking out the sun for a long moment before disappearing again.

"I hope that that was just a cloud," Twitch said, panic forcing his voice higher than it had been as an adolescent.

"Just keep moving, Twitch." Violet tugged him along beside her, fighting against the churn of the water every step of the way.

Another shadowy beast passed overhead.

"That was huge! What was that?!" Twitch asked fearfully, willing his legs to move faster. His calves felt like they were dissolving into jam.

Struggling to keep her tone even, Violet took a deep breath. "Even tiny fish look massive when they are close to the surface. Just focus. We're close."

As they approached the bubble, they felt the eyes of something linger, watching them intensely. Pushing through the barrier, a surge of water forced them inside, spitting them forcefully onto the dry sand.

Twitch and Violet gasped violently as their gills resealed and their bodies gobbled up the briny air.

Twitch screamed, scrambling backward, away from the barrier. Violet clutched him tightly, using the wyl as a shield.

Towering over them, a giant sand-colored dragon held its face against the barrier, glaring at them wickedly, an oceanic nightmare of a beast. Its huge nostrils puffed, sending powerful jets of water all around the barrier, percolating the water until it bubbled and boiled all around. Twitch could feel the heat in the dome rise instantly.

The dragon's orange eyes illuminated the slick dinner-plate-sized scales of its narrow face. Its lizard-like mouth curled to showcase a snarl that made Twitch's legs feel like they were liquefied. The dragon's pupils were larger than the wyl's torso, its focus darting between the tasty-looking live prey as if it were deciding who to lunge at first.

The dragon's body went rigid, shoulders hunching as its snout slammed against the barrier, rocking the foundation of the humble bubble-encased village, nearly toppling the structures within.

"Grandfather!" Violet screamed in terror.

"Quistix!" Twitch shrieked.

The mountain of scale and muscle launched against the barrier again. Spidery bolts of lightning shot in every direction through the dome, stemming from the point of contact, illuminating the dragon's daunting size with the brilliant flash of light.

As if he had been painfully zapped, the dragon crumpled into a clumsy ball, a tangle of limbs and tail splayed atop the giant bubble-shaped structure.

His fangs sank into the barrier, its mouth suddenly alight with another pulsing, painful current. Recoiling in pain, the dragon shook his head, erupting in a roar that vibrated the sand beneath them. Columns shuddered, teetering on their bases. Glass crashed distantly behind them. Mounds of clutter toppled.

A pair of scrawny, bare feet padded past Twitch and Violet. Parnix stood at the dome's curved wall, staring up at the beast with wide eyes.

"*By the Gods, it's you*!" the worried wizard whispered, voice dripping with amazement and terror. His age-spotted hands trembled at his sides. "What have I done?"

The crazed old man teetered forward, frizzy curls bobbing against his shoulders. He narrowed his eyes, eyes that now showed a bit of lucidity and recognition. "Do not fear me, old friend. We are both children of these waters. You couldn't possibly remember, but you and I have been acquainted for nearly ten years. I found you nearly a month after I left Apex to come down here for my research. I found you outside of that town over there, where the merfolk wanted to eat your yolk and let the snails slurp away at your shell to strengthen their own. I bought you for three bushels of oysters."

Parnix cackled, tickled by the memory of it all. "Oh, I cared for you when you were but a fractured egg! I poured wax on your cracked shell to seal it closed and used a warming spell to incubate you for *weeks* until you were ready to greet the world."

He clutched his head in pain and winced and then reached out and stroked the surface of the dome lovingly, inches away from the water dragon's snorting snout.

"Why, I even taught you how to fish! We're old chums, you and I."

A growl rumbled deep inside the dragon's chest. It swiveled its head slowly from side to side, assessing Irenas's acquaintances.

"Easy now, Kackaroth. Never mind them. Look at me. You know you can trust me," he added softly, pressing his forehead against the barrier between them.

"Grandfather, don't get so close!"

The dragon's reddened eyes glowed bright, two beacons in the murk.

Parnix squinted. "Your eyes, Kackaroth. They're red as blood! Are you hurt? What happened to you?"

Bearing a mouthful of pale teeth, the length of the former professor's legs, the dragon crouched. Tiny whirlpools of water formed around the creature's webbed crown of spikes as he lowered his head. Long, glimmering protrusions rose in the water along his spine. The small bones inside flexed and twisted, stiffening as the dragon propelled itself upward with all four powerful legs. The mammoth beast used its webbed feet to swim off, dragging its elongated tail behind.

In seconds, the monster had disappeared back into the depths of the dark turquoise abyss.

Quistix approached, voice laced with disbelief. "Was that... a water dragon?"

"Yes," Omen said with a shiver, following closely behind from the direction of Parnix's home. "Ghastly things, aren't they?"

Parnix shot Omen a menacing glance. Omen put his fiery hands up in surrender. "Sorry."

"Where the Nether did he *come* from, Pops? You didn't seem a bit surprised to see that... *thing*." Omen grimaced.

"Kackaroth is not some mindless monster drifting through these waters. I *raised* him. He has a grasp on basic commands and learns very quickly," Irenas growled.

"Are there more like him?" Twitch asked.

Parnix snickered. "Yes. Just not in these waters. They never make it this far inland. Usually, they stay in the deeper spots. There's a wide, cold water channel that runs around the perimeter of Asera where they are more often found. The waters here are usually too shallow. They prefer more frigid temperatures, and their eyes are sensitive. Even the light can't exist where most of them live. Kackaroth is an anomaly in many ways."

"Is that why its eyes glowed? Because they're usually in darker waters?"

"Precisely. Normally, they glow white, but his eyes looked like they were full of beet juice. Something is certainly wrong with him."

"Your eyes are pretty red, too. I'm not sure you have room to talk," Violet joked, nudging an empty conch shell with the toe of her boot.

"So why is that thing here if they're normally found around Asera? We are a long trek from there, I'd imagine," Quistix said.

Parnix stared off into the gloomy blue waters. "I found his egg in a shipwreck nearby, along with some other illegal goods. Someone was trying to smuggle him into Destorian waters. Or at least *through* them. As for why anyone would have a use for a smuggled water dragon, I'm afraid I can't speak to their motivations. It was likely someone with more coin than common sense."

"So, what was that you were saying about you accidentally setting that beast free?" Quistix placed her hands on her hips.

Parnix looked around, genuinely confused. He ran his frail hands through his messy mop of white hair. "I can't seem to remember that part. But I'm the only one who could have *possibly* let him off his chains. They were magically fortified. Complicated spell, you see. Very advanced.

Not something these snot-nosed kids at the Apex institute could undo as some sort of prank."

Twitch grabbed Violet's hand and held it for a beat too long, staring at her with a look of genuine concern. "Are you alright? That thing gave us a fright."

"Yes. I'm fine." She smiled, giving his hand a gentle squeeze. "You're sweet for asking."

Omen rolled his eyes and stepped between them, turning back toward Parnix. "Any other secrets you've been keeping from us, Pops? Have you taken a mermaid for a wife? Perhaps found a cure for the Aseran plague?"

"I am still working on that one." Parnix shoved his hands in his robe's pocket and leaned toward Quistix. "It's much easier down here for me to experiment. Down here, I'm far away from the litany of restrictions and those greedy, coin-grubbing bureaucrats on the Destorian Council."

Violet glanced up at Twitch, then at her shuffling grandfather. "How have you never mentioned a water dragon to any of us in ten years?"

Parnix ignored the question, licking his chapped lips. "By the Gods, I'm parched. Come, Little Bean. Make us some tea, would you, darling?" Parnix looked at Quistix. "Violet makes the best seaweed tea. Delectable!"

Violet rolled her eyes at the nickname. "You know I hate it when you call me Little Bean."

Twitch hoisted the burlap bag onto his shoulder and turned to Violet. "What exactly does he drink down here? I know it's ironic to even ask, seeing as though we are surrounded by it, but does he ever just drink *water*?"

"Yes. All the time. He was given a *Scroll of Desalination* when he was sent down here to do his research. With a couple of words and the flick of his wrist, he can remove every grain of sea salt from a whole basin of water. Then, he runs it through a particle filtration contraption so that it's crystal clear."

"Wow." Twitch stared at her, studying the delicate curves of her face.

Violet smiled. "What?"

Twitch tore his gaze from Violet's pillowy lips and shook his head. He adjusted the heavy bag of dripping seaweed on his shoulder. "Nothing." He looked onward. "It's just... I could use a drink."

14

Dungeon of the Ruby Palace
Desdemona, Willowdale

Even opening Werner's eyelids took massive effort. The guards had not brought him his measly daily portion of gruel or his cup of murky rainwater. He had lost hope that any were coming. The guards must have forgotten him again. Or maybe they'd been avoiding him intentionally, starving him out. The acts of violence that had landed Werner in the Ruby Palace dungeon had solidified a reputation as one of the most dangerous prisoners Willowdale had ever known.

The fight had left his body long ago, the same night that rage and fury had overtaken his mind out of seemingly nowhere. Before that, his worst offense had been knocking out a eaflic's tooth in a saloon fight in his youth, and the man had had the altercation coming for months.

Werner's filth-caked clothes hung off of his emaciated landigo frame. Past sunken cheeks and chapped lips sat a tongue as tacky and rough as the feral feline who prowled the halls to keep the rodent population at bay.

The cold seeping in from the stone walls made his heart slow to a quiet, occasional thud, causing him to weave in and out of consciousness.

Without food and water, death was finally imminent. Every time he closed his eyes, he feared it would be the last. He bobbled limply, his chin drooping toward his chest.

He didn't know if it had been hours or minutes, the darkness always blending into one maddeningly long, eternal night. Werner awoke, snorting fearfully as his shackles clicked open. His hands flopped limply to the floor. His shoulders burned, forearms completely numb. If he'd had an ounce of fluid to spare, he would have sobbed tears of relief.

His tongue stuck to the roof of his mouth, requiring too much energy to move. He mumbled, hoarse, but it came out as a tired mess of nonsensical syllables.

Starting from the mere thickness of a porcupine quill, a light flickered in front of him, its width thickening as it swirled in blinding circles. The sudden appearance of light after months of darkness made him recoil in horror. The hiss of a lit fuse echoed ominously off the rock walls of his cell as a portal, rimmed in light, expanded before his squinted eyes.

Inside, a quichyrd stood, staff in hand, on the edge of a picturesque pond sparkling with reflected light from all three moons. A symph howled in the distance, chasing one another from its flock through the crisp night sky.

The amethyst globe atop the quichyrd's staff glowed, illuminating the smirk on her beak. Her hand stretched toward him, plum robe drooping off her thin arms.

"Come, Werner. We've much to discuss," Ceosteol hissed.

Werner tried to rise to his feet and collapsed. He crawled toward the portal, collapsing again in the tall grass on the other side, mere feet from the water his body ached for.

For the first time in months, Werner managed the hint of a smile. If he were to die now, at least it wouldn't be in a cell.

Unless this was all a cruel dream...

Closing his eyes, he pressed his fur-covered face against the roots and dirt. A cold, alarming splash of water splattered against his face. He couldn't muster the energy to respond with a shout. Instead, he lapped at the chilled liquid, a primal part mindlessly giving him the strength to crawl toward the source.

Standing at the water's edge, Ceosteol stood, empty wooden mug in hand. "Wash yourself, Werner. You smell foul. Bathe. Drink your fill. After, you can join me for dinner."

She gestured to a blanket laid out on the bank, covered in an array of fresh food, lit by four floating orbs of light, one hovering above each corner of the fabric. Werner caught a whiff of fresh bread and pickled noubald feet, and his senses came alive. He pried his eyes open further, wide enough to see a steaming roast, mashed potatoes, and some kind of over-stuffed fruit pie. Cherry, by the smell of it.

Werner scrambled to the edge of the pond and hissed as he slid into the freezing water to his throat. He drifted like a beaver, pushing off the bank with his toes to propel him out toward the middle of the water, guzzling cupped handfuls of water down.

"Go slow," Ceosteol warned, taking a seat on the blanket. "Wash first. Then, you can have more. You mustn't vomit."

Nodding, he slurped another mouthful before dipping below the surface, scrubbing away nearly a year's worth of urine and grime. The chill of the water made the sores on his back and wrists sting, a mix of acute pain and soothing relief that finally broke him. His sobs came quietly at first, tears mixing in with pond water. Then, they grew more audible as evidence of the torturous days and weeks sloughed off, shedding the dank, abysmal conditions of his cell.

After the rejuvenating soak, Werner dragged himself from the pond, his soaked, oversized clothes nearly slipping right off his body. As a breeze whisked through the meadow, Werner trembled.

"Here. You must change into something more appropriate than that atrocious criminal garb. A man of your prior stature belongs in something more *elegant*."

She summoned a growing orb of light in the palm of her avian hand, waited until it grew to the size of an apple, and then tossed it in his direction. Once the orb of light made contact with his fur, warm energy shot through him. The light swirled in narrow circles around his torso and extremities. In seconds, her spell had transformed his baggy prisoner's uniform into a fitted, formal suit with smooth lines made of royal purple velvet fabric. It bore the crest of Taernsby over the right side of his chest. He rubbed the warm, dry fabric as the last of the orb's energy dissipated into the grass beneath him through the soles of his polished black boots.

He felt like himself again, only frail and malnourished, sanity fraying.

"Why?" he croaked. It was all he could manage to get out, his muscles weak.

Ceosteol cawed a strange laugh. She tossed a grape in the air and burst the tender fruit between the halves of her beak. "Why *what*? Why *here*? Why *me*? Why *tonight*? Come, darling. You were always one of the most well-spoken on Exos's council. With that silver tongue, I expect more from you. Out with it, Werner. Mind games do get tiresome."

Werner made his way over slowly and took a seat on the far edge of the blanket, casting a weak glance at the floating light orbs above, a form of magic he'd never fathomed possible.

He eyed the food, hesitating to eat despite his stomach's ravenous growls.

"Eat." Ceosteol gestured to the food. "You'll need your strength."

"For what?" he managed.

"Don't worry. It isn't *poisoned*, if that's what you're thinking."

Bits of the night that his life had gone awry flashed before his eyes.

Council members lunging at each other like feral beasts...

The shrill screams of friends he had served with for years...

Grayson's stubby fingers pressing into a pair of eyeballs until they burst...

The orc boy who calmly watched the massacre unfold, his glowing gaze the same shade of toxic green as the quichyrd's in front of him...

"Why would I bother freeing you if you could not trust me? If I were going to execute you, Werner, I'd have spared myself the trouble and done it in your cell. I'd have simply strangled you to death with a noose of braided magic threads and made your demise look like one of natural causes."

Werner scarfed down a roll, too hungry to question her logic. Next, he grabbed fruit and stuffed it in his maw, too, before he had fully swallowed the sourdough.

"I assure you, this is much-needed sustenance that you've been deprived of for far too long."

Werner sat a little straighter, washing down a hunk of cheese with a goblet of peach wine. "Enough chatter. If there's something you need from me, *get on with it.*"

Ceosteol threw her head back and squawked a chuckle, the likes of which made the landigo's body tense. "Being an outcast for so long, myself, has made me eager for discourse. But that's fine. I'll cut to the quick. I want us to become... *allies.*"

He snorted, violently ripping off a drumstick from the baked chicken and indelicately shoving the wad of meat between his cracked lips. After crudely chewing and hastily swallowing, he said, "Have you not seen where I reside now? I wield no power anymore. My future is as bland and boring as the seasoning on this fowl." He spat a bit of bone into the grass.

Ceosteol was grateful that, unlike humans, her beak could hide her grimace. "Cooking is not a strength of mine, I'm afraid. I set my sights on higher ambitions, something far greater."

"Like what?"

"Like prestige, progress, *power.*" The last word rolled off her tongue like viscous molasses.

"Power, huh?" His eyebrows furrowed in confusion. "What *power,* exactly?"

"Brilliant minds like ours are wasted in cells and hovels. We are meant to shed light in the crevices of humanity. We don't follow a path. Instead, we are the ones *paving* it."

Werner tossed down the cleaned chicken bone and sucked the grease from his finger pads.

"You know Destoria," she continued. "You were once highly revered."

He laughed at the preposterous notion and then choked down another roll, eyes full of shame.

"You made but one mistake, Werner. No man is perfect. In time, Destorians will offer forgiveness. The isle's aches soothe with the passage of time."

She turned her attention to the night sky, the endless stars reflecting in her green eyes. "The sun rises and the moons chase it away, day after day, despite our desire for the sand in the hourglass to halt. We arrive in this world naked, lawless creatures. Then, we impose rules. We follow blindly. We trust that the society before us was wiser than we are. But who truly governs our behavior, our thoughts, our minds?" The corners of her beak twisted into a wry smile. "We do. Everything in this life... the rules, the expectations, the relationships, the respect... it is all fluid. In a morphing existence, the only constant... is *change* itself."

Werner grumbled, "Enough. Speak plainly. Tell me what you desire of me, or send me back. At least in my cell, there was silence."

Ceosteol shook her head, irritated by the brazen disrespect. "You need me. I can get you out of that dank dungeon."

"And what of you? Surely, this must benefit you in some way, Ceosteol. In all of my years of being acquainted with you, I can safely say you are not known for your charity."

"I need your connections," she barked, bluntly.

He laughed. "You truly are mad. I *have* none." He sucked in a deep lungful of night air, his eyes taking in the majesty of the blue-black sky for possibly the last time. "Return me. Power-hungry diplomats wouldn't dare speak with a criminal like me. Such an association would end their careers, surely."

"What if I could have royalty issue a formal retraction of all of your charges?"

Werner perked up and narrowed his eyes, trying to figure out if she was serious.

"What if I could have your reputation somewhat restored? I've already been using some connections to plant seeds of disbelief among the locals in Willowdale."

"How?"

"I have my ways, Werner. You don't lurk in the shadows of this isle for as long as I have and not pick up some tricks along the way. It wasn't hard."

"I don't understand how that's possible."

"It's simple, really. Nearly everyone who bore witness to your crime that night is dead. Most died in the massacre. The few remaining witnesses have been sworn to secrecy."

"How do you know? You weren't there." His eyes shot open as something suddenly dawned on him.

The orc child's green, glowing eyes...

"You *were* there. Weren't you?"

Ceosteol looked away, her practiced composure unwavering. "We'll remold your image and paint you as a lone survivor, a hero who tried to save your fellow council members, a wrongly-accused prisoner who suffered months of abuse in the dungeons. We can say you went on a hunger strike, kept alive by a need for true justice."

A glimmer of hope flickered behind Werner's eyes, only to quickly be snuffed out by reality. "You cannot *possibly* have that sort of influence. I feel like your wicked intent is to crush the remains of my spirit with some twisted game of the mind."

She placed her delicate hand on him, lowering the roll in his grasp back down to the blanket. "No trickery. Simply a mutually-beneficial arrangement. A simple trade. Freedom for allegiance."

"I refuse to become some morbid pet for you, sitting and speaking on command. I still have my pride."

With a flick of her wrist, the portal ripped a wide circle out of nowhere, and his dungeon cell reappeared in the chilled night air before him. His shackles hung against the wall, tufts of his spotted fur still caught in the hinges. It was a welcoming entrance back to an abysmal existence full of pain, starvation, soul-crushing boredom, and torment.

He recoiled, the food curdling in his stomach at the sight of the cell. The whirling ring of light framed his other option.

Finally, he managed to look away and speak. "What are your terms?"

Ceosteol closed the portal, once again severing the ties between the meadow and the grim reality of the Ruby Castle dungeon. Her voice was soft, like a mother lulling an uneasy infant back into a peaceful sleep. "Life will be better than it ever was, Werner. We will make it so, together."

A symph fluttered toward the quichyrd, perching on her shoulder. Its wolf-like face and colorful wings were barely discernible in the moonlight, but its howl set off a chain reaction with all of the other noisy symphs nearby. Soon, the calm meadow hummed with their tiny wails. Ceosteol petted the symph on her shoulder with a crooked claw, tickling its chin in the perfect spot to make its hind paw thump with satisfaction. She held her talon up to the symph's wet nose to silence it. The others quieted, too.

She stared at Werner with a gaze so intense that he leaned back. "Don't let your dark deeds stop you from becoming what Destoria needs. Not all deeds are rewarded or punished. Sometimes we must exist in the gray." She held out her scaly claws. "I can send you back now... or you can give me your palm."

"Why do you need my palm?"

"We must bond our souls," she hissed.

Hesitantly, Werner leaned forward and offered her his whole arm. She grabbed him, her talon quickly slashing through his flesh. He hissed and tried to jerk away, but her knobby fingers wrapped around his wrist and forcefully pulled him back toward her.

He looked into her eyes, disarmed by her suddenly calm demeanor. She gouged the thin skin of her own arm and drew her inky, black blood upward. She pointed at his open wound and whispered, "*Vide ut vidi.*"

The blood darted inside his wound, as if the liquid itself were sentient.

Werner's head swung backward, and he screamed, symphs mimicking him until their voices were a chaotic cacophony.

Swirling in from the corners of his eyes, the blackness swallowed up the whites, enveloping them fully. For a moment, he panicked, fearing he'd gone blind. Then, after a flash of brilliant green, he could see again.

Only this time, he saw his own body, his frail landigo form trembling in the quichyrd's clutches. He viewed himself through the glowing eyes of Ceosteol...

Before everything dimmed to black.

15

The Lagdaloon Saloon
Lagdaloon, Silvercrest

The darkness was an abyss, one Werner had fallen into. There was no light. No sound. Not one chirp of an evening cricket. He screamed into the void, the nothingness, but no sound came from his mouth. As though he were bound with twine, gagged with a wad of cloth, all he could do was watch flaccidly as a pinprick of light came into view like a single star on a blanket of black.

Soon, the light expanded and engulfed him, blinding him for a moment. As his vision cleared, Werner realized that he was watching the world through the eyes of a young child, one who came up to the waist of the eaflic walking beside her. Though the youthful eaflic boy couldn't be more than ten years old, his large hand seemed to swallow her tiny claws.

Near them, donik trees flexed in the wind, leaves fluttering in the humid, spring air. Several rambunctious roses clustered together beneath trees, dodging the eaflic's wide feet. Lazy lilacs drooped, emitting a scent so wonderful it could cause even the most alert mind to doze. The brooding sky grew dark with spring rain, clouds dimming Werner's view of the rickety wooden building through the young quichyrd's eyes as the body he was tethered to approached the saloon door.

He could sense her dread and experienced the pain shooting through her leg with each limping step. He felt his heart race -- *her heart* -- beneath their small, feather-covered chest.

He could sense her thoughts, too. As the leaves on the trees rattled, the child, whose body and soul he was inhabiting, recalled the sounds of crashing waves on the coast a year prior, before she was sent back to live with her mother. With every *whooshing* gust, she felt a wave of tranquility wash over her until a small smile played at the corners of her beak.

Her downy feathers, not yet toughened by years in the elements, flitted as cool air rushed between them, relieving her momentarily from the stifling warmth of her cotton gown, whose long sleeves and high neckline made her feel suffocated most of the time.

The plump eaflic looked down at her and gave her a smile, one that felt wholly insincere, as if he knew an unfortunate fate awaited her. His chubby fingers wrapped around the metal handle, and he opened the door to the saloon.

The pungent smell of fresh-cut tanook intermingled with the floral perfumes of the various courtesans in a noxiously sweet blend. Werner's eyes adjusted to the dim lighting, the child's gaze seeking out a familiar form, a woman draped over a table. Her mother.

Werner's eyes turned up to face the eaflic. His mouth opened, and a child's voice came out, the recognizable lisp of Ceosteol, only far younger.

"Isn't she beautiful? I wish I looked more like *her* than my father."

Young Ceosteol's clawed feet clacked against the floorboards as she hobbled.

Her mother, a giggling elf that bore no resemblance at all beyond her striking green eyes, was sprawled vulgarly across the tabletop between two drunk barbarians and an ewanian patron. Clad in a skin-tight velvet gown, her wavy blonde tresses dragged across the mead-soaked tabletop. She froze the second she caught sight of Ceosteol, her tan cheeks blushing to a pink the color of salmon meat. Her flirtatious smile evaporated, and she politely excused herself, gracefully sashaying toward Werner. She grimaced.

"Bref, why is she here? You know she is only allowed out after dark!" Ceosteol's mother growled quietly. She forced a phony, pleasant smile and waved back at the gaggle of men she'd been entertaining.

Bref was meek. "Sorry, Lady Broadrick. She was crying. We were pretending to be pirates. She fell off one of the crates in the basement and landed too hard. She says her leg hurts. She's walking strangely. I'm afraid she might have broken something."

Lady Broadrick sighed. "And what am I supposed to do about that, Bref?"

"She's in pain, m'lady."

Lady Broadrick leaned closer to Ceosteol and Bref. "This is our chance at a better life. Nobody wants to wed a mother. This coin and these men... they could possibly change *everything* for us. But, I can't have them knowing about my bastard quichyrd. At least... for *now*."

The eaflic nodded and squeezed Werner's hand through the rejection.

"Take her across the street to the apothecary. See if they can do something for her. Then, take her right back to the basement next door. I'll be down later to check on her." She dug in the flattened coin purse tied to her thigh with two garter ribbons.

"Here. Now, off you go." She shoved the coins into Bref's free hand and walked back to the table without looking back.

Werner felt the pang of disappointment grip the quichyrd's chest as her unsympathetic mother left.

The ewanian spilled mead on his fancy, white tunic with polished agate toggles and shouted, "Your kindness knows no bounds, Lady Broadrick, but you shouldn't feed the beggars. They're like rats. Once you feed them, they'll never stop coming around for more."

Ceosteol's mother acted as though the ewanian had told the funniest joke she had heard in ages. "Oh, Darling, I've been told more than once that I am *far* too giving for my own good. I think I just need a man who can support my generous heart."

The barbarian beside her purred, "Your inner beauty is only rivaled by that enchanting face."

The vision warped in Werner's eyes, transporting him to another memory of Ceosteol's.

Digging in the dirt, his hands unearthed a brown potato. His quichyrd claws were larger now, more callus. He felt older, taller, as he rose and wiped the excess loam onto the filthy skirt draped over his legs and took a bite of the vegetable. Werner could taste the iron-tinged flavor of dirt. He could feel the starchy crunch as she mashed it between the halves of her beak.

She hobbled through rows of tall corn as she made her way to another part of a farm, hunching low to avoid detection by the farmer tilling a ridge for cabbage nearby. She skulked through a patch of tomato vines, propped by tripods of donik sticks and twine. Halfway through, she halted abruptly.

Lying in the dirt at her feet was the fluffy white form of a raakaby. Its rainbow-colored ear feathers bristled in the breeze. Werner stared at it through her eyes, waiting for its chest to rise or fall. After nearly a full minute of stillness, of silence, she was positive the creature was dead.

Werner felt its cold body in her dirty avian hands. Tears stung her eyes as the creature's head lolled, body limp in her hands. Its pink nose had gone pale. Its white whiskers were speckled with soil. She traced its mouth with her finger to wipe away the mud and sliced herself on its razor-sharp front teeth, leaving a streak of her blood on the protrusions poking out of its stiff lip.

She bunched her skirt and nestled the dead creature in the cloth cocoon. She turned away and scuttled back to the main road.

As she reached the well-worn path, something knocked against her thigh. With a furrowed brow, she carefully opened the bunched fabric and looked down at the raakaby.

It appeared to be alive, struggling to right itself. Werner felt Ceosteol's eyes widen in amazement as its face turned to look up. He had never seen one up close before. Its eyes were unlike anything he'd ever seen, shining back the same glowing green hue as Ceosteol's. The raakaby thumped its hind legs, using its clawed front paws to shred a path up the front of her dress.

Ceosteol shrieked fearfully, trying to shake it loose from the fabric, but the critter nestled against her neck, perching on her shoulder. She reached up and stroked its fur gently. It burrowed closer, as if it needed more contact.

Ceosteol laughed and limped toward town, eager to make her new companion at home in the dank basement of the

Lagdaloon Saloon, the underground stone pit she had called home for most of her childhood.

The landscape morphed again, and the pond came back into view. From the intensity of the forceful time shift, Werner panted, struggling to focus on the blanket beneath his spotted legs.

"Take a moment. Breathe," Ceosteol said.

Finally, he caught his breath and scooted away onto the grass, desperate to put some distance between him and the quichyrd. "What was that? What did you do to me? How?"

"I was showing you my memories, Werner. I want you to understand."

"That raakaby... it was dead. How did it...?"

"That was the day I discovered my ability to blood bond. From what I have seen, it's among the rarest of skills. Though there *was* someone, they say, over a hundred years ago with blood like mine."

"Where is she now?"

Ceosteol flashed a morose smile. "They burned her alive. Chained her to the gates of the Ruby Palace and lit her up like a torch, dear Werner."

Werner's blood felt cold.

"She had a son a few years before they killed her. I have reason to believe he was my father."

"So something in your blood has the ability to bring things back from the dead?"

She nodded. "We share a bond now, too." She pointed at the blood on his forearm, the wound already scabbing over. "My memories can be yours now. You share my history. You can share my thoughts. And I, yours."

He stared at the grass, trying to wrap his mind around it all.

"I know what you're thinking right now, and to answer your question, yes, while my blood can bring beings back from the dead, they are not exactly *living* when I do. They become... an extension of me.

They still exist. Their ideas and memories are still real, still their own. But their existence is dependant upon our bond. A piece of me resides in them, a sliver of them in me. I feel their pain, taste their food, and feel the touch of their lovers. But if I ever choose to sever our bond, they cease to exist once again," she hissed. "Death is but a suggestion with a friend like me."

"So, you can force me to see your memories? Does that mean you see all of mine?" Werner swallowed hard.

"Afraid not. I can see through the eyes of any being I share a soul bond with, but only in the present."

"Are... *we* bonded now?"

She nodded.

After a long silence, Werner whispered, with tears in his eyes. " *Why me*?"

"Everyone deserves a new beginning." A breeze swept through the meadow, and Ceosteol ruffled her dark feathers, puffing out her chest. "You and I... we are not so different. We've both been cast aside, misunderstood. We've been doomed to the cellars, the dungeons, the underground darkness, cast out of society for far too long. It is time for *our* day in the sun, Werner. It is time for a *revolution*."

16

Irenas Parnix's Home
The Radiant Sea

"Have you sailed through Ravenspell Bay?" Parnix sang, strumming a hunk of twisted driftwood as if it were a lute. "*The sparkling water is black as the night. A mirror of the sky where hope takes flight.*" Parnix leaned over, beard hair singeing as it brushed against Omen's flaming skin. "*When the candles dim, and there's no sun in sight, she parts her legs and shows him the light!*"

"Wow," Twitch howled, slapping his hands on a towering stack of books beside the chair he was lounging in. “How do I not know this song?”

Omen grinned, turning his face toward Parnix, almost nose-to-nose with the old man. “I do not need to be this close to your face.”

Parnix leaned away, wobbling toward Violet, who sat, trying to reorganize the books that had been blown off the shelves in Parnix’s earlier tirade. Irenas plucked a book from her hand and tossed it on the floor. He yanked her to her feet and spun her around in a clumsy attempt at a ballroom dance.

Parnix sang until he started to go hoarse, his lyrics devolving into utter nonsense.

Violet pulled away. “Grandfather, rest your voice. I’ll get you some more water.”

“Hey,” Omen barked, unfastening a flask from his hip. “Fill me up, too, would ya?”

Omen’s flask sailed toward her, but was deflected by Twitch, who swatted it away in the nick of time. Violet smiled and gave the wyl an appreciative nod. "Thank you."

"Don't mention it." He glared at Omen. "Only an *animal* would throw something at a beautiful woman."

Violet returned from the kitchen with a glass container of water and a full flask moments later. She handed the container to her grandfather, and he chugged the contents as if he were dehydrated. Then, he lobbed it onto the floor and whirled in large circles, arms out wide like a child. Soon, dizziness overtook him, and he slammed into a bookcase.

"Ugh, this is just water," Omen said, grimacing as he took a sip from his flask.

"What did you think it was, genius?" Violet spat back.

"I don't know. I thought he had wine or spirits or... something in there."

"He hasn't touched the stuff in a year, Omen."

"The water here tastes even nastier than usual." Omen started to pour out his flask on the floor beside his chair, making faces at the taste.

Twitch watched in disbelief, his eyes locked on the blatant act of disrespect until Parnix slammed into a table, hard enough to break bones. The candle on it toppled over into the puddle of water on the floor.

Instead of extinguishing the flame, the water acted as a fuel. It *woofed* high in a brief, bright ball of flames. It simmered and bubbled, the puddle roiling as flames danced on its surface.

"What the..." Quistix rose from her stool, eyes locked on the puddle.

"What was *in* that?" Aurora asked, shaking her drowsy eyes and blinking hard from her spot on the floor. She carefully rose onto her hooves to examine it closer. The esteg sniffed the liquid and recoiled.

"It's just... water," Violet said, pointing at the bucket at the edge of the kitchen.

Aurora turned toward the wizard, eyes locking with the man's massive pupils. "When did you start feeling like this?"

"Like what?" he asked, gesturing so wildly he knocked his arm into Violet's chest. "Oh! Sorry." He turned back to Aurora. "I feel the best I have felt in ages. No more creaking knees, no more aches and pains."

"How long have you been feeling this... spry?"

"Can't rightly say. It's like a wave of relief just sort of washed over me a few weeks back. Even the ocean floor residents have seemed at peace lately. Mating habits, dominance rituals, even feeding patterns have all seemed a little... slower. Less aggressive."

"I think I might have an idea what's going on. On our way down here, we saw a ship. Any idea what it was hauling?"

Parnix thought for a moment. "I'm not entirely sure. I know which one you speak of, too. I've been documenting the mating and migration patterns of the glitterfish near there. I'd never been able to get very close to them. They're so skittish, you see. But ever since that thing went down… they *have* been much more curious. Playful with me, even."

Omen rose, concerned. He looked at Quistix. "You guys up for paying that shipwreck a visit?"

17

The Ruby Palace West Wing Bedchambers
Desdemona, Willowdale

Quistix Daedumal of Bellaneau,

As you can see from the royal seal, this is a genuine correspondence from the royal queen of Destoria, her majesty Vervaine Brius.

I am afraid this message is of a very private and urgent matter. Someone who has spent decades in the shadows has bestowed upon me a "gift." I cannot divulge the details of it in my correspondence, lest this letter be intercepted on its journey to you.

With your magical abilities, you have become an almost mythical figure among the commoners. That is precisely why I pray you'll be willing to overlook your past with my sister; may her soul rest in peace. You are the only one who knows the deepest truths about my rise to power.

I understand you may not trust me. If roles were reversed, I'd have likely burned this letter the moment I saw the royal seal. I can only hope you will show more mercy than my family has shown you. I never desired to see you rot in my dungeon. After the esteg healed me fully, I had plans to pardon you all.

There are murmurings in the streets and alleys of a revolution on the horizon. I beg of you, we must work together before this isle is left in ruins.

I wish to extend a proposition: three formal pardons. In exchange, you must agree to meet so that we may discuss a certain necromancer who plagues us both.

I pray this letter finds you quickly. I fear I am not long for this world. One attempt has already been made on my life. Time is of the essence.

On the third day of autumn, meet me near your family home—

A taloned hand drifted in from Vervaine's periphery and grasped the piece of parchment. Ceosteol crumpled it, smearing the damp ink on the queen's wooden desk.

Vervaine was pinned beneath a glowing, green stare that froze her like a scruffed kitten. Tears pricked her eyes as she stared forward, across a war room with a wide table with maps pinned down by the corners with marble statuettes. The God of War sat in his stone glory, sword hoisted high in celebration, grieves glinting, his boot resting on two bodies stacked atop each other.

Vervaine's eyes affixed to the ceremonial axe hanging over the fireplace, one that felt miles away. She flinched when Ceosteol's robe came into view beside her.

"Why must you repeatedly test me? Hmmm?" Ceosteol asked before lighting the parchment on fire with the flame of a nearby everburn torch sconce. She let the flaming pieces of it fall to the stone floor, watching each blacken into soot.

Vervaine's heart sank at the sight of it. Every careful word, nothing but embers.

"Your sadness is my own. Your joy, your heartache, your fury... it all belongs to me. What you see, I see. Every scheme that pops into that little head of yours, I'm *there*."

Vervaine's eyes watered, tears threatening to spill. Ceosteol ran her talons through the silky strands of her chestnut-colored hair and lightly stroked the queen's back through her thin dressing gown.

"Free will in exchange for life."

"Life without freedom is not life at all. It is merely *existing*. I never asked for this trade. I'm not Exos. This wasn't something I wanted. I would have never agreed to your terms!"

"Would you have preferred I leave you in that prison to be tossed around like a rag doll between those crimson soul reapers? There wouldn't have even been enough of that pretty little face to bury." Ceosteol cackled.

"Instead, I'm being used like a marionette with someone controlling my every move. I would have preferred the reapers!"

Ceosteol's lips turned upward. "Is that so?"

Tears finally fell, weaving down Vervaine's face. "As far as I'm concerned, I *did* die in that cave that day. You just keep bringing me back. It's like suffering through layer after layer of the Nether."

"You are so ungrateful. You've received the greatest gift one can offer, and you spit in my face."

Vervaine's lips flattened into a tight line, her cheeks flushing with anger. "You're just as sad, old, *lonely* buzzard who has to *force* people to be around you. You're sick!"

Her eyes flicked again to the axe over the hearth.

Without needing to look, Ceosteol spoke again. "Go ahead. Grab it. Cut off my head. Better yet," she reached inside the folds of her robe and produced an emerald-encrusted dagger, "hurt yourself. This time, I will not rescue you."

Vervaine searched Ceosteol's face, trying to decide if she was bluffing. She stood and walked toward the fireplace. Light danced on the axe's golden handle. She gripped it in her hand and plucked it from the wall.

"On with it, then," Ceosteol hissed, storming toward the map table in the center of the room. She bent at the waist, stretching out her elongated neck over a corner of the table, eyes boring into Vervaine.

The look was a challenge, one Vervaine gladly accepted. She stomped toward the quichyrd and swallowed hard while raising the axe high overhead, staring at Ceosteol's neck. Arms trembling, she peered down at the old woman who had caused her so much heartache and yet was the reason she was still alive. The woman was a spectator to every thought and feeling in her mind, her heart.

She screamed and swung the axe, pinching her eyes to avoid the gore.

Before the blade could make contact, it was as if the weapon froze in place, her arms seized mid-air, forearms burning from waves of resistance. Warping heat radiated from the quichyrd's feathered flesh and the blade hovered, stuck in place mere inches above Ceosteol's spine.

Ceosteol slithered out from beneath the weapon, green, glowing eyes wide with shock.

"I can't believe you were really going to do it," she squawked. "After all I've done for you, you were actually going to cut my head off!"

Ceosteol took a few steps away, Vervaine still holding the immovable axe in mid-air.

"Our bond does not sever your soul. It melds *ours together*. My blood called you back from the Ethereal Sanctum and anchored you here for more time!"

She traced her sharp talon along the healed skin of Vervaine's cheek hard enough to leave a pink stripe down it.

"You grieve a life you once knew, but nearly everything you were still exists! I feel it, that ache in your chest, that tender spot in your soul. Life is granted without *anyone's* consent, my dear. From our first breath, we are here because someone else forced us to be. How is what I've done *any* different?"

Ceosteol released her hold on the axe and let the blade of it smash hard into the table.

Vervaine crumpled to the floor and sobbed. “Because... now I am under your control! So is Arias! Our choices are not our own. Our will is not free. Why can’t you understand that?!”

The quichyrd said as she started toward the door. “You never asked for this gift. Yet, I gave it freely, at the cost of my own sanity and strength. I could’ve let you die for good, either time, but I *know* Destoria’s future is brighter with you.”

“You just want to use us to push your insane agenda! A brighter future? How is that possible once this isle is overrun with all of your unholy abominations, crawling with the undead? You picture yourself as some kind of God! But I have enough of those! I’ve seen how you live, what twisted creations your mind comes up with while you play with things meant to be laid to rest. You play with us like toys!”

Infuriated by the queen’s back-talk, Ceosteol raised her hands high, as if summoning something. Two whirling voids opened up out of nowhere, one at Vervaine's feet, one above her head. From the darkened voids, decayed hands with flayed flesh reached out, gripping Vervaine by the ankles, locking her in place. She screamed, and another hand slid down and clasped over her mouth.

More hands grabbed from both portals, fingers digging into her flesh, chipped nails gouging, palms leaving smears of dirt and old blood on her pale skin. The hands above gripped her hair, tangling and twisting for a better hold. The ones around her ankles yanked forcefully downward. All of the extremities pulled in various directions. Vervaine felt the pull in her stomach as they tried their best to rip her in two.

"The people of this isle treat the dead like they are trash to be discarded," Ceosteol yelled, hearing boots clattering in the hall. She rushed over and bolted the lock on the door. "Your father was different. That's why I was always so drawn to him. He spent most of his life seeking a cure for death.

Turns out, I had it all along. But you Tempests never did listen to me. You'd still have a mother if your father had trusted me. Wouldn't life have been better if she'd been around?"

Vervaine's muffled screams died in mid-air as a chunk of her hair was tugged from her scalp and sucked up into the portal above. She whimpered and tried her best to nod.

Ceosteol's anger softened. Clasping her hands together, she forced the portals to close, severing two of the slowest hands like sideways guillotines.

Behind her, the door to the war room thundered. A voice called out. "Queen Vervaine! Open the door, your majesty!"

Another voice with an accent Vervaine couldn't place spoke. "Break it down!"

Wham!

Wham!

Wham!

The sounds of the battering ram, clattering armor, and groaning wood hammered through the room as Vervaine struggled to compose herself, unable to pry her eyes off the severed set of hands at her feet, unable to ignore the noxious scent of decayed flesh rising up in her face.

Ceosteol approached her, restrained fury percolating behind her glowing eyes. "You have two choices. You can either stop waging war against me and comply..."

"Or?" Vervaine asked, trying her best not to sound defiant.

Ceosteol kicked one of the severed hands toward Vervaine's slippered foot.

"Or you can end up like one of them."

The threat from the unhinged quichyrd chilled Vervaine to the core. The door burst open. Several guards tumbled atop one another in the entryway.

"Are you alright, my queen?" one of the guards asked, rising from the pile.

"We heard screaming," another said.

A third man sniffed hard, glanced around, and gasped as he saw the severed hands on the floor. "By the Gods, what happened?"

"What are you talking about?" Ceosteol's eyes swirled, and she flapped the folds of her purple robe. The hands vanished in an instant. "Have you men been eating tainted meat? Do you all share some sort of fever? No one was screaming. There are no hands."

The men looked around, confused for a moment.

"Men, get down to see the royal apothecary. You might be sick, though likely not from anything a tincture and good night's rest can't cure. Isn't that right, Vervaine?"

Vervaine thought about the severed hand that had touched her moments before and nodded.

"Rest assured, soldiers. I'm alive and well," she lied.

18

East Wing of The Ruby Palace
Desdemona, Willowdale

As voices boomed through the militia's sleeping quarters, Rebecca Glenshire of Apex summoned a blue soul gem, one that emitted a faint sky-blue glow on the dark stone walls of the hall outside, its cool shade wrestling for dominance with the warm orange of the everburn sconces on the wall. Then, she focused her steely eyes on the pinched fingers of her other hand as she spread them, summoning a pink orb of light. She affixed it in the air, too, and smiled. She glanced around her chambers, now painted in multi-colored lights that reminded her of the way the sun hit through the stained glass windows at the Institute of Magic back in Apex. Despite being an isle away from everything she'd ever known, she suddenly felt at home.

A loud thud resonated from the shared stone wall beside her, followed by several men's cheers, and she gasped. Just as her heart's pounding began to slow, a gruff knock sounded again, this time at her door.

"Is… it a medical emergency?" she asked, her honeyed voice slightly meek.

"No, but I'm hoping you might make an exception for your king."

Her eyes bolted open wide. She smoothed her powder-blue robe, embroidered with the institute's symbolic eye. Opening the door, she froze at the sight of the akiah king flanked by two guards standing at attention.

"I'm sorry to disturb you at this hour." Arias's voice was drowned out by another burst of shouts from the barracks next door. "I'm afraid we have not been properly introduced."

"Professor Rebecca Glenshire." She shook her head and let out a nervous chuckle. Then, with her thick Apexian accent, she corrected herself. "No, sorry. I guess it's just *Rebecca Glenshire* now that I'm here. Old habits are hard to break."

"Certainly. You came highly recommended. The headmaster sang your praises and assured me you have achieved quite an impressive list of accolades during your tenure in Apex." A smile formed through the short fur on the akiah's face. He held up a satchel with a bunched length of netting hanging out from the top flap like a white rope tongue. "I'm going on a little late-night filibrat hunt. Would you care to accompany me?"

She glanced out at the window at the darkness beyond and then back at him. "You're serious?"

Arias gave a hearty laugh and nodded. “Yes. I am afraid I am.”

“It’s the middle of the night.”

“Filibrats are nocturnal. They’re becoming quite the menace around here. They came in on the Asera’s trade ships and now they run rampant, breeding like damned raakabies. They’ve been decimating some of the local crops, and there are rumblings that they have spread a nasty fever among the dwarf population. One even reported that he’d gone blind because of them.” He motioned to the guards next to him. “These men seem to know where they have a nest nearby.”

“I am sorry, your majesty. I’m a healer. It isn’t in my nature to kill.”

“None will be slain tonight, I assure you. They are to be captured and studied. Think of it, instead, as an opportunity to learn about a new species and potentially figure out a treatment or tincture of protection for the dwarves.”

Reluctantly, she nodded her head.

"Excellent. You're going to want to bring your cloak. The air tonight is brisk."

The crickets chirped their nightly song. Distant symphs howled, breaking the otherwise eerie silence of the grounds.

Rebecca walked and waited, unsure if she was allowed to speak first or whether she should wait until spoken to. She decided to err on the side of caution and glanced upward, wishing she could count the stars until she fell asleep, just as she had as a child.

"Are you cold? Or just uncomfortable?" Arias asked.

She gave a kind smile, touched that a man of his stature would dare try to understand such nuance.

"I suppose I'm a touch uncomfortable. I hope people won't talk about you being seen with me at night like this. You know how rumors can spin out of hand and cause unnecessary frustration."

"I appreciate your consideration, but I'm capable of snuffing out nonsense.

People will always talk. However, I trust these guards with my life, quite literally. They have been nothing but discreet since I have held the throne."

Nearing a hole in a mounded pile of dirt on the ground, Arias kneeled. "Guards, hold the net here, just outside of the opening. I'll root it out from the other side."

The guard nodded, his voice muffled beneath the lip of his metal helm. "Your majesty, forgive me for my bluntness, but are you sure you don't want the guards and staff to eradicate these? It feels reckless to allow you to have contact with such vile vermin. Surely, you have more important things to trouble yourself with."

Arias stood. "A hunter must keep his mind sharp, always. There's no sense in losing my skill and agility simply because my seat now comes with a cushion. One mustn't become complacent."

The guard nodded respectfully at the king and his new, royal physician.

A bulge of dirt suddenly rose through the grass and raced in a winding path through the courtyard, churning the soil effortlessly in its wake. The underground creature came to an abrupt stop and spewed loosened loam into the air near the castle's East Wing entrance.

Arias bolted toward it, as fast as his akiah legs would take him. Rebecca watched as he skidded onto the ground beside the hole and plunged the fiery end of his torch inside.

"He's coming!" Arias laughed, his breath visible.

The bulge followed its new path back toward Rebecca. A guard slid on a pair of thick gloves from the satchel, and he pinned the net loosely over the hole with both hands and knees. The other guard stepped away with his torch, allowing the animal a dark exit.

"Rebecca, come!" Arias waved her over to him, and she followed obediently, careful not to mash down the bulged path of grass. Once she arrived by his side, he smiled.

"Ms. Glenshire, are you the philosophical sort or do you prefer cold, hard facts?"

"I suppose a bit of both."

"Excellent. And you are a wielder of magic?"

"Restoration magic. Yes, your majesty. I think you'll find I'm highly proficient."

He nodded, waiting for the furry mass to emerge into the guard's net on the other end of the burrow. "Do you believe in dark magic?"

She swallowed hard, unsure if she should answer. Finally, she did. "Of course, your majesty. Every monument of strength casts a shadow. Light cannot exist without the presence of darkness. But such magic was outlawed a century ago. Fortunately, it's nothing you must concern yourself with now. Even most of the texts about it have been eradicated."

"*Most*?" Arias asked.

Rebecca didn't elaborate. Instead, she stared out at the guards across the lawn. "Why do you ask? Has there been some sort of... incident?"

"No," he laughed, an obvious lie. "Certainly not. But, humor my hypothetical for a moment, would you?"

"Alright."

"Anything yet?" Arias yelled toward the guard.

The guard swung his head from side to side, still kneeling on the net. The one standing shrugged.

"Alright, stay vigilant!"

"It's probably hiding in the middle. I'll bet their sense of smell is keen," Rebecca volunteered.

"True." Arias thought for a moment and then peered up at the sky. "Suppose it did exist still."

"Dark magic?"

"Yes. And suppose things such as resurrection were possible."

"You mean necromancy?" She chuckled. "Oh, now *that* would be highly unlikely. Though resurrection magic would certainly make *my* job easier," she joked.

"If they existed, resurrected creatures would be classified as *what,* exactly?"

"The undead. I think that term would be most appropriate. But when a soul vacates and then later re-assumes its vessel, surely there would be consequences."

"Like what?"

"Surely a myriad of things. I'm just speculating, but I'd imagine their memories couldn't be fully trusted. There will probably be continued bodily decay. Maybe even some spiritual ties a reanimated corpse might bring back from the other side. They could return as something else entirely. This is the downside of ancestors burning the texts about necromancy during the purge of the libraries. We will never truly know."

"Quite right." Arias tried not to think about how his undead existence was all uncharted territory.

Arias pulled the torch out of the hole and eyed its depths. Suddenly, with the absence of fire, the lump in the earth moved again, this time toward the king.

"Why do you ask about this? I can't help but sense this outing is more than just a meet-and-greet."

"No," he waved her away. "Simply my curiosity in overdrive. It is not every day I meet such a decorated Apexian with a wealth of knowledge in things I am not well-acquainted with. That's all."

"He's headed your way, m'Lord!" one of the guards shouted.

A pink snout poked its nose out from the hole beneath Arias. He sat patiently, stone-still as the vermin sniffed the air and finally started to clamber out of the hole. It gripped the mound of soil with its five-fingered hand, each with a wicked-looking nail that clacked like long teeth. Its fur was the color of sand. It spun around blindly, trying to sense any movement before sticking its neck from the hole.

With a lunge forward that made Rebecca yelp, Arias snatched the small creature by the neck and ripped it out of the hole. One of the guards raced over with a mesh bag made of braided metal wires, and Arias dumped the creature in. It scrambled and thrashed, trying to gnaw through the steel, all the while making a horrific squeal of fear.

"Calm down," Arias mumbled to the creature, through the netting. Then, he nodded at the guard and smiled at Rebecca. "One down."

Rebecca glanced back at the animal, its belly plump from feasting on the nearby vegetation and insects. The filibrat opened its mouth, exposing a pair of gnashing flat front teeth, rodent-like, with two snake-like fangs retracted up into holes beside them. The animal's eyelids flew open, exposing fogged eyes, the same shade as the king's. The filabrat screeched again, the sound so sharp Rebecca had to cover her ears.

Finally, it gave up thrashing as the guard tied the metal ties at the top to a thick stick. He slung it over his shoulder. The animal dangled in the net behind him, hyperventilating. As the armored guard turned to leave, Rebecca grabbed him by the bicep. "Wait! What will you do with it?"

"Me? Nothing." The guard chuckled. "Its fate is in the hands of a quichyrd who is keen on experimentation. You'll see her around the castle. Look for the ugly bird limping around in a purple robe. You can't miss her. This week, she's been keeping an eye on the queen, after her... *mishap*. Now that you've arrived," he jiggled the stick and the filibrat screeched again, "this ought to keep the old coot busy."

"Does she have a name?"

"Ceosteol."

Rebecca's eyes widened, having heard the name before, never for anything good.

"Now that you're here, she's been promoted to Vervaine's and my new advisor." Arias glared at the guard, a silent warning to stop talking. “She’s been the resident apothecary for some time here at the Ruby Castle. I’m sure once you get settled in, she’ll introduce herself. After all, you will likely be working together.”

Rebecca nodded. “She won’t hurt it, will she?”

“She might,” Arias stated plainly. “I don’t like to interfere with her process. She has such a... *curious* mind, after all.”

“Can’t she study it alive?”

“For a while, surely. But sometimes, to understand how something works, one must get inside and see what makes it function. The health and livelihoods of Destorians are worth more than any single life, wouldn’t you agree?”

“Well, of course, but...” Rebecca’s eyebrows rose with concern.

Arias snatched the net with the filibrat off the guard’s pole and offered the squealing animal to her. “Am I to understand you are volunteering to keep such a filthy thing as a pet?”

The blind creature sniffed at her through the wires, its snout wiggling over fangs that dripped viscous drool.

"Actually, if I may, your majesty... I'd like to request that *I* keep it and study it in my chambers. Surely we can find a crab trap or something to keep it in with the wharf so nearby."

"You... wish to... study it?" Arias looked like he'd just eaten something rancid.

"Yes. That liquid it produces... It's interesting. I'd like to do some tests with it of my own, and I can't do that if it is killed."

"I can simply get you another one. They're running amok on these grounds. There's enough to go around."

"Do you recall the spine-back lizards of Evolt?"

"Yes," Aries answered, shifting the weight from one hip to the other. "What of them?"

"They originally began in the city of Enewain, where they were destroying the vegetation, uprooting the flora."

"Right."

"Then, you might also recall they were gathered up and transplanted into Evolt to kill off that horrendous infestation of burrow flies, the ones infecting people with their larvae?"

"...And your point?"

"One province's problem is sometimes another province's solution. Perhaps we can utilize these vermin in a different way, a helpful one."

Rebecca didn't have the heart to warn Arias about Ceosteol's rumored penchant for toying with carrion. She didn't have the nerve to explain that, if what she'd heard about the quichyrd was true, the animal was no more than decaying cannon fodder in her possession.

Arias nodded, "So be it. I'll have my men start to gather them in the raakaby hutches outside the castle walls until you find a better place for them. They cannot be left to breed and run rampant."

"Yes, your majesty." She glanced back at the animal.

"Don't get too attached. Not all life is meant to be saved. Not everything has a purpose," Arias murmured. "At dawn, please see to my wife. Make sure she is still healing alright."

"Healing? From what? If she's hurt, shouldn't I see about her now?"

"No," Arias said calmly despite the low thrum of panic in his gut, recalling the image of her bloodied corpse in his arms mere days before. "She's... resting. See to her in the morning." Then, he looked around and waved the other guard over to them.

"Yes, sir?"

"Escort Ms. Glenshire back to her quarters, please. It's getting a little too cold out here, and we still have a few more of these things to catch tonight."

"Of course, your majesty."

Arias turned back to Rebecca, his lips curling into a polite smile. "Thank you for humoring me. I don't get many opportunities to philosophize these days. It was a pleasure."

Rebecca forced a smile.

"If the guards in your wing are being too loud, don't be afraid to show them your teeth. Manhandle them with some of that legendary Apexian magic, if need be. Just make certain they can still wield a sword at the end of it." he chuckled.

"Will do." Rebecca nodded solemnly and followed the guard back through the courtyard to the drawbridge.

Arias watched her leave, gritting his teeth, his wine-colored eyes following her the entire time.

19

The Lost City of Elathia
The Radiant Sea

"Twitch, stop the damned humming. We need stealth," Quistix grumbled, gliding buoyantly along the ocean floor, irritated eyes darting around in search of hazards in the water around them.

Beside her, Twitch snickered and spun with abandon, creating small vortexes of water along his path. Violet walked several paces behind, trying hard to stifle her giggles. Aurora struggled from the rear, awkwardly kicking and galloping to make headway forward, her magic-imbued gills fluttering wildly with her exertion.

A school of fish darted by. Crustaceans crept drunkenly along the sand, burrowing seemingly at random. Invertebrates passed, some tiring easily, some experiencing a burst of manic energy. Some seemed confused, some fearful.

An octopus squirmed nearby, jetting in a zigzag before head-butting the ocean floor. There it lay, stunned for a moment, tendrils wiggling loosely with the current.

Aurora was in awe. Most of the species were ones the esteg had never read about. A flutterswarm darted between her kicking legs, swirling around her neck in a somewhat-unified pattern before dispersing clumsily in many directions.

Most of the animals seemed disoriented or ill, some sluggish, some anxious. A spider crab lay upside down, lazily kicking all of its legs in a haphazard attempt to right itself. Nearby, a species of red and gold fish with shiny scales spiraled awkwardly along the ocean floor, bumping their noses against the sand and then changing course at random.

Nearly missing a confused blue fish the size of her torso, Quistix glanced back at Aurora. The behaviors of all of these aquatic species struck Quistix as odd. They were all moving like Parnix. Disoriented. Despite the wonderment of the underwater world around her, Quistix felt the uncanny feeling that something the ocean's depths stalking them. She was out of her element, like an ewanian amid an Evoltian blizzard. She searched for Kackaroth, feeling vulnerable to an attack from any angle, fairly powerless to defend herself.

Twitch hummed again, a jaunty tune from his youth on Wyl Isle.

"What are we looking for exactly?" Violet asked with a shy smile, playing with the ring on her necklace.

Quistix turned, her bloodshot eyes locking on the jewelry in Violet's hand before noticing something peculiar over the girl's shoulder. In the distance, a dark shadow drifted along the ocean floor. She stiffened and grabbed Twitch by the arm.

Grinning, he spun her around playfully. "Oh, darling, has our day finally come?"

Angry, Quistix pressed a finger to her lips, the signal for him to shut up. But in his amorous, discombobulated state, he misunderstood completely, taking it as a sign that she finally wanted to kiss. It was, after all, a romantic setting, he supposed.

He angled his snout toward her plump lips and kissed her.

Violet's heart sank at the sight. Quistix recoiled in horror, her red eyes wide with shock.

Twitch pulled back, lips spreading into a bemused smile. "That was... not quite what I had imagined." He giggled, stepping away. "I always imagined we'd have chemistry. Don't worry, darling, with practice, I'm sure we can improve."

"You imbecile," Quistix growled and wiped her mouth roughly with her arm, "I meant... shut... up. Turn around and look!"

He started to turn and tripped over a half-buried conch shell. In slow-motion, he floundered, kicking up sand and silt as he tumbled. He giggled so hard he wheezed, struggling to stand.

Soon, contagious laughter overtook them all, drawing chuckles from the rest of the confused group despite the ominous shadow growing in the distance.

Soon, a full-blown cackle plagued Quistix, too. She was unable to quiet herself, resting her hand on Aurora's back to hold herself steady.

"That kiss... was long... overdue," Twitch managed, fumbling his ability to take two steps.

Delirious, Quistix muttered, in between uncontrollable snickering, "Kiss me again, Twitch, and I'll put my emerald-encrusted dagger right through your throat when I get it back."

Aurora watched the shadow move closer, seized in terror, unable to move.

"You're all threats and red hair, my love. All bark. No bite. But, you should know," he laughed again, "I adore a little biting every now and then."

"Wait, so they're not together?" Violet whispered into Aurora's ear.

Aurora shook her head so hard she nearly knocked Violet over. "No. By the Gods, could you imagine?!"

"We must...focus." Quistix tried to contain her giggling.

"On what, again?" Twitch asked. "I'm having trouble remembering."

Quistix opened her mouth to respond, but felt panic rise. "I... can't remember."

Aurora chuckled, feeling a mixture of giddiness and anxiety. "We're looking for the... the thing."

Violet's playful expression suddenly turned flat. "Guys, how do you all feel right now?"

"Great!" Twitch shouted, doing another spin on wobbling legs.

Quistix focused on Violet, panic growing. "I feel... strange. Like my muscles are humming."

"I feel... light," Aurora said, a large grin plastered on her face. "I think maybe I like it down here."

Violet shook her head, youthful face wrinkling with worry. "Something's wrong. Whatever is happening to my grandfather seems to be happening to us. Right now, we are all a wreck."

The word jogged something in her mind. Quistix snapped her fingers, and bubbles rose from them, rising toward the surface above. "The shipwreck! That's what we were looking for."

"Ah, that's it! The shipwreck. The... thing."

Aurora nodded, her legs suddenly heavier and harder to control. "Yes, let's pick up the pace."

Quistix hesitantly led the way as if the sand might part at any moment and let the ocean floor swallow them whole. The underwater realm felt wrong, as if Destoria had been suddenly tilted on its axis. As her laughter dissipated, an overwhelming sense of dread fell over her like a veil.

"Aurora?" Quistix gasped suddenly. "The spell isn't working! I can't breathe!" She clutched her chest and stumbled. Her breathing grew erratic. Her gills flapped wildly. She gritted her teeth, feeling the intense urge to bolt toward the surface.

Twitch grabbed her by the arms and stared into her eyes. "Q, you're breathing just fine. Just focus on my voice."

"I... I... can't. I'm... drown...ing," she wheezed, her words garbled by the rapid gasps.

Aurora stared at Quistix's functioning gills. "You're breathing. You're just panicked. Try to relax."

Twitch hugged Quistix to his chest as she hyperventilated, softly stroking her back to calm her. "Look up."

A pudgy paddle-shaped creature wiggled out of the sand and scrambled away hurriedly. Quistix looked up at the glittering light of the surface, high above, the ocean's push and pull rocking her as a mother would a newborn.

"How many people can say they've seen anything even remotely as beautiful as this?" The wyl's voice was calming, his soft tone soothing the prickling sensation on the back of her neck. "The world is so calm and quiet here."

Her breathing slowed, panic slowly dissipating.

Violet watched their embrace from a distance, once again feeling like the outsider she'd always been. Evidence of their colorful history made her wish she could be part of a found family, too. Instead, she felt more alone than ever.

Her eyes darted away, unable to watch any more. She felt the longing and jealousy within her grow. Spinning around, she gasped and pointed to something ahead. "Guys, I think that might be what we're looking for!"

With her breathing returning to normal, Quistix's red-rimmed eyes bulged when she saw the hard edges of the stately ship through the seaweed-striped murk, its size enormous, the splintered vessel cracked almost perfectly in half in the middle.

"By the Gods," she whispered.

As they approached the wreckage, thousands of slivers of sea glass glimmered on the ocean floor.

A swarm of bulbous, black fish emerged from the gaping opening of the ship. They were covered in an oily substance that seemed to leave a pearlescent trail in their wake.

Closer still, Violet eyed the jagged wood, ones that seemed like wicked fingers coaxing them all into danger.

A trail of black liquid carved a wiggly line through the water. The chubby fish gobbled it eagerly, sucking the pollution through their small beak-like mouths and expelling clear water from their gills.

The light above was snuffed out, leaving them all in the darkness.

"What is that?" Quistix asked.

"I don't know," Aurora said. Then, the sun's rays appeared again, and the large shadow drifted away.

"Was that Kackaroth?" Twitch asked, speech slurring.

"I hope not," Violet whispered.

They grabbed the splintered planks near the gash in the ship and swam inside. Quistix led the way, shrieking when a swarm of dizzied glitterfish pelted her like loosed arrows in the darkness. They slapped against her clumsily and ricocheted in every direction until they bumbled their way back outside.

Twitch looked at Violet and smiled through the dim remnants of the light. "You've got something on your cheek."

He wiped the oily substance and stared at the residue it left on the pads of his fingers. Then, his hand went numb. "What the...?"

"My face has gone numb! What is this stuff?" Violet was alarmed.

Twitch's eyes widened. "Quistix?" When she didn't respond, he said her name again, this time with more urgency. "Quistix! I think I know what's making ol' Parnix go all cuckoo."

Taking a step forward, Quistix's legs nearly collapsed. She braced herself against Aurora's back. When she approached, her eyes widened in horror. The wyl was standing in front of a pile of busted crates, their contents scattered recklessly, most of the all-too-familiar bottles busted. She lowered to the floor, gills flapping wild in panic. She picked up one of the few bottles containing the black pearlescent liquid that was still intact. She turned to face Aurora.

"Oh no. Please say it isn't so," the esteg muttered.

"Dikeeka." Quistix could barely get the word out, the insidious one that eventually cost her husband his life.

"Do you mean to tell me, a whole ship transporting drugs..." Violet trailed off and looked around at all the shattered glass, some growing green with algae.

Quistix allowed the glass vial to roll around in her palm. Then, she glanced over at what looked to be the skeletal remains of the captain, his bones picked clean by hungry ocean dwellers. "This ship was loaded with drugs."

Quistix made her way back out of the gash in the starboard hull and looked up at the rippling sunbeams to try to collect her thoughts.

Violet and Aurora soon joined her.

"Which direction is this?" Quistix asked, pointing toward the tattered stern of the boat.

"Northeast, I believe," Violet answered, looking back at the lights over the distant underwater city of Elathia.

"What's that direction?" Twitch used an unbroken bottle of dikeeka to point in the direction the bow was facing.

"Knight Harbor, probably," Aurora said. "That means that unless it spun when it sank, the shipment was coming from a southern port in Asera for a delivery in Destoria."

"Exos." Quistix shook her head in disgust. "This has Exos Tempest written all over it."

Violet scrubbed the oily substance off her numb cheek. "What is this stuff?"

"It's a drug," Twitch answered. "People started using it for pain, but then, people started abusing it, taking it for fun, for escape. It's highly addictive. Exos made it legal for apothecaries everywhere on the isle to distribute it. She taxed it to re-stock the treasury so she'd have a surplus to bribe."

Aurora added, "Now, many Destorians find themselves in the throes of addiction."

"To the Nether with the people who use it! For honest reasons or not." Quistix took the vial out of Twitch's hand and hurled it. It went a few feet forward before slowly settling down in the sand in an unfulfilling way.

The sight of it caused another fit of giggles to spark among them all.

"It's not funny," Quistix said. "This garbage sunk its claws into my husband and eventually robbed him of every shred of dignity he had."

Twitch's giggles stopped cold. He cleared his throat to compose himself.

Quistix thought of Rowland, a pang of pain resonating through her tingling body. Gone was the man who picked her wildflowers after his shift in the spring, or the man who held her when morning sickness racked her body the winter she carried Danson. His soft eyes full of love had changed into the sunken stare of a man possessed by the end. In his final days, he no longer resembled the man she'd married. He was a husk, his identity devoured by addiction. The drug itself had not killed him, but the need for it had taken his life all the same.

In the distance, the massive cloud of darkness reappeared, a forest of seaweed distorting it. The pudgy, dikeeka-covered fish scattered ominously in a moment.

Aurora went rigid as the creature came into view, beams of hazy light refracting off its enormous body. Two black nostrils flexed as the mountain of beige scales glided toward them.

Quistix glanced back in the direction of Elathia, their domed barrier too far away.

"In the ship!" she shouted. "Everyone, get in the ship!"

"Are you sure? Shouldn't we swim for the dome?" Violet shouted.

The others followed the order, swimming back into the less-than-promising wooden sanctuary. On his way in, Twitch grasped Violet's hand and pulled her along. "Trust Quistix, Violet. She's gotten us out of some pretty harrowing messes before."

"It's Kackaroth! Shhhh," Quistix hissed, positioning herself between the busted hull's opening and a full, undamaged crate of dikeeka.

The water dragon cruised above them, blotting out the light until they were all submerged in full darkness. Quistix felt around, grasping at broken shards of glass along the planks. She clenched several of the broken bottle scraps between her fingers like a makeshift filabrat claw, one with razor-sharp nails. She was poised to swipe, never having missed the feeling of Swordbreaker at her side more.

Twitch and Violet huddled together behind some crates. He wrapped an arm around her.

A sudden rush of water jostled the boat's halves, and the sun rays reemerged through the gap as the dragon drifted away. Quistix's shoulders slumped as the form disappeared in the distance, relief palpably washing over her like cool, soothing waves on scorched skin.

"That thing is huge! Bigger than it looked in Parnix's dome," Twitch offered breathlessly.

Quistix nodded between ragged, panicked breaths, "Massive."

Darkness fell over them again. Quistix leaned toward the gap in the hull.

Suddenly, the mouth of the behemoth appeared, its snapping rows full of yellowed teeth engulfing the ship's opening with a deafening wooden crunch.

They all screamed as the ship rose through the water and shook violently. They bounced around, teeth piercing through the starboard side, threatening to crush them the instant the saturated wood finally caved. The dragon's jaws opened and bit down again, chewing the vessel like a wolf with a noubald bone.

Paddling, Quistix grabbed the nearest support beam, avoiding the flying crates of dikeeka slamming back and forth. She muttered a silent prayer and then looked around frantically.

"What do we do, Q?!" Twitch shouted.

The boat shook harder, and Quistix nearly lost her hold. "Kick the crates into the gap!" she screamed, launching a crate with both feet toward the opening to illustrate for the others.

Sharp teeth punched through a nearby spot in the hull, fracturing the wood by her head. She screamed.

Twitch and Violet put all four of their feet on one of the full crates. Twitch nodded, and they kicked it away in tandem. The crate hurtled toward the gap and smacked open against the wall. The dragon's massive tongue slid in, plugging the hole, trying to scoop the bottles out of the gap.

CRUNCH!

The walls caved in a little more, trapping them in a space half the size. Aurora jammed her head against a sliding crate and shoved it toward the reptilian tongue with a guttural scream. It hit the wall hard, and the tongue retracted in pain. The crate bobbled and then tumbled into the black pit, wedging in the back of the dragon's pulsing throat. The dragon gagged and thrashed hard, trying to breathe, trying to unstick its teeth from the wood.

"More!" Quistix screamed, and everyone forced another crate toward the opening.

The dragon hacked and thrashed its whole body, spinning the gang end-over-end inside the busted barge. Violet and Twitch were slapped against the fractured wall. Aurora's hooves scrambled to find purchase on the moving walls.

Violet shrieked as the wall behind her cracked wide, nearly splitting in two.

Tumbling and swirling, the last unopened crate slammed against the beams, breaking open, sending projectiles of shattered glass and dikeeka swirling through the water. One of the bottles sliced Violet's arms before burying one of its points into Twitch's thigh. A splintered piece of wood drove into Aurora's side, forcing a bubbled bugle from her mouth.

Quistix pinched her eyes shut as glass pieces embedded in her skin. A wooden plank popped off its nails, flying off what was once the floor and smacking against her, driving more broken glass shards into her skin. She let out a growl like an enraged bear.

Suddenly, the teeth broke free, the thrashing stopped, light broke through the gap, and their bodies tumbled.

CRASH!

The boat smashed against the ocean floor, the force pounding their bodies. A plume of sand rushed in, a cloud of granules filling their lungs with every gasping breath. As the grains settled in the darkness, they realized the boat had landed on its opening, encapsulating them inside. The punctured tooth holes allowed only thin slivers of light to permeate the wooden tomb.

Quistix released her grasp on the pillar. In the shadows, she could barely make out the silhouettes of the others, Aurora's hooves swinging like a lazy pendulum from a bowed plank above.

"Is everyone alright?" Quistix shouted breathlessly.

"Define *alright*," Twitch muttered, a hint of sarcasm in his tone.

Violet hissed, the saltwater stinging her cuts. Aurora tumbled to the sand, rolling on her side to expose a stake the size of a dagger's blade wedged in her.

Violet tensed, her body shape-shifting into a glitterfish. She swam over Aurora and cast her bio-luminescent light on the wound. Twitch watched Violet with wonderment, trying to fathom the miraculous event of her changing forms.

Quistix watched, mouth open in shock. "Violet, did you just shape-shift?"

The glowing fish bobbled as if nodding.

"That would have been handy to know before right now," Quistix said. Then, she rolled her eyes. "Alright, Aurora. Talk to me. Tell me what I need to do."

Mewling, Aurora tensed to brace herself. "Remove the offending implement before I can heal ar—"

Quistix grasped the wooden shard and yanked it out of Aurora's side. A shrill scream tore from Aurora's throat and her body heaved. The nubs of her horns glowed bright green.

Dizzy, Twitch fainted at the sight of the open wound, his body flopping hard on the floor. The glitterfish swam to his side, hovering above his closed eyes.

The open wound beneath Aurora's fur pulled itself closed, and the seam sealed. She sprouted new hair and, in a miraculous matter of moments, her body looked unscathed. Then, the esteg bucked violently.

Quistix whirled just in time to miss Aurora's hoof as it whizzed by, narrowly missing her chest. "Whoa! What in the Nether was that for?"

"That was because you didn't let me finish what I was saying before you pulled that thing out!" Aurora was furious. She rose onto all four hooves, glaring at Quistix.

"What would waiting have helped? This way, you didn't have time to dread it!" Quistix snapped. "You can kill a person with a kick like that, you know!"

Aurora turned away and muttered something beneath her breath.

"Wake up, Twitch," Quistix said, slapping the wyl's muzzle.

Still, he remained unconscious.

"Wonderful," Quistix muttered. "Not only do we have to dig ourselves out, but we'll have to drag this delicate little princess along with us."

Violet's fish form flit through one of the tooth holes, and her light vanished as her body changed again, this time into an octopus, identical to the one they had passed on their trek to the boat. Her body molded and slid through the hole until she was outside. Quistix watched from another tooth hole as the octopus slid down toward the ocean floor and out of sight.

Beneath her feet, the sand started to shift, and tentacles appeared. Quistix kneeled down and paddled sand out of her end like an eager dog until there was a hole beneath. One of the tentacles reached in and pointed to Twitch.

Quistix dragged the unconscious wyl to the small opening. The tentacles wrapped around his arms and pulled. The boat creaked, and Twitch slid through the sand hole outside.

Violet's tentacles pulled out more sand, and then one pointed to the esteg.

"Looks like you're up, Aurora." Quistix paddled out more sand, widening the tunnel. "Once you go through, I should be able to slide out no problem."

Aurora didn't respond. She just lay down in the pit and waited. Moments later, Violet's suction-cupped tentacles slid around her throat and the creases of her front legs, and the esteg was dragged through the tight sandy tunnel.

Quistix dove through the hole and scrambled toward the light. On the other side, one of Violet's tentacles scooped her out.

Once out, Quistix looked around and startled when she saw Kackaroth, lying on his back in the sand in the distance. His tongue lolled out the side of his mouth, and bursts of bubbles surfaced at regular intervals as if he was breathing slow and steady. The drugged creature squirmed around, knocking plumes of silt into the air.

"We may not have much time before he comes to. Can you help with Twitch?" Quistix asked the octopus.

Violet's rounded head bobbed in affirmation, and her tentacles spun out, two grabbing Twitch, two grabbing Aurora, and another grabbing Quistix. Once they were all securely in her grasp, Violet launched through the water toward the dome with big forward bursts of motion.

20

The Ruby Palace
Desdemona, Willowdale

It was about Quistix. It had always been about her, but what made her so special? Why had Exos and Master Tempest tried so hard to find her? Sure, exceptional magic was highly sought-after, but their destructive hunts for the half-elf bordered on madness, Vervaine thought.

In the otherwise empty Great Hall, the queen felt her stomach wrench as she recalled the women who'd claimed the throne before her.

Her *sister.* Her *mother.* Her *grandmother.*

Sadly, it would all end with her. Without being able to produce an heir, Destoria would one day belong to another family, halting her royal lineage for good. She rubbed her stomach, imagining her womb empty and inhospitable beneath. *Dead.* Decaying from the inside since the moment she first perished in that prison cell.

Vervaine wondered, if it were even *possible*, what sort of an abomination would be born to two undead parents like her and Arias. She shuddered at the thought.

A burst of childish giggles rang out from beyond one of the stained glass windows. Vervaine approached quietly and peered through at two children playing just beyond. With quick strides, Vervaine trotted out of the Great Hall and out the nearby door to the castle courtyard. A pair of guards followed her, waiting just outside the door to give her space. Vervaine strode toward the young girls, one of whom was making a burlap rag doll dance along the parapet for the other's amusement.

The smaller girl lunged for the toy, her brunette curls swaying just enough to reveal her pointed elven ears. "Let me try!"

"Once I'm done! It is still *my* turn!"

"Give it!" The little one cried again.

Despite a small height difference, the girls looked remarkably similar, sisters in matching black ankle-length dresses. The elder of the two, roughly eight or nine years old, made the doll walk back and forth in front of her sister, jerking it away every time her little hands reached for it.

"You know, sisters are supposed to stick together," Vervaine finally said, startling the children. The oldest let go and dropped the doll over the other side of the wall.

"No!" the youngest shouted.

Vervaine approached, leaning over the wall. The doll was neatly nestled in the branches of a hedge below.

"Sorry, your highness," the oldest uttered uneasily before ramming her sister with her shoulder.

"Yes, sorry for disturbing you. We were just playing."

Reaching over the ledge, Vervaine used her magic, coaxing the doll back up through the air with white, smoky tendrils.

The youngest leaned out and grabbed it from the air, clutching it to her chest, eyes full of wonder and excitement. "So, it's true, you really *are* magical!"

"What else can you do?" asked the eldest.

"There's much I can do. And much that I can't. Why don't you give me a suggestion?"

The eldest rocked back on her heels and looked at her sister conspiratorially. "Can you make us another doll just like this one so we can play together at the same time?"

"What's your name?" Vervaine asked with a soft smile.

"Belinda."

"I'm Sophie."

"Well-met, Belinda. Sophie, may I have the doll for a moment?"

Hesitantly, the girl handed the doll over, glancing at her sister for reassurance. Vervaine clutched it, covering it completely with her palms. She closed her eyes and whispered something. Then, she opened her eyes and pried apart her hands to reveal the same doll.

Belinda's shoulders sagged as Vervaine handed back the doll. "Thanks for trying anyway."

"Look behind you." Vervaine flashed a broad smile. The girls turned to find a second, identical burlap doll on the parapet.

"*Whoa*," Sophie whispered in amazement.

With her toy in hand, Belinda wrapped her arms around Vervaine's waist in a tight hug. "Thank you!"

Vervaine cherished the warmth and affection. "Now," she kneeled and asked quietly, "how would you like to see something *really* amazing?"

Wandering around the castle, Arias stopped in front of the towering Great Hall doors, ones with half of Desdemona's massive tree symbol scrawled into each.

"Is my wife in there?" the akiah asked one of the guards waiting patiently outside.

The guard nodded dutifully.

The sound of a horse's neigh and childlike laughter coming from beyond the doors made Arias grin. "What is she up to in there?"

The guard stifled a smile. "Best if you see with your own eyes, your majesty."

Arias nodded, and the guard opened one of the doors for the king. The Great Hall was transformed, lively with a whirlwind of playful chaos. His wife and two children were seated in the eye of it all. Each large stained glass window was now covered by a thick tapestry he'd never seen before, blocking out all light beyond.

Several royal horses trotted in place, each wearing a fanciful dress instead of a saddle, rainbow-colored hooves *clomping* on the stone floor. A tornado of symphs circled the edges of the room like a cyclone, one barely missing Arias before starting another loop around the dim room.

Arias startled when a full-grown raakaby in a regal hat tried to claw its way up his boots. He kicked it off and stepped inside the room, stumbling over a scurrying filibrat before catching himself on the back of a huge noubald with each of its waggling tentacles covered in hand puppets. The creature groaned and stalked away. Petals from rambunctious roses lay scattered around the floor like confetti.

Arias stepped closer and was nearly gored by the tine of a galloping esteg. A pleom fluttered past. He swatted it away and finally made eye contact with his wife.

He wanted to be angry at the mess, at such a flagrant display of her magic, but he simply couldn't. Her genuine smile warmed him. It was the happiest he'd seen her since she was alive, all those months ago. It felt like it had been an eternity since he'd heard such carefree laughter from her lips. Her jade-green eyes were full of mischief and whimsy. Her giggles evaporated his frustration in an instant.

Arias bowed. The girls curtsied back at him. "Excuse me, ladies, but the queen and I are late for a very important engagement."

The sisters let out a groan of disapproval.

Vervaine snapped her fingers, and the curtains dropped from the windows, the fabric disappearing into the seam in the floor grout, allowing the tangerine and violet hues of the sunset paint the walls. The beasts and their costumes vanished, leaving nothing but the vague smell of wild animals behind. She snapped again, and the petals and symphs disappeared, too, leaving no trace beyond a single, falling symph feather. Vervaine plucked it out of the air and tucked it behind Sophie's pointed ear like a flower.

"Run along now, girls." She winked.

The sisters smiled and started toward the door with their matching dolls.

As she passed, Belinda grinned up at Arias. "The other children are never going to believe this!"

The second the Great Hall doors closed and they were alone, Arias helped Vervaine off the floor. "You must be exhausted after all of that."

"I will sleep well this evening." She wrapped her hand around his muscular forearm.

"Soon, you're going to end up with every child in Willowdale begging you to put on a show."

"Sorry we're late," Arias said, addressing the chamber full of people while flashing an accusatory glance at Vervaine.

"The king and queen cannot be late, your majesty. Everyone else can only be too early," Alvanak stated in jest. Then, he took his seat at the long council table, adjusted the elegant dinnerware, and said, "We've got many matters to discuss tonight. I propose we get started right away."

"Right." Vervaine looked around and settled into her chair. "Who would like to begin?"

Ceosteol raised her clawed hand. "Might I be the first?"

Alvanak cleared his throat. "No need for hand raising."

"My apologies," the quichyrd hissed.

"As an honored guest at this council meeting, I don't expect you to know of our protocols. Typically, we start by addressing the needs of the many over the needs of the few, and the few will be addressed at the end, and only if time permits. Is this about the overall quality of life in a particular providence, or the isle as a whole?"

"Yes, Taernsby," she said, feeling the eyes of the most influential people in Destoria boring into her.

Arias cleared his throat, irritated. "You may have the floor, Ceosteol, but please make your address as concise as possible. Our docket is unusually full tonight."

She clacked her talons on the table. "I believe we should pardon Werner and reinstate his position on this council."

The council gasped, erupting in murmurs of disapproval.

"That's preposterous!" one shouted.

Ceosteol spoke again. "New information has come to light. He's an innocent man."

One of the guards flanking the chamber's entrance stepped forward. "Pardon me for speaking out of turn, but I was there that night. I saw Duke Grayson gouge a man's eyes out myself. I still have nightmares about it. Werner was there. He participated in the massacre."

"Thank you." Alvanak sneered. "That'll be all from you." The ewanian waved the guard away dismissively. "Might I be so bold as to say that if you're still having nightmares about such an occurrence, perhaps you are in the wrong line of work?"

The guard stepped back into position and reset his gaze on the stone wall across the room.

"Werner was poisoned. I have proof," Ceosteol said. "He drank an enchanted elixir in the council's wine that night. They all did." She reached inside the folds of her robe and produced the bottle, setting an empty glass jar on the table.

"How do we know that *that* is what caused their madness? And how can we be sure where this vial was found?" Arias asked.

"I visited him in the dungeon. I believed I had seen this sort of behavior before. It's a simple concoction, really, one with some very *gruesome* side effects." She looked up to the guards beside the door. "I tested the remnants from this bottle on some filibrats last week. Just as I suspected, they attacked each other… to the death."

Arias's voice came out as a boom, reverberating off the stone walls with a force that made the hair on everyone's neck stand at attention. "Where did you find the vial?"

"One of the staff members who cleaned up after the event said she found it discarded behind a cask of wine the evening's carafe had been filled from. She said she went to Exos about it the day after the attack, but the matter was either ignored or lost in the shuffle. The bottle has the tell-tale scent of the potion *Requiem of Rage*."

"Requiem of Rage?" Arias repeated, the words bitter on his tongue, like the memory of a rancid meal.

"It was originally created by one of my apothecary predecessors for the great King Forsighth nearly eighty years ago. The potion was created with a potent seed of the biago berry, which, when crushed, stimulates the mind in such a way that unbridled rage is nearly always the result. Its original purpose was to be administered to soldiers to give them a boost of bloodlust in battle. However, during the trial, it was banned because the soldiers maimed *themselves* when there was no one left to fight."

The council sat quietly, mulling over the brutal image that her words conjured in their minds.

Alvanak thumbed the open ledger in front of him, its pages still frustratingly empty. His intense gaze settled on her. "Werner cannot be pardoned. It is a matter of security."

"I assure you, Werner has not shown a single sign of aggression in our meetings. I would bet my life that he is rehabilitated now that the potion is out of his system."

Alvanak turned to Arias. "Please do not tell me that you are seriously entertaining the idea of releasing a murderer back onto the streets of Desdemona."

Arias stared down at his plate of food and said nothing.

Vervaine offered an apologetic glance to the council members around the table. Then, her eyes changed from jade to something far brighter as Ceosteol inhabited her mind. Her lips moved against her will as she said, "Pardon granted."

"Thank you," Ceosteol said smugly, her gaze turning to Alvanak as Vervaine's eyes returned to their normal shade.

Alvanak shook his head, his webbed fingers splaying out across the donik wood table on opposite sides of his ledger, a long list of matters still untouched. "I would like it noted that I wholeheartedly disagree with this decision."

"Noted," Vervaine said, feeling as if something horrific had crawled across her bare skin. She shivered.

Arias spoke up. "Our worst behaviors in times of weakness should not define us. This isle began as the home to Asera's prison colony, after all. As Destorians, we created our own second chance. Given this new information about the landigo, it would be a gesture of goodwill to release him if he is no longer a danger to others."

"I suppose... at least we won't have to use taxpayer coin to *feed* the freeloader if we let him out," Guarin, the Silvercrest representative, said. "Let him be someone else's burden." Then, he looked at Kleego. "Maybe we'll get lucky, and he'll catch a wagon ride down to Obsidia and waste away quietly like everyone else in that drug-smuggling wasteland you call a province."

Kleego whipped his head toward Guarin and narrowed his eyes. "Right. Because Silvercrest is *perfect*," he spat sarcastically.

"Enough," Arias grumbled sternly, in no mood for pettiness. "Sabet, how are things going in Taernsby?"

Sabet straightened and swept a feathered forearm over her forehead. "Two more perished in the streets today. Children. Young girls."

Vervaine frowned, thinking of the sisters she'd spent the afternoon with. "May they rest in peace in the Ethereal Sanctum."

"Yes," Sabet said softly. "I have been receiving updates about the vegetables, meat, and milk for the interim. Some of the wagons are set to arrive as early as tomorrow.

Vervaine perked up and turned toward the quichyrds. "I think I may have an idea that will help. Ceosteol?"

"Yes, your majesty?"

"You possess the power to change the weather, do you not?"

"Yes, of course. But it is draining. I can only manage for very short bursts, my queen. Why? What would you like me to do?"

Turning back to Alvanak, Vervaine's eyes widened with excitement. "Seeds. Order seeds. Lots of them. Take coin from the treasury and buy them in bulk from Asera. Have it delivered on the next incoming cargo ship."

Blinking wildly, Alvanak nodded. "Of course."

"Order seeds for crops that'll grow rapidly, ones that would be prolific in Taernsby's growing conditions. Have them expedited." She turned back to Ceosteol. "Once the seeds have been planted, I'll need you to cast rain over the crops. Even for short bursts each day. At least until some Apexians can arrive. Their botanical program is top-notch. Surely, the institute can spare some young mages who can work the fields for a few months in exchange for school credit. With all of this happening in tandem, we can have the starvation of those in Taernsby under control within a few short weeks."

"But Vervaine, that will require me to stay in Taernsby for possibly weeks," Ceosteol protested.

"Yes, but you'll be viewed as a hero. It will be good for your reputation around the isle. It wasn't that long ago that you were a fugitive like Werner, after all."

Vervaine and Ceosteol locked eyes for a long time. Finally, the quichyrd smiled and sat back in her chair. “Very well, your majesty. As you wish.” Her glowing eyes glimmered mischievously.

“How soon until the seeds arrive?” Vervaine asked Alvanak.

“Five days. Perhaps a week, at the latest, if I send the request via symph tonight.”

“Do it.” Vervaine nodded decisively.

“Very well.” With a scarlet frumlan feather, Alvanak dipped the shaft in his inkwell and scribbled notes in his ledger.

21

Irenas Parnix's Underwater Dome
The Radiant Sea

Beneath Parnix's protective dome, Quistix squeezed saltwater out of her hair and walked slowly around the ruins of a building that reminded her of her old home in Bellaneau. She thought about Geoffrey, Danson's burlap doll, still in a satchel somewhere in the Ruby Palace. It was there somewhere, rotting away in a chest alongside her emerald dagger, Swordbreaker, Hadina's full complement of armor. The last sliver she had of her son was far away, a loss she felt deep in her bones.

She looked down at the floor, imagining herself holding Danson in the rubble as the life drained from his body. His loss was a pit she would never escape from. As much as she tried to forget, to dull her senses with muscadine wine and distraction, the hurt always seemed to return with a vengeance.

She staggered away, watching the waves above dance and sway to a silent song.

“Quistix!” Twitch howled from somewhere in the dilapidated city, his volume thrown by the curve of the dome.

She squinted, trying to focus her blurry eyes. Ahead of her, something darted from one building to another.

Taking a few steps forward, her eyes strained to focus. Still intoxicated, Quistix staggered forward and tripped. She slammed to the ground, hissing as some of the sand clung to her fresh cuts.

"Quistix!" Twitch yelled again from the shadowy street in front of her as he padded to a clumsy stop a few inches from her. "There you are! I was looking for you," he slurred. He struggled to stay rooted in place, his hind legs flexing with every wobble as he wavered buck-naked before her.

Quistix sat for a moment, eye-level with the wyl's crotch. "I see you're finally up." She glanced at his privates again, a little longer this time, then at his face. "No pun intended."

He hissed with laughter, doubling over, his tail wagging wild. He rolled onto the ground by her and draped a piece of flotsam over his groin. He stared up at the top of the bubble, irises massive.

Violet approached, her damp nightclothes hugging her feminine figure, wet curls leaking onto the silk. "Sorry, he finally came to and just... ran off. I see he lost every stitch of clothing somewhere along the way."

“Come! Sit!” He patted the sand beside him. “The moons are putting on a show.”

“No, *your* moon is putting on a show,” Quistix muttered. “Put some damned clothes on.”

“I should go,” Violet said, blushing as she turned back toward Parnix’s dwelling.

“No! Please, don’t go,” he whined.

“Come with me. We will put you in some of my grandfather’s clothes.”

Twitch rose, unsteady. “Oh, Violet, where have you been all my life? You’re so beautiful. I would follow you to the ends of the isle and never tire of your face.”

“Careful,” Quistix muttered. “He really will follow you forever. He’s quite obnoxious like that.”

Twitch stuck out his tongue at her childishly. “Don’t fill this angel’s mind with your nonsense.”

“Oh, stop,” Violet said, blushing again. “I’m no angel.”

Twitch draped an arm over her shoulder and stared at her as they hobbled away. “Gods take my sight this instant! I want this gorgeous face to be the last thing these eyes ever see.”

A smile spread across her cheeks, crinkles forming in the corners of her eyes.

“Hey!” Omen’s dual voices shouted in unison. “Get away from Violet!”

Wobbling like a drunkard, Quistix stood and swayed. From the shadows of the street, Omen’s head cast a blue glow on the dilapidated buildings. His flaming bare hand shoved Twitch onto the sand, flames singeing the fur on his chest with the contact.

“Leave him alone!” Violet shrieked, shoving Omen away, careful to keep her hands on the leather of his jacket.

“Stay out of this.” Omen snarled, then turned his attention back to Twitch. “Lay a single furry finger on my sister and I’ll burn it off!”

Violet took a step forward and Omen stepped too her unflinchingly, the heat from his flames dangerously close to scorching her. "Violet, you and that old man are family." He pointed in the direction of Parnix's dwelling. "The Nether will freeze over before I allow you to mess with a buffoon like him."

"Allow?" She narrowed her eyes at him. "You don't allow a damned thing in my life."

"Hey!" Quistix shouted, wavering on her sandy bare feet. "Touch the wyl again and I swear to every God in the Sanctum that I will make you regret it. You may be immortal, but I will make you pray for death, I promise."

Omen spun around, trying to compose himself before speaking again.

"That naked idiot over there is my best friend," she continued. "One of my only friends! The damned fool has saved my life more times than I can even count." She looked at Twitch, then at Omen. "She could do a lot worse than him."

Omen stared at her for a beat too long before looking away again. He pulled his enchanted leather gloves from his pocket and pulled them on.

"Quistix..."

"Don't thank me." Quistix waved him away.

"No," he said, fear in his voice. He pointed.

Quistix followed the direction of his claw and turned to the side.

Beside them all, from the murky depths emerged two flared nostrils expelling twin currents of water, followed by two enormous bloodshot eyes.

Kackaroth.

The scaly beast studied them. As it blinked, a transparent eyelid closed vertically over its pupils before the second pair of lids closed horizontally.

Quistix felt her heart thud.

"Irenas," Omen shouted in an almost bored tone, "your pet is back. He looks hungry."

Ambling hurriedly down the path, the aging wizard shouted angrily, "Kackaroth, I'm so sorry, old friend! I will fix this somehow. Just give me time!"

As if it understood, the monster turned away, slinking back into the darkness.

Rage had bubbled up inside of Parnix, the origin of which he was unsure. It was as if the air itself was abrasive, irritating every nerve ending in his body like gritty sandstone. His stomach burbled with nausea, his wrinkled head pounding. His parched mouth searched for words to explain his fury, but none came..

Suddenly, Twitch growled and lunged at Omen. Omen leaned back, unsheathing the emerald dagger at his hip. Quistix kicked the blade from Omen's hand, her yellow eyes flashing bright white. She screamed and hurled herself at him. Twitch joined in. Violet struggled to pull the wyl away.

Aurora approached to investigate the noise, a helpless spectator. "Something is wrong with them! Irenas, you must do something! They're going to kill each other."

Parnix shoved his palms against the ground. The sand juddered as subtle vibrations grew to violent quakes. Half-broken pillars toppled. Bricks rattled loose in walls. The fish outside the dome stilled.

The group stopped fighting, each one staring at the ground as if it would soon split open and swallow them whole.

Lifting his palms, the quaking stopped abruptly, and the enraged wizard bellowed so loud that Violet shook with fear. "That is enough! I've seen sea worms with more civility and sense than you all possess right now! Now, what exactly did you find out there today?"

"Your little pet brought down a huge transport ship full of dikeeka," Quistix said. "It seems to be poisoning the fish and that... thing... just like it's been poisoning you."

"What's dikeeka?" Parnix's brows pinched together.

Omen spoke. "I forget how removed you are from the isle and its politics down here." He cleared his throat, his voices low. "It's a drug. One that the last queen made legal in Destoria during her reign."

"My mouth is as dry as the deserts of Obsidia. Does anyone have any water?" Twitch looked around. Everyone ignored him.

"It's legal in Asera now, too." Quistix wanted to double over and scream into her hands.

How many others would lose everything to the drug? How many more men like Rowland had to die before it was abolished?

"Seriously, guys. Water. I'm dyin' here."

Omen nodded solemnly. "The legislature recently passed in Asera shortly after the king there found out how much Exos was making off the taxes on it."

"What is it? Maybe if I know what is in it, I can find something to counteract its effects."

"It's a mixture of two parts biago berry seeds, one part raakaby venom, and one part diced tulip bulbs. Add in one part potato liquor and you have one vile concoction," Aurora said. "Side effects are impaired judgement, poor coordination and balance..."

"Basically, Twitch on a normal day," Quistix joked, a moment of levity to soothe the percolating irritation among them.

"Still thirsty here," Twitch added.

"Hey, you just threatened me for—"

She interrupted Omen. "I can abuse him. You haven't earned the right, yet."

Aurora looked perturbed. "Might I be permitted to finish?"

Quistix nodded, her rare smile fading.

Twitch slapped his naked thigh, still cupping his groin in the other. "By the Gods, I'm invisible, I say!"

"Twitch," Quistix shouted. "We hear you! Shut up for a minute!"

"Other side effects include numbness, delirium, headaches, and nausea, to name a few."

The mage's pallor turned slightly green. "This stuff sounds absolutely noxious. Why would anyone use it?"

Twitch interjected, "The numbness, old man. The numbness is why people take it. Some for physical pain, some for mental anguish. The same reason drunkards drink themselves into a stupor. It makes you feel good. Invincible, even. Like nothing in the world can touch you. Like you could watch everything you love go up in flames and it would all be alright."

Quistix grimaced at his choice of words.

"Some shifty street peddlers even lie and claim it cures everything from hair loss to the *plague*."

"Oh no." Irenas shook his head and stomped back toward his dwelling, shoving past Omen on a mission.

"Oh no, what?" Violet asked.

They followed Parnix down the corridor and into the building. He breezed through the library and into the kitchen. He stopped there, examining his glass contraption, he noticed his water filtration system for what seemed like the first time in weeks.

"When I came here to Apex, I was given a Scroll of Desalination to take the salt out of the water. From there, I just run it through a particle filtration contraption that I made."

"And?" Violet asked.

Twitch dunked a goblet in the bucket of filtered water and raised it to his dry lips. Parnix smacked the cup out of his hand. It clanged loudly around the room.

"Grandfather, what has gotten into you?!"

"I'm trying to tell you that it's my water! The water here isn't safe to drink!" He looked at her with bloodshot eyes. "The scroll only removes salt from the source. Nothing else. If that disgusting muck is concentrated out there, it doesn't do me a lick of good against that! If it's in liquid form, it'll go right through the filter."

Violet and Aurora looked at each other, eyes full of alarm.

"How long ago did the ship go down?"

"No telling," Quistix answered honestly. "Any ledgers inside would be waterlogged and illegible. When did you start feeling this way?"

"A while." Parnix smacked his head hard. "By the Gods, I've been drinking it for weeks!"

"Are you sure it's tainted?" Quistix asked.

He popped his head up like a gopher. "There's a way to test it!" He scurried over to the cupboards and found a clear vial with a cork top. He plucked it out of the cabinet, filled it with water from the bucket Twitch was staring into longingly. Then, he rushed off into the library with it. The others followed.

"The water may look clear, but there is a book that can—"

Aurora gasped. "The *Experimentalist's Guide to Purity?* You have a copy?"

Parnix stopped for a moment to flash Aurora a smile of approval. "Your depth of knowledge astonishes me, Aurora Formens Lucem."

The sound of her full name made her ears twitch. She shied away bashfully so he would not see her smile.

Parnix stood on a wobbly stack of books and plucked a specific text off the eighth shelf. He blew the dust off of it and hopped back down to the ground. He flipped open to a page in the middle, riffling through a few more until he found the one he wanted.

"Aha, here it is. The water may appear clear, but when you hold it against the page..."

He pressed the vial against the parchment, and the clear liquid showed a vibrant purple.

"Ah, see that? The color of a ripe muscadine. Let's see what that one is." He flipped through a few more pages. "Muscadine purple." He jammed a finger aggressively at the page. "Raakaby venom."

Quistix felt sick. The liquid she'd hated for all of these years, the same one that tarnished Rowland's legacy, was now coursing through her. She thought about retching to get it all out of her body as soon as possible, but without a source of drinking water, dehydration could become a problem.

"I take it you are all feeling the effects of this drug after having been in the water?"

Quistix nodded.

"The ingredients you listed, they're all potent poisons except for the venom, which is a hallucinogenic. It's a miracle we are alive at the rates we've been ingesting it." He thought for a moment and looked at the esteg. "What are the detoxification symptoms as it leaves one's system?"

Quistix answered before Aurora could, vividly recalling Rowland's behaviors.

"Perspiration, violent rage, severe exhaustion, extreme thirst, vomiting, hallucinations..."

"All ways for the body to rid itself of poison." Irenas nodded.

"The bouts of rage seem to be the worst of them," Omen said. "There have been a lot of murders since its legalization, many from brawls and intimate combat."

Irenas jogged back to the cabinets in the kitchen. "I have something that may help. I used it when I dealt with snakes and raakaby's for my classes. Someone would always inevitably get bitten."

Grasping a jar of green leaves suspended in brine, he popped off the lid and dumped it in an empty pot. He disappeared and returned with a pinch of fireplace ash. He ground it up and sprinkled it into the bottle.

He glanced at Quistix, his expression gravely serious. "I need you to go back out there."

"No. Absolutely not. I don't have a death wish, Parnix."

"You must! I need one more item, a specific fish."

"What fish?"

"It's what I call a billaguppy. They are a previously undocumented species. I have a drawing!"

Parnix rushed out of the room.

Quistix looked at Omen and rolled her eyes. "Oh, great. He has a drawing. Your grandfather is going to get us killed with this nonsense!"

Irenas whisked back in, drawings in hand. He stuffed them in Quistix's hand. "There. That's what they look like. They're round, with a long narrow snout and webbed claws. They're a light tan shade and blend in well with the ocean floor. Bottom dwellers, these things. They burrow in small dens in the sand."

Twitch scoffed. "You think a fish is gonna fix this?"

"These particular fish have a potent gland inside of them that would be a perfect counter-toxin. It feeds on all of the poisonous fish that skirt the ocean floor. It has to frequently rid itself of the toxins somehow. If I could just get a couple of them, I think it would suffice. They won't be hard to find, you've likely stepped right over one of their holes and not even known it."

"We've seen them," Quistix interjected.

"A lot of them," Twitch confirmed. "I think they were gobbling up dikeeka at the shipwreck."

"That's exactly what we are going to do to lure them in," Parnix said, snapping his fingers. "They are attracted to toxins. I have some puffer fish organs that I think would work well as an attractant in this case. I have been ethically harvesting their organs and poison glands for a while now."

He grunted as he pulled a large glass jar from a nearby shelf between two leaning stacks of tomes. Inside the jar were lumps of tissue bobbing in yellow liquid. He offered the jar to Quistix. “There’s a blade in the kitchen. Use it to slice them into thin strips. Be careful. I’ll cast a barrier spell between your hands and the organs so you don’t absorb any toxins. Out there, you’ll wiggle the strips like worms by their dens and draw them out. Use this,” he mumbled, pulling down a large burlap sack from one of the cluttered corners of the room. It was folded neatly and covered in a thin layer of dust. He set it in Quistix’s outstretched arms.

“Can’t wait. Sounds like a great way to spend an afternoon,” Quistix grumbled sarcastically.

Parnix wagged a finger at Twitch. “I’m going to need vials, too. They’re plentiful over there in Elathia. Take Violet. She can shape-shift to blend in with the merfolk. They don’t trust any of us, you know. For good reason, too. They only trust their own. Once you’ve shifted into one of them, ask for some vials, as many as they can spare. Oh, and casks! We’ll need casks. If we are going to counteract this nonsense and share the antidote with others on land, we need containers. The vials will be for us, in case we need more than one dose. It would be wise to keep some on hand for the future."

Twitch looked around. "We aren't seriously considering this, are we?"

"You need to hurry. We are going to start feeling the effects of dehydration soon."

"If I have to go back out in that stuff, I'm drinking this! I don't care!" Twitch shoved his whole face in the bucket of filtered water and chugged. Omen watched, making a sour face.

Twitch wiped his palms down his soaked face, tugging at the fur under his eyes, dragging his jowls down with his claws. "Ohhhh, that is refreshing!"

22

Knight Harbor Wharf
Desdemona, Willowdale

The savage sunlight seared the greenery-laden cliffs of Knight Harbor, waves of stone towering over the wharf. Bent grass trailed through the cliff's face to a watchtower full of patrolmen with bugles working revolving shifts, the path leading to it tamped down by the stomp of heavy boots over the years.

Through the ages, the wharf was the target of many opportunistic sieges, either led by rogue pirates or Aseran sea captains with lofty aspirations to claim land by force. Due to the sparse workers in its employ and close proximity to the Ruby Palace, for years, many Destorians had considered Knight Harbor a threat to the kingdom, a weakness, an open door for nefarious invasions.

Those were just *some* of the reasons that Emma Aerendyl was confused about why she'd been summoned to such a place.

A pastel blue exoskeleton with a multitude of legs wove through sand smoothed by the lowering tide. Using her calf-high leather boot, Aerendyl toed away a curious crustacean. The two plates of its outer shell parted to reveal a set of pincers large enough to hold a sovereign gold coin. The pincers snapped onto the toe of the tip of her shoe. She shrieked just as a sword's tip sliced down through its shell, snapping the creature in two. As both halves wriggled in agony, Madam Aerendyl looked at the patrolman who stabbed it and nodded in appreciation.

"Careful. These things are everywhere during low tide," he muttered, before kicking the thing off his blade and continuing on his path.

What was she doing here?

Did they know she was the one behind Quistix's escape?

Had they come to arrest her? Torture her?

Emma imagined being hauled off to the half-elf's very dungeon cell in magic-resistant shackles of her own design, an ironic fate on many levels. Still, a summons from the royal court simply could not be ignored. She rushed to Knight Harbor the moment she received the correspondence bearing the royal seal. Now, Emma stood, sweating in the sun, baking in a purple robe with the embroidered symbol of the Apexian Eye, pondering her fate.

Pebbles skittered down the beach, followed by the sound of boots pounding in sand. She watched as several guards led the way for the regal king and queen. She bowed reverently as they approached, as did the merchants and fishermen milling around the wharf.

Arias and Vervaine stopped in front of Emma, and the guards moved out of the way. Several patrolmen and spotters crept out to the edge of the cliff, watching the exchange from above.

"Your majesties!" She faked a smile, waiting to see whether their response would be warm. "To what do I owe the pleasure of this meeting?"

"Ah! Well met, Madame Aerendyl," Arias bellowed, his voice echoing off the stone cliff beside him. "It's good to see you. We have an important matter that needs your immediate attention."

Emma swallowed hard, suddenly overcome with a feeling of unease. "Your majesties, whatever you need, I'm at your service."

Judging by Vervaine's soft smile and the tone of Arias's voice, they couldn't possibly suspect her of what she'd done.

"Are you familiar with a Quistix Daedumal?" Vervaine asked.

Emma's mouth felt dry in an instant. Her fingers twitched. Every muscle begged for her to run. "Yes, oddly enough, she was my late husband's daughter. I've never met her, so I'm not sure how much help I can be."

Just then, Emma could have sworn she'd seen Vervaine's eyes flash an eerie shade of green. An *unnatural* color...

Arias stepped closer and lowered his voice, his tone a clear warning. "Madam, I advise you to choose your next words very carefully."

They knew, she thought.

Emma readied herself to summon a portal back to Apex. Before she could, a guard closed the gap between them, and she felt the cold bite of metal slip around her wrist. The metal shackles were imbued with an oily sheen that made her feel suddenly exhausted.

Vervaine's eyes seemed to return to their duller shade, and she mouthed the words, *I'm sorry*.

Arias shook her shackles. "Just a precaution I assure you. Can't have a mage like you using your tricks to get away, now can we?"

Emma stared at him, barely able to keep her eyelids up.

"So, what was that yarn you were just spinning me about how you'd never met your step-daughter despite numerous reports of her being educated by your institute whilst you were headmaster? I find it quite peculiar that you'd somehow had no idea who was partaking in your curriculum, considering how coveted acceptance at the institute has become."

Emma couldn't manage to form any words.

Arias motioned to one of the guards, who hoisted Aerendyl over his armored shoulder with a grunt.

"Come, Emma. I feel like we have much more to discuss once you're feeling more like yourself." Arias scooped the crook of Vervaine's arm into his and marched back in the direction of the castle.

23

The Wilds of Bellaneau
Bellaneau

Rumbling along the same path he'd traveled down hundreds of times, Gregor's slick eyelids drew heavy. The hefty ewanian bobbled in time with the gentle rock of his carriage, tacky green hands gripping the reins of his horse whose low-slung head signaled it was time for a break. He guided the horse and carriage into a clearing on the outskirts of Bellaneau, in the wilds south of Vrisca. The sun's light had begun to tuck behind the horizon, bathing everything in the sapphire hues of impending nightfall. The night air bit at his slippery sage-green flesh, sending a shiver that shook him so hard his portly belly jiggled.

He spotted some deadfall and decided it was time to build a fire. Hopping down from his seat on the carriage, he gathered broken branches and sticks, tossing them into a messy pile.

Behind him, he heard a soft scrape, one that sounded like claws against wood. Glancing at his carriage, he noticed the crates, nailed shut, full of Assassins Guild victims. He recalled the red-headed wild woman in the woods he'd met long ago and the nearly-dead wyl she'd emancipated from his cargo before robbing him. He stiffened, wondering if she still lurked in the woods. Since that day, the guild has taken more precautions. Their dead had now been separated, limb from limb, the mismatched extremities packed tightly into the crates for transport and burial.

The scratching sounded again, emanating from the carriage.

He whispered to himself, "*Not again.*"

Pulling a small, lackluster dagger from his hip sheath, he grumbled incoherent curses and quietly approached the cart, waiting for the sound to return.

He rapped his slick knuckles on the outermost crate, his eyes locked on it as he waited for a reply.

Silence. Even the crickets had ceased their song. *But when?*

The sack below his neck pulsed as he called out hesitantly into the night. He looked around, his senses in overdrive. "H-Hello? Is someone there? If you're looking to rob me, you must know... I-I'm armed!"

Nothing.

"Dammit, make the sound again, you coward!" he yelled, desperate to prove he wasn't losing his wits.

He scoffed, annoyed by his own overreaction.

It finally sounded again.

Scriiiiiitch.

He raced toward the back to the edge of the cart and swung the burlap cover off the nestled layer of coffin-shaped crates.

"Which of you morons didn't have the decency to die, huh?"

As he lifted a foot to climb up, he heard something hiss beneath the cart. He felt the sharp pain of thin spikes pierce his flesh and looked down to see the head of a snake, fangs burrowed into him. He screamed, falling to the leaf-littered gravel path. The snake unlatched and retreated beneath the cart.

Gregor screamed into the wilderness. Lowering to the ground, he peered beneath the cart wheels, his thundering heart beating as a large pair of glowing eyes stared back from the darkness, ones too large to belong to the snake.

A moment later, they were joined by a second pair. The creature's hoarse growls and gnashing teeth made Gregor forget the reptile's bite altogether. He scooted away frantically to expand his distance from them.

Ducking out into the moonlight from its spot beneath the cart, a tailed infernal unfolded. It creaked and popped, its joints cracking as it unfurled. Both decaying wolf-like heads snarled menacingly, and its stitched-on snake tail hissed again.

Gregor frantically scanned the area for something bigger than his dulled, puny dagger to protect himself with. Spotting only dry twigs and gravel, he reached for one of the apple-sized stones at the edge of the dirt. As his plump fingers clutched the rock, the infernal encroached, striding closer, teeth dripping with noxious-smelling drool.

Gregor's throat sac throbbed in time with his rapid heartbeat as he hurled the rock at one of the infernal's wolf heads, striking one in one of its four glowing, foggy eyes. The creature stumbled back and let out a terrifying sound, roaring into the night air as fluid dribbled from its punctured eye.

The second head turned to examine the wounded head and snarled. It turned back, hunched lower, and lunged at Gregor. Overgrown nails shredded through the dirt and gravel, and in a second, both sets of beastly teeth sank into the ewanian's throat.

Gregor's rasping screams shattered the silence of the wilderness. Beneath him, a growing pool of Merlot-colored blood expanded, soaking through the gravel into the dirt below.

Their hunger never satiated, they dispatched the wagon driver and retreated into the woods to do what they do best:

Stalk. Devour. Repeat.

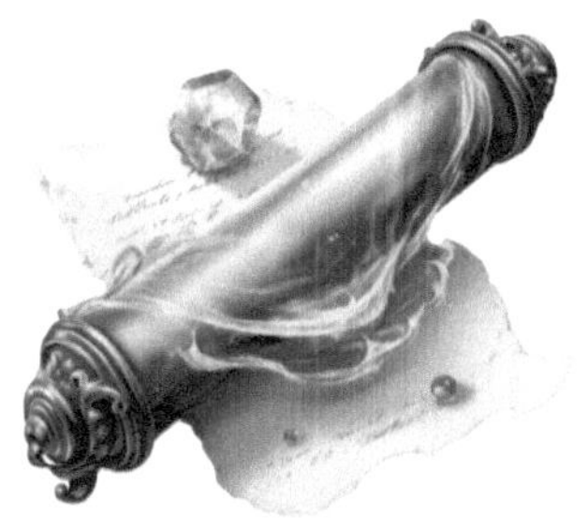

24

Outside the Lost City of Elathia
The Radiant Sea

Omen grunted, dragging a cask full of Parnix's home-boiled antidote through the sand with a rope. "Why couldn't Violet turn into a whale or something and drag these out?"

"She's busy… helping Parnix fill the vials."

"She could have helped us first."

"Stop… complaining!" Twitch growled.

Omen narrowed his eyes at the wyl and stopped to take a break. He used his mired barrel as a seat and let the ropes dangle in the current.

Twitch yelled to Quistix, who was far ahead, nearly out of sight. "Q! *Torch Boy* needs a breather! He can't hack it. He needs a break."

Quistix shook her head and continued marching into the murk.

"How is she so strong?" Omen asked, impressed.

"Because she doesn't have other people doing all of her fighting for her," Twitch fired back like he'd been dying to get a dig in. "Come on. We're gonna end up as sea dragon scat if we sit around out here in the open all day."

"I just need a second," Omen huffed. The irritation in his voices made the hackles on Twitch's back raise.

Twitch stopped to catch his breath, too, hoping that if he stayed close enough to

Omen, he could push the man into harm's way to save himself if Kackaroth came back.

Omen pointed in the direction Quistix had disappeared. "She sure is a bristly one. I don't know how you manage to travel day in and day out with someone so hot-and-cold like that."

Twitch turned to face Omen. "That woman has been through a lot. She's been beaten down, hunted like a dog, survived loss, and she still has the balls to get up and face every new day despite it all. That woman is a legend. She's got more fight and dignity in her pinkie than you've got in your whole flammable, sad excuse for a body."

Omen ignored the insult. From all he'd seen and heard, the wyl was right. "She mentioned Rowland. I didn't realize she's married," Omen said quietly.

"She's not. Not anymore."

"Was it... recent?"

"No. Happened before I met her. He was a city guard there in Bellaneau. She had a son, too, back then."

Omen looked away. He knew exactly what had happened to her boy at his behest, and about the revenge she'd exacted. Soren Everbleed was a poor excuse for an Emerald Bandit, one Omen deeply regretted recruiting years ago. His gaggle of men went from hand-picked hunters to pathetic pillagers in a matter of weeks. Embarrassments, every one of them.

"If you're asking because you're thinking about taking a run at her, I'd have a real problem with that." Twitch glared at him.

"I'm not. But," Omen laughed, "if I were, I certainly wouldn't let a wyl, of all things, stand in my way."

"This is far enough away!" the voice yelled in the distance. "Get them over here!"

Twitch motioned in her direction with his head. "C'mon. The lady beckons."

"You always do what she says?"

Twitch simply laughed and yanked the cask back out of the sand by the ropes.

Minutes later, their casks were clustered together, each full of Parnix's noxious billaguppy antidote blend.

Just as Twitch had stepped back to nod at the octopus behind him, a gargantuan figure emerged from the murky forest of seaweed and cruised overhead, blotting out the sun.

"We've got company," Omen said quietly.

Kackaroth circled back like a shark, its tail wagging from side to side like a rudder. He dove deep near them, stirring up a plume of sand that obscured his view. As the silt and granules settled, they saw his bloodshot eyes lock onto them.

"It's showtime," Quistix mumbled. "Give me the dagger." She held her hand out to Omen.

He ignored her and walked over to the barrel himself, stabbing the blade of his emerald dagger into the wooden top of the largest cask. He struggled to yank it out.

When he did, green fluid seeped out of the hole, up into the water.

"How long did Parnix say it would take to neutralize this stuff?" Twitch asked, never taking his eyes off the dragon.

Quistix shrugged. "He's a madman, Twitch. It's hard to tell if he's gone crazy or if he's just an intoxicated genius."

"I'm hoping for the latter," he replied. The octopus slid a tentacle around his furry shoulder. He smiled and patted it tenderly.

Omen stabbed the second cask and released the fluid. He poised to stab the third and looked at Quistix. "Ready?"

Quistix nodded. The octopus did the same.

"It's time for the fish, then," Omen said. "I'm going to pry this one open completely on the count of three. One... two..."

The octopus used a free tentacle to hurl a net full of dead fish into the air. It slowly fell onto the first cask.

"Three!" Omen pried the lid off the third barrel, bending the blade of his knife in the process. Thick tendrils of speckled green liquid oozed out, dissipating into the waters around them.

Kackaroth shot out from the seaweed at full speed, his massive jaws chomping.

The trio stood side by side, and the octopus slid a tentacle around each of their bent arms and jetted away from the barrels, using every muscle to propel them through the water toward the dome in the distance.

The dragon studied the net full of fish and sniffed deep, drawing the rancid-smelling green antidote in through his nose.

Kackaroth roared and bit down onto one of the barrels, gnarling the fish-covered wood with a deafening crunch.

Twitch stifled his scream as they rocketed through the water, the dome approaching too fast for his liking.

With a flourish of each extremity, the octopus shook them loose, and they tumbled to the ocean floor, each making a run for the dome.

As they gasped for breath inside the dry bubble, waiting for their gills to transition again, Quistix watched as the octopus performed its miraculous shape-shifting feat back into Violet, as they had come to know her.

Twitch greeted her with the folded robe from the bench just inside the clear dome wall, and she covered her naked body with it.

"That sight never gets old," he said with a smile.

"I know. That's what everyone says the first few times they watch me transition." She grinned.

"Oh, darling. I was talking about you." He winked.

She blushed.

Twitch handed out small, personal-sized glass vials of Parnix's antidote among them. Quistix squeezed saltwater out of her long red braid, staring out at Kackaroth in the distance, devouring the casks, lapping at the liquid with its humongous tongue. The sleek, sand-colored creature shifted uneasily on its webbed feet, glancing around like a pet in search of its master. Something in its eyes seemed frightened.

"Fear makes monsters of us all," Quistix muttered and chugged the contents of her vial, wincing violently as she finished.

As the others drank their antidotes, Kackaroth grew tired of gnawing at the crates. He cruised closer, his movements less erratic, more tranquil. He swam to the bubble and pressed his nose almost to the dome, staying just far enough away that he wouldn't be zapped.

Taking a step toward the barrier, Quistix reached out her hand.

Omen grabbed her wrist. "Kackaroth isn't a pleom. It's a dragon, one of the largest of its kind."

"Wow, I never would have guessed," Quistix snarled. "Thank you for the clarification." Jerking her wrist from his grip,

Quistix glowered at him. “Unburden yourself, Omen. I do as I please. I answer only to myself.”

Taking a step back, Omen raised his hands in defeat. “Your funeral.”

Pressing her hand gently through the domed barrier, Quistix held her palm up flat near one of the dragon’s nostrils. Dwarfed by its sheer enormity, she couldn’t help but be in awe of its size. Her entire sideways body wouldn’t even be the width of its snout.

The dragon breathed in her scent.

Twitch and Violet watched in silence.

Kackaroth inched closer, surging warm water through her fingertips with every breath. She leaned out further, until the barrier was at her shoulder. She winced, ready to pull back at the slightest hint of animosity. It was powerful, but it was also gargantuan, and she felt she had speed on her side.

Aurora approached quietly from the shadowy edge of the street.

"Be ready to heal her when she draws back a stump," Twitch said to the esteg, shaking his head.

Quistix giggled in amazement as the dragon allowed her to pet the tip of its nose. Its eyes shut and it sprawled in the sand like a loyal dog beside the dome, breathing out a contented puff of water.

"That thing's supposedly gone from murderous sea monster to domesticated filabrat that quickly? I don't buy it," Twitch said.

"I do. That stuff is nasty, but I'm already feeling better. Less clumsy. More coordinated," Quistix said, never blinking, unable to tear her citrine eyes away from the sea dragon. Kackaroth batted his four eyelids, and she could see the whites around the edges of his reptilian eyes, areas that were once irritated and red.

"Your grandfather told us he released it. He wasn't thinking very clearly because of the dikeeka." Quistix pulled her hand back and walked over to Violet. "Why was it locked away in the first place?"

Parnix's voice arose behind them, seemingly out of nowhere. "It was an honest misunderstanding."

Twitch startled. "Ugh! Wizards! Mark my words, I'm sewing a bell onto your robe so I can hear you coming!"

"A while back, a shipment went missing off the coast of Asera. A torrential storm came through and fractured the ship. It took on water and sank to the ocean floor. The vessel was a fishing boat, seemingly on its way back to the mainland, containing thousands of fish. When they didn't return, a rescue attempt was made. The captain of that ship located the boat... along with Kackaroth, who had scarfed down every last fish he could get his little webbed paws on. They blamed him for the ship's capsizing. They tried to net him and shoot him with harpoons, but he tore through. His tail whipped their ship and nearly sank them, too. Once they made it back to dry land, they had one of the professors at Apex summon me, since aquatics is my specialty. The Aserans asked for my assistance in clearing the ship route between Asera and Destoria. I spent weeks pretending to study him, trying to buy myself time to figure out what to do, as if I hadn't known him since he was a mere egg!" Parnix looked out at the dragon. "He's really a gentle creature. He just eats so much..."

Twitch laughed. "As someone who has been in a ship he was snacking on, I can safely say that's an understatement."

Parnix went on. "One day, while I was on the Aserans boat, a horrible storm sent the ship's sails hurtling right into me. Knocked me overboard. Kackaroth saved me and took me to Elathia. That's when I discovered this little nesting spot of ruins just outside of the city. I created the barrier, made up a few tall tales on land about how I needed to do more research in private, but assured them that they would have no more troubles from him."

Aurora stepped forward. "Being on the cutting edge of such knowledge, I'd love to read any of those research materials if you still have any."

Parnix's lips quirked up into a smile. "Splendid! Maybe you can help add to it."

Aurora's fluffy white tail wagged back and forth excitedly, doe eyes widening. "Me?"

"I could use another pair of eyes on some of my older work, especially if they belong to someone as well-read and intellectual as yourself. I think you'd be especially interested in a study of jellyfish that I did years back. Truly stunning creatures."

"That would be such an honor, Irenas."

"It's nothing! I'd love to discuss it with you. You're so well-read that perhaps I could rack your brain for a few things myself."

Aurora stuttered. "I-I'm at your service!"

"Parnix, you said when we met that you let Kackaroth loose. How do we recapture him?"

Parnix smiled softly and looked at Quistix. "I have no plans to recapture, my dear. He has a right to freedom just as every living thing."

"Wait, you're just going to let him run amok?" Twitch asked, shocked.

Parnix sighed and swept his silvery locks over his shoulder. "Kackaroth was never supposed to be contained forever. It was just a temporary solution. There's an abyss nearby, a pocket leading to fathoms of darkness, the depths of which are still unknown. After the Aserians hired me to clear the trade route, I knew I had to do something or else they'd kill him. I lured him to the abyss with a net full of his favorites, octopus and squid. I tossed it into that endless pit, and, like the trusting soul he is, Kackaroth followed it down. Then, I cast a barrier spell over the top to keep him there. I worried constantly, but it was for his own protection, you see. It was a risk in itself, not knowing what could be in those depths with him, but those damned Aserans were searching! They were ready to hunt him down. Kackaroth was down there for a year, at least. A large chunk of every day has been spent gathering food for him, ensuring he stayed well-fed. It was the very *least* I could do."

Parnix's gaze drifted solemnly to the floor. "I visited him multiple times a day until he started showing signs of deep sadness. Towards the end, he wouldn't even come up to the barrier to see me anymore. He'd just sulk down there." His voice cracked. "Makes me want to cry even talking about it."

"Sounds like a horrible way to live," Quistix said.

"It's not living at all! I wanted to protect him so that he could enjoy a long life. But even though I had the best intentions, the whole thing was cruel. He deserves freedom."

Parnix stared off into the distance for a moment, seemingly lost in thought. His voice came out as a whisper, "I think part of me also kept him around because… I needed him. Life isn't meant to be lived in solitude."

Twitch glanced at Quistix. He had told her that countless times. She had always brushed it off.

Parnix sniffled and wiped his cheeks. He smiled and whisked Aurora toward the street in the direction of his hovel. "Come now. Enough of our woes. I have a pot of fish stew boiling. You all must be ravenous after all of that."

Omen nudged Quistix. "Sounds disgusting, but his kettle-simmered flounder is sublime."

She nodded, close enough to smell the well-oiled leather and scent of bonfire smoke emanating from him.

"I'm going to go get washed up for dinner." Violet poked Twitch playfully on the snout with her finger and turned to join them.

He watched her walk away, staring at the sway of her robe-clad figure as she made her way down the street.

Twitch and Quistix stood together in the silence for a moment, watching the others chat and laugh as they made their way back to Irenas's home.

"Violet's cute," Quistix finally said. "She likes you, you know."

"She's lovely."

"You should go for it."

Twitch smiled, but a moment later, it dissipated. "Be honest."

"Always am."

His ears drooped, heart aching slightly. Finally, he managed to get the words out. "You were never going to give me a chance, were you? Not really."

Her face softened, her annoyance at his persistence transforming into sympathy. "No, Twitch. I tried to tell you a million times."

He sighed and nodded, trying to act like it didn't crush him to hear her say it honestly. "For a while there, I thought you were just playing hard to get."

She shook her head. "I was never playing. After Rowland and Danson… there's safety in keeping people at arm's length."

The once-mischievous look in his eyes dulled.

The sharp, never-dulling throb of loss bit at her. The pain was always there. Lurking. Every laugh was tainted. The act of enjoyment felt like a betrayal of her son's and husband's memories, as though their lives could be so easily forgotten. But they would always be there, only visible in the corners of her vision, haunting her like forlorn specters until they were reunited in death.

She gave his shoulder a reassuring pat. "Now, are you going to feel out Violet, or do I need to use you as sea dragon chum?"

"Omen would never allow it," Twitch said weakly. "The Violet thing. He'd love to see me as chum."

"I'll punch Omen in the throat if he gets in your way. You've been at my side through thick and thin. Rest assured, I'll be by yours."

"Because you love me?" His ears perked up. His smile was teasing.

"Because you're my best friend." She planted a tender kiss on his furry cheek. Then, out of nowhere, she smacked his forehead with her flattened palm.

"Ow!"

"Now, turn on that wyl charm or become Kackaroth's antidote palette cleanser. Your choice." She shoved him away and started walking backward toward Parnix's place.

Kackaroth raised his head and stared at Twitch. He swallowed hard and started toward the house. "Wouldn't want that beast to have to cough up a furball, now would I?"

25

Knight Harbor Pier
Desdemona, Willowdale

Saddled, Arias set the pace with his Palfrey as Vervaine's horse trotted closely behind. From the rear, several guards followed behind on their well-groomed Rounceys, keeping their distance, as requested by the king.

Vervaine whispered to Arias, "*I miss the days when we could be alone without a dozen eyes watching our every move. These fools would faint watching me dive from the cliffs of Obsidia.*"

"Go easy on them." Arias smirked, red eyes focused on his destination ahead. "They want to protect you. They've vowed to die in the pursuit of your safety."

Tugging the reins, Arias slowed his horse. Vervaine followed suit. They dismounted, and the guards behind them tied the animals to the trunk of a nearby tree, one twisted and leafless from the punishing, unimpeded Northern winds.

Arias wrapped his wife's waist in his arms and turned her around so that she faced the steep rock wall instead of the townspeople crowded in front of the crashing waves.

"Wait, are we not here to give a speech?"

"No." Arias smiled and nodded at one of the patrolmen standing halfway up the steep path. The man scrambled, racing up the face of the mountain toward a gaggle of others. Twelve more patrolmen stood at the base of a monumental figure covered in sewn-together sheets of tattered burlap, each a different shade of brown.

"What is going on?" Vervaine smiled. "You know I hate surprises."

Arias scooped her long hair over one shoulder and kissed the exposed side of her neck. "You hid your face for so long, that beautiful face that I loved all my life, long before it was ever healed. You are beloved, my darling. Not just by me..."

"What have you done?"

"I wish I could take credit, but this was none of my doing. Our people, *your* people, they find you inspiring. You have something your father and sister never did."

"What's that?"

"The respect of the isle." Arias raised his hand to the readied men above, a signal for them to proceed. In unison, they tugged the ropes tied to the bottom and unveiled a sleek soapstone statue of Vervaine in a billowing gown on the cliff above. The sculpted version of her stood in a regal posture, grace and beauty personified. Tree roots wound around the figure's outstretched hand and up its stone wrist.

Tears flooded Vervaine's eyes. Arias intertwined his fingers through hers.

"A statue? We can't afford this after all we are doing for Taernsby, Arias."

"Not to worry. This didn't cost us a single sovereign. It was made by the people. Artists have been chiseling away at it for weeks. Surely, it was a long, exhaustive measure just to get the raw soapstone *up* there."

"I don't know what to say."

"You needn't say anything. Not to me. This is a gift from them, an expression of their gratitude for the way you've ruled with kindness and mercy. Exos bled this isle dry to stock her own treasury. You've gone above and beyond to stimulate the economies of the provinces and make sure that children are not starving to death in the streets." He turned her back toward the people clustered around the wharf, all smiling, some wiping their eyes. "They did this."

"The statue is beautiful!" She hollered to the commoners around the wharf.

"You're a walking miracle!" one woman shouted.

"Yes, truly a miracle. Such a monument befits someone who has died and come back to life!" barked an elderly wyl man with a muzzle full of gray, wiry hairs.

"What?" Vervaine's smile vanished.

"We heard about the stabbing and your demise at the hands of Haldrin," another shouted, his mouth full of rotted teeth. "Glad to see necromancy is on the rise again! My wife will be *thrilled* once we bring her back!"

"Truly a miracle!"

"Yes, truly! I never thought I'd see it legalized!"

"My brother died in the battle fighting at your sister's behest, your majesty. Can you make bringing him back a priority?"

Arias positioned himself between Vervaine and the overjoyed crowd. He gritted his teeth. “Time to go, my darling.”

26

Desdemona, Willowdale

Staggering through the streets, Werner swerved like a drunkard, stumbling over his own feet as he bumbled through town. He dunked his head in a nearby wash barrel in front of a modest home and vomited violently beneath the surface as a dwarf woman stared in horror from the window above. He gasped for air and wiped the water and bile from his spotted face and whiskers. He glanced down at the murky liquid, a color unlike anything he'd recently consumed, which wasn't much. For days, everything he had ingested made him feel ill.

Werner began to hyperventilate, jerking as a large man snatched him up by his soaked shirt. The slate-gray eaflic grimaced. "Vomit on your own property, you drunkard! We don't need you stinking the place up any more than you already have!"

The pudgy man's expression shifted from anger to concern.

"Hey... you alright? You look like you're just this side of death."

Werner stumbled away from the eaflic, catching himself on the dwarf's splintered fence. With the last of his strength, he made his way back onto the cobblestone thoroughfare bustling with activity.

Inside one of the shops, a reptilian shop owner held up a pearl necklace for a kleax woman. The baiya stood slack-jawed as he watched Werner scuttle clumsily past his window, soaked and sickly.

Though an autumnal chill was in the air, sweat roiled off of Werner's furry temples. The towering walls of the nearby buildings seemed to shift, warping and bending, arching over him, boxing him in. The ground shuddered beneath him, making simply walking a troublesome feat. Every sound amplified. Carts rumbled, symphs chirped, and the trivial chatter made his head throb, his ears ache. Colors seemed muted, everything draining to various shades of gray. His chest constricted, robbing air from his strained lungs like a fish thrown ashore.

The world abruptly lurched to the right, sending Werner stumbling into an unsuspecting family of ewanians before slamming into the stone wall of another local merchant.

Gripped by the shirt, Werner was swung around like a doll by a scrawny barbarian. He growled, "How about you go home before I knock those fangs down your throat?"

Werner's colorless pallor made the barbarian release him. He backed away from the landigo slowly. "What in the Nether is *wrong* with you? You smell like death."

Wobbling off, the remaining distance to the inn seemed like an insurmountable trek. As its distant sign came into view, he tumbled down onto the cobblestone and convulsed, his furry limbs curling inward until he was in a ball on his side. The ground beneath him trembled, and then suddenly the world broke apart, the ground shattering into pieces that swirled around in a cyclone.

The worried voices of the townsfolk faded away, and moments later, the shaking stopped. A pleasant warmth spread through him. Relaxing, the last of his consciousness slipped away as the black void of death enveloped him.

Werner gasped, his lungs nearly exploding, the weight of his eyelids too heavy to bear.

His freezing body shuddered, teeth clenched.

"By the Gods!" a woman exclaimed.

Finally, Werner mustered the strength to open his eyes.

A pale ewanian's neck sac swelled. Staggering in her black, ankle-length coat, her body crumpled, smacking her forehead against the stone slab where Werner was laid with a nauseating *crack*. Unconscious, she lolled onto the stone floor.

Werner stared at her in horror, recognizing her garb, the uniform of a Willowdale undertaker.

Still shaking, he glanced around. There were body parts in jars, suspended in yellow liquids. Tools were scattered on a nearby table, saws with biting metal teeth, sharpened scalpels. Dangling from his skin hung a long, curved needle and a length of thread. He shrieked at the absence of organs in the empty cavern of his torso. Sawdust spilled out of him instead, pooling between his legs.

His breaths were ragged as he watched the tips of his expanding lungs bob out from beneath the undertaker's cuts.

He wondered how he could be alive. How could they have thought him dead? How long had he been swimming in the darkness?

Before him, the wall of jarred organs began to morph and move as a portal ripped through the fabric of space. Nothing seemed real anymore. He wondered if perhaps this was all a delusion, a dream caused by whatever was ailing him.

Through the blackness of the portal came a beak and two familiar, glowing, green eyes. The curled claw of the mad quichyrd beckoned him.

27

Irenas Parnix's Coral Library
The Radiant Sea

Parnix sipped tea from a green sea glass mug in the coral library, watching the steam rise as he stared up through the domed roof. There was such a peaceful tranquility that existed in the Radiant Sea. The silence wasn't like any he'd ever experienced on land. It afforded him greater focus.

Beside him, Aurora stood, shifting her weight gently as she read from one of his old texts. She glanced up at him, a silent request to turn her page. He smiled and flipped the parchment to the next. She continued on, her ravenous intellectual appetite raging with the same passionate fervor as his own. She seemed truly happy, the silent company of the former professor providing her a respite from the incessant chatter and inconsequential babbles of those not devoted to higher learning or academic research.

The sound of a slamming door made Irenas nearly drop his glass, splashing his robe with steaming liquid. Shoulders hunched, gray hair still mussed, eyes heavy with puffy bags, he flashed the intruders a look of irritation. He clutched his head.

"By the Gods, I feel like absolute rubbish and you come in here banging about like some demolition crew!" he grumbled.

"Oops," Twitch mumbled, pulling the pad of his hand off the door like it had scorched his skin. "My apologies."

"Can we talk, Parnix?" Shielding her eyes from the light, Quistix's repentant expression softened Irenas's rigid nerves. Despite the antidote speeding their recovery, it appeared they all felt like garbage as their bodies expelled the last traces of dikeeka.

"Yes, yes. Come in."

Stepping inside, Twitch looked around at the coral and flotsam shelves loaded with brown, leather-bound books. Slivers of light filtered in from the open dome above, bathing them all in rippling shades of blue.

Omen and Violet entered behind them. Violet rubbed the sleep from her eyes. Omen was dressed for war, as always.

"Parnix, do you know a quichyrd by the name of Ceosteol?" Quistix asked, slinking into a stone chair in the corner.

"Oh, of course. I'd be surprised if any educated mage in this isle didn't know who she was. She's deplorable."

"Ah, so you really do know her," Quistix mumbled.

"She and Omen are bonded. His eternal fire is a custom curse of her making."

Twitch fondled a large tome with gemstones on the binding.

"Put that down," Aurora growled.

Twitch slid it back onto the shelf and stuck his tongue out at her as she went back to reading.

"What, specifically, do you wish to know about her?" Parnix asked.

"Everything you can share. She's building an army of the undead. I need to know everything I can. I plan to stop her... or die trying."

"I don't think you know what kind of power you're going up against." Omen's voice was firm. "I know who she is and what she can do." He pointed to his face. "If you don't wish to spend eternity on fire, I'd advise you to pour your skills and energy into more worthwhile endeavors."

Twitch took a step toward Omen. "Her creatures are all over this isle. We saw them in Hadina's crypt. We encountered them in the wild. We saw those monsters. Floating skeletons in robes, wolves sewn together with snake tails. And we're supposed to... what? Turn a blind eye? People are dying!"

Omen raised his voices. "Many more will die until she gets what she wants!"

"Please, Omen, I beg of you..." Parnix waved his hand and clutched his temples again. "Quiet yourself."

Quistix leaned forward. "What does she want exactly?"

Omen's handsome face grinned. "She wants you, Lux... Alba."

All eyes turned to Quistix.

"You've taken many lives, but her interest is in how you can give them."

"I don't understand."

"You're the Illuminator. She followed your father's research on immortality with great interest."

Violet raised a brow. "But you're immortal. So she can obviously make things live forever without Quistix."

"He is cursed, Violet. He was cursed while he was living. They are speaking of the revival of a being after it has been dead. Pulling a corpse's soul back from the Ethereal Sanctum to inhabit a body again. These are very different things," Parnix retorted. "Curses are black magic, too, and are therefore just as forbidden. If anyone caught a hint of such magical disobedience, they would ideally be exiled or imprisoned. There is no room for black magic in an isle of civilized people. Allowing it would lead to utter chaos. Apex watches over these matters closely. Master Tempest, however, constructed a cavern to conceal Ceosteol's experiments, below the Obsidian palace."

"We've been," Twitch said curtly.

"Ceosteol is one of the isle's most notable practitioners of black magic. Her escapades with dead wyl children were what got her imprisoned the first time. For decades, she stood alongside Master Tempest, carrying out various experiments on corpses. Necromancy, that's what they called it. Master Tempest announced to anyone that would listen that he had found the solution, the Illuminator."

"That's her." Omen and Twitch said in unison, both pointing to Quistix.

Parnix's jaw dropped. "By the Gods... I never in a million years imagined it would be a person." After a moment of staring at Quistix, he pulled a red leather-bound book off of one of the shelves and handed it to her. "There's some interesting information in here about necromancy and the undead. It also has some musings about soul bonds as well."

"Soul bonds?"

"Yes, dark magic practitioners can tether other lives to theirs with a soul bond. It binds one to a person person that has offered a piece of their essence. Once the binding takes place, the bonding party can inhabit the recipient. When this happens, they become a host that can harbor them temporarily. It is rumored that Ceosteol has bonded to a lot of beings over the years. She, in theory, can become anything. Wyl, human, symph... it doesn't matter. If a piece of her has been offered and accepted, that being is now under her control whenever she chooses to inhabit its mind. Thank the Gods she's behind bars. She'd be a menace on the streets with that kind of power."

Twitch tapped his claws on a stack of tomes. "Ceosteol was pardoned. By Exos Tempest. She's been freely walking the streets of Destoria for months, Irenas."

Parnix clutched his chest. "What?!"

Quistix looked at Omen. "Wait a second, Vervaine!"

"Was there a question in there somewhere?" Omen asked.

"Vervaine Brius... is she one of these undead soul-bonded things you're talking about?"

Omen hesitated for a moment and then nodded, his tefly leather squeaking as he folded his arms. "Yes, I think so. Arias, too, from what I've heard from some of the rumblings around the palace. He died the same night as Exos, I believe."

For several long moments, the only sound was the swish of water against the dome, like a quiet heartbeat inside a mother's womb. Oblivious sea life darted around the open waters above them, dappling the light from above.

"So... the isle is... being run by the undead?" Irenas croaked.

Omen nodded. "Well, it would be more accurate to say that it's being run by Ceosteol. The former prisoner. The mad quichyrd."

"No," Parnix said quietly. He trembled as he lowered himself onto a stool, needing to sit down at the news. "You have to stop her. It'll be bedlam..."

"Now, she's untouchable," Omen said. "She has the king and queen in her pocket. She can write her own pardons. She can do anything she wants with the majority of the isle at her command. It's only a matter of time before she pushes to legalize dark magic again. I imagine that's the end goal here. To bring her toys out into the light of day so they can walk, and rot, with freedom."

Parnix added, "She always wrote about wanting to create a superior being, 'children' of her own making, as she called them. Her creatures will overwhelm, overpower, and outnumber the living. If she is allowed to practice openly, the isle is as good as damned. All that would soon be left to do is abandon Destoria. Take a few boats to Asera and pray that those things never learn how to swim."

Twitch spoke. "Destoria deserves better. I won't abandon this place. It's my home. There are innocent beings here, like Aurora and Frok." The name stole the air from his lungs for a moment. Finally, his emotions settled enough to speak again. "I'd rather bleed my last drop of blood on Destorian soil knowing that I tried than to live as a coward anywhere else."

"It's too late to stop her," Omen said flippantly. "The bird is already in power with a king and queen in tow. That's check and mate."

"Irenas," Quistix said. "How can we stop her?"

Parnix wobbled his head. "She's a very powerful sorceress. With those soul bonds, she can appear anywhere, be anyone at any time."

Quistix rose from her seat with urgency. "Then... we need to be everywhere at once." Looking at the wizard, her yellow irises flashed platinum-white. "We need a call to arms. How can we possibly contact Destorians across the map, ideally without having Ceosteol know about it? You taught at Apex. Is there some sort of spell you could do to manage a sort of... mass alert?"

Twitch's eyes bulged. "Can that be done?"

Parnix stuttered, "I-I don't..."

"What about some sort of... symph carriers or a spell to make people hear an announcement?"

"Hmmmm. Perhaps... no."

"What?! Tell us."

"Well, maybe I could enchant a scroll with a message. It would only appear for a short time before disappearing for good."

"That would work!"

"But... Ahhhh." He waved the idea away.

"What?" Quistix's eyes shimmered.

"The one I have in mind, I've never actually done it. I only taught it as a theory. But if we bound it to you specifically, it would go out only to people that you have met. You'd have to be able to think about them first and concentrate hard for the scrolls to find their way to the recipients. *In theory.*"

Quistix stared at Parnix for a long time, her intense gaze making the wizard squirm. "Irenas. Tell me it can be done."

28

The Rusty Ogre Tavern
Vrisca, Bellaneau

A blow to the face, that was all Bea could recall. A serving platter launched from her hand as she was knocked to the ground. The barroom brawl surged on, having started like the flaming flash in a cooking pan out of nowhere. Her thoughts meandered somewhere just beyond consciousness.

A vocal roar exploded through the silence, filling the tavern, vibrating the floorboards with its timbre. All fell still, balled fists poised to throw another punch.

In front of Bea, two hind feet stopped. Their claws clicked against the wood as Barnabus kneeled down. The white towel he used for cleaning glassware dangled from the apron strings around his waist as he scooped her up in his arms. In a few quick strides, they were back at the bar. He swiped the top clear and draped her on it.

Bea was dizzy, her mind retreating like a roach into darkness.

"Whose bar is this? Is it *yours*?" Barnabus shouted, jabbing a claw into one of the dwarf patrons' chests. The dwarf stumbled backward. Barnabus waved his hands, gesturing to everyone else. "Did any of *you* buy these mugs and tables with *your* hard-earned coin?"

The patrons lowered their fists, trying to diffuse the livid barkeep's anger.

Barnabus's face scanned the room, his mane swaying. "What do you have to say for yourselves? Hmm?"

"He started it." A dwarf tattled, pointing a chubby finger at a wyl.

Graying around his reddened muzzle, the wyl lowered his head in shame. "Sorry, Barn. I'm not in a good place."

"You've been lookin' for trouble ever since that thing took your wife!" the dwarf shouted.

"My bar is no place for your aggressive nonsense! You wanna brawl? Go outside! There's a whole *world* out there. And you owe Bea an apology, plus some sovereign from that coin purse of yours."

"Sorry, Bea," the wyl mumbled, untying the coin purse on his belt. He set some gold pieces in the human's hand. As a wyl, it pained him to give up coin, but he'd struck her, a woman, in front of a kleax no less. He considered himself lucky for being allowed to leave with his limbs intact.

Barnabus pointed to the dwarf and the wyl. "*Both* of you are banned. To the Nether with you! Get out!"

As the men started out the door, a glimmer of light appeared before them, something shimmering like gold flecks in the sunlight.

“What the...?” the wyl mumbled.

A magical scroll unfurled before the faces of several people in the establishment, all at the same time. The people without scrolls looked around at each other, confused. A scroll even hovered, horizontally, in front of Bea’s face as she struggled to gain consciousness.

On each blank scroll, words started to appear, neat words in cursive written before their very eyes.

Barnabus swatted at his, but his hand seemed to go right through it.

Each letter said:

Irosday, fourth of Autumn

Dearest Destorians,

The isle is in danger. The time has come to rise up in revolution against a practitioner of dark magic who walks freely among us, a sorceress quichyrd who has the queen’s ear.

Her name is Ceosteol, a dark magic mage pardoned for the crimes of experimenting on dead children and attempting hideous mutations with animals.

These creatures are now terrorizing our isle from the shadows. Many lurk in her subterranean lair. I have seen them with my very eyes, these tailed monstrosities, reapers, and black-eyed beings, all necromanced creatures of her own design.

Our isle is in grave danger. Royalty can't be trusted. They are being manipulated like puppets by this sick woman. It won't be long before we will be forced to kneel and watch as a race of abominations roam free.

She plays with the bodies of our loved ones, altering their legacies with her nefarious intentions.

Dear friends, I implore you to join our revolution. The future of the isle depends on you. We must stop the madness. Soon, we will wage war.

Join our forces. Fight with us. We meet on the second Nismisday, the eighteenth of

Autumn, in the capital city of Taernsby at the pier.

At the bottom of the page, the magical writing halted for a moment before the final words signed themselves:

Sincerely yours,

Quistix Daedumal of the Harbingers of Hope

As soon as the last word was inked, the scrolls all started to smolder, starting at the top edge. Sparkling with lit embers, the papers engulfed slowly in flames before turning into no more than floating charcoal flakes.

"The *Harbingers of Hope*?" the old wyl repeated aloud, confused.

Carefully, Bea blinked a few times and sat up. She slid her feet onto the floor and steadied herself. She smiled at Barnabus and nodded, her eye already starting to turn purple around the edges. She started toward the door.

"Where are you going?" Barnabus shouted.

Bea looked around at everyone and gave a weak smile. "I know I got hit hard, but surely I didn't just imagine what we all saw."

"No, but..."

"You've seen them, haven't you? The soul reapers? Those demon dogs with snakes for tails? The children who play in the woods at night with the eyes that..." She trailed off. "We can only turn a blind eye for so long before someone gouges it out altogether. I promise, if you saw the aftermath of what those things had done to my sister, how they'd left her carcass to rot in the middle of her farm, her body wrung out like a rag... You wouldn't hesitate."

"Bea, think about what you're doing. What if this is a hoax? And, even if it's not, you're just a regular person. You don't even know how to fight."

"Sure. I'm just some idiot barmaid in Bellaneau, right? That's what you all think. But watching you animals tear each other apart in here for years, I'm sure I can handle that. I am not going to stand around when I have a chance to fight back, Barnabus. Because it only takes one little pebble to disrupt even the finest of cogs. Who knows. Maybe I'm that pebble. And, perhaps, there will be many more pebbles just like me when I get to that harbor."

"Bea!"

"I knew her, you know. I knew Quistix. Her grandfather used to send her here to bring him back bottles of mead when she was just a wee-little elven child. I watched her fight in here, too, many years later, as an adult. She defended me. She sent Vetrove and that gaggle of unwashed thieves running for the hills after they messed with me." Bea smiled and shook her head. "She's not a bad horse to hitch your wagon to."

"Don't leave, Bea. You have a job to do."

Bea chuckled and grabbed the door. "Then, I quit."

She walked outside, and the saloon doors wobbled shut. The men in the tavern looked at each other, and several followed her out the door.

Barnabus groaned and hurled his wash rag into the basin of the sink. "Alright, everyone out."

The patrons filed out, and Barnabus plodded out to the tavern's raised porch. "Bea!"

Bea stopped in the dirt path and turned on her heels to face in his direction.

Barnabus sighed. "You'll need a ride. I've got the wagon. We can take the barrels off and go together."

Bea grinned and started back toward the tavern.

The graying wyl elbowed Barnabus and held out a handful of coins. "Hey, Barn, twelve sovereigns if you have enough space in that wagon for one more."

29

Gardens of the Ruby Palace
Desdemona, Willowdale

Vervaine forced herself to take a deep breath. "You *can't* be serious."

Arias nodded, leaning against the wall, looking out over the royal garden strewn with leaves. Pink budding autumnal vines, Vervaine had named *Frolics of Frok,* in honor of the fallen pleom, climbed the etched spires of a stone pergola. Timid tulips and rambunctious rose bushes dotted the winding path, seemingly unresponsive to their presence. Swaying heather lined the walls. Vervaine sucked in an exasperated lungful of perfumed air while Arias watched a cluster of symphs migrating south, their howls a symphonic echo.

"Serious as death itself," Arias said.

Guards stood nearby, scanning the grounds for potential threats.

"Gentlemen. Who delivered this letter to the palace?"

"A local woman, your majesty. Several of my men claimed to have seen the scrolls before they vanished. A group got together and wrote down the gist of it. I believe they had the intention of distributing it *en masse*, your majesty."

Arias pointed to the parchment in Vervaine's hands. "I was told it showed up in front of many people, wrote itself somehow, and then disappeared as if the scroll never existed."

"By the Gods..." Vervaine shook her head.

Arias stepped next to her, whispering quietly. "*My love, were you... involved in this*?"

"What?! Absolutely not."

He stepped away and popped the head off a rose, watching it fall onto the grass. "It was signed by your favorite ginger and the *Harbingers of Hope,* whatever that means."

"She's trying to stop Ceosteol."

"I know." Arias leaned back against a pillar of the pergola, eyes downcast. "If she is gearing up for a civil war, it might be wise to call our men back from the other provinces and keep our resources here, defending these walls. We can't allow the palace to remain under-protected with such a threat looming."

"Maybe I should see if I can arrange a meeting to talk to Quistix."

He scoffed. "*Yes,* like she'd readily just meet with you after all you've been through. You, the woman who fairly recently had her imprisoned in that very dungeon." He pointed to the base of the castle.

"I had no choice. How would it have looked, Arias?"

"I know. I'm just saying that she may not see it that way. She may be out for blood, *your* blood, despite you and Quistix both desiring the same thing."

There was a long silence. Finally, Vervaine opened her mouth again. "And what, pray tell, issss *that*?" she hissed, Vervaine's eyes suddenly turning a toxic shade of green.

30

The Dreaming Bard Inn
Voria, Taernsby

When Werner awoke, he wasn't sure if it had been moments or months since the horrific incident with the undertaker.

"It gets much easier," the quichyrd's voice said.

Werner looked down at his chest, where garish stitches held his skin together. He felt his stomach, feeling packed sawdust where soft intestines should be. His shoulders sank. He hadn't been dreaming. "What have you done?"

Her waifish frame pressed down onto the bed beside him.

"I made you something beautiful. Something far more permanent."

Werner's face burned, rage blooming through him, burning hotter than the great fires of Willowdale. "*Beautiful*? You've marred me! I'm like a doll, stitched up and poorly stuffed!"

He got out of bed, wincing at the feeling in his belly. "Look at what you've done to me! Look, damn you!"

"I am," she said firmly.

"Why am I still alive?"

A pair of fists pounding on his door startled him. "Shut up in there! Some of us are tryin' to sleep!"

Ceosteol stood. Taking a step toward him, he noticed her eyes looked... *kind*. Worried. She looked at him like a mother would. "We are family now, Werner. I think of you as one of my own children. Loneliness is a curse you are free of now. Soon, I shall introduce you to your siblings, too. But first, you must heal. We have much to accomplish together. I need you to rest. Regain your strength."

She fished in her robe's pocket and pulled out a jar of powder and a kleax mane brush. She dipped the bristles in the container and strode to him, dabbing the brush along his sewn-together wounds. Beneath the stitches, the seams and incisions sealed shut and slowly disappeared.

"What is that?"

She cawed and smiled. "A little ground esteg horn, timid tulip pollen, and some other things. I can't have you walking around looking like a corpse, now, can I?"

He looked down, examining her work. Where there once there were incisions, now there was cold, seamless, furry skin. Werner felt the flesh, amazed that all traces of mutilation had vanished.

He narrowed his eyes at her. "I would have done what you asked in exchange for freedom. You didn't have to kill me!"

"You might be right. I could have taken that gamble. But why do it if I don't have to?" She stared at him, studying his reaction.

He didn't give her one.

"Dark magic is a gift. Even necromancy has a cost, and I have generously paid it on your behalf. You should be thanking me, Werner."

"A gift?" He scoffed. "Excuse me if I have trouble seeing this as such."

She smiled. "Whether you believe me or not, it is. And what we do with this gift together will be *extraordinary*."

Werner pulled a folded robe off the chest at the foot of the bed, donned it, and strode over to the small, fogged window.

"Where are we?"

"An inn. I thought my lair would be too jarring for your recovery."

He scoffed at that.

"The innkeeper is one of my many children. He kindly offered the room for free." She stepped behind him. "You will soon discover there are many others like you on this isle. Some in the light…"

She peered out the window.

"…And many in the shadows."

He bared his fangs, trying his best to calm his anger.

She watched a starving child out the window as it begged passersby for food scraps in the street, his bedraggled mother barely able to hold herself up. Several people passed by without making eye contact.

"Your wounds were fresh enough for the powder to work, but many of my children, especially my first hundred or so, were much too decomposed for that. Until the isle allows dark magic, many of them cannot roam freely in the daylight as you can. This must be remedied. Every single one of them deserves to experience all the beauty this isle has to offer."

She took a deep breath and let it out slowly, her glowing eyes finally prying from the sickly child's face. "I dream of a future, Werner, where the Institute of Magic in

Apex teaches necromancy as a valid part of their curriculum. I dream of a day when the legendary figures of our past can share a slice of crumb cake with their great-great-grandchildren."

Werner softened. He thought of his mother and father, both long gone.

"With your help, we can eradicate the brutal finality of death, my friend. Life can be the gift it was meant to be, and not the short-term contract none of us ever voluntarily entered into. Legacies can continue. They can *evolve*. Loved ones everywhere could return."

"So you want me to somehow help make dark magic legal? Without a council seat?" Werner asked, his eyes unfocused, distrustful.

"Yes." She patted his back softly and quietly hobbled toward the door to leave.

"How?"

"You're clever, Werner. I watched you manipulate kings and queens for years. You were tenacious. Whenever you wanted something, you always got it." She opened the door and stared at the dusty floor planks in the hall for a moment before glancing back at him over the shoulder of her robe. "I'm sure you'll figure something out."

31

The Ruby Castle
Desdemona, Willowdale

Laying awake in the middle of the night, Arias stared up at the ceiling. Tonight, it was not the state of Destoria that preoccupied his mind, but something much more personal. Looking over at Vervaine's sleeping face, he smiled. Her smooth skin glistened in the moonlight, her brown hair in a neat braid, her body pressed against his.

He imagined a different outcome for them, one that did not involve sleeping in royal bedchambers with guards mere feet away, the weight of an entire isle resting upon their shoulders.

Instead, he imagined an alternate reality, one in which their lives were simple.

One where they were *happy*.

One where they were both *alive*.

From the darkness beside the bed, a light sparkled, swirling and spiraling into a circle of pitch-black.

Ceosteol whispered in Arias's mind, *Perhaps we should talk.*

Reluctantly, he slung his legs over the bedside and stepped into the dark void.

In a mere moment, as if the world had flipped, the other end of the portal opened horizontally, dropping him three feet down onto his chest. He didn't have time to brace for impact. The force stole the air from his lungs.

Ceosteol covered her smiling beak with a wing. *Sometimes they have a mind of their own.*

I see, he thought.

Arias grunted, righting himself. He'd been summoned to a mountaintop. The frosty wind whipped, tearing at his skin.

The moons were impossibly large overhead, casting their brilliant light across the isle's terrain. A winding river glittered in the distance.

I come here from time to time to clear my mind. I could tell yours was racing. I thought the fresh air would do you good.

That's right. He looked out at the river. *I never get to have an original thought anymore without you being privy to it.*

I'm afraid that isn't true at all, she thought. *I have hundreds of children whose minds I can inhabit. Imagine what it is like to be me, to hear a crowd in my mind, chattering away. I have to tune them out. I had to learn how to listen for certain words and then hone in on a single voice. Many of my children are animals. I had to learn to tune their desires out completely. It took me years. It was driving me insane. People like you, though, that is where my fascination for inhabitation lies.*

Arias walked over to a bare tree. Its veins of copper told him he was among a forest of tanooks.

I feel like a slave to your every insane whim, he thought. *You have welcomed yourself into every crevice of Vervaine's and my life. You must know how invasive you are. Can you not afford us even a modicum of privacy?*

She shook her head. *Sometimes a parent must read their child's diary as a last resort. Learning to trust takes time.*

I don't understand what you're getting out of this, why you won't let the dead simply... be.

Arias, you work, you live, you learn, and then you die. Your slate wipes clean. Experience, expertise, memories, love... they're all erased, buried in the dirt while everyone around you moves on. But I found a way to change that. I found a way to return the gift of life, yet I'm branded a monster for being the first being brave enough to look death square in its face and question it. Had I not intervened, you would be a buried pile of bones and rotting flesh. Instead, you lead a kingdom, she thought. *So ungrateful.*

This is not living, he thought. *I cannot sacrifice my life for a cause I believe in. I have no freedom. No choice. No privacy. No heirs..*

And there it is. There is no need to reproduce for fear of extinction anymore. She beamed. *Family. That's what this is about, Arias. You need no heir to carry on your lineage, your legacy. You have the ability to do that for yourself now, and I think that truly scares you.*

Arias stared at her for an uncomfortably long time and crossed his arms. *I believe we are finished here. I wish to return now. I've a long day tomorrow.*

Sure, she muttered. She sighed and took a seat on the edge of the mountaintop, her clawed feet dangling off the perilous edge. *As you wish.*

Moments later, Arias had been returned to the warmth of his bedchambers, the portal shrinking out of sight in the blink of an eye. He looked at Vervaine, still sleeping peacefully. He studied the curves of her face and the silhouette of her body beneath the embroidered blanket.

He climbed beneath the covers and faced her. In the silence, he dared to imagine a child with her. He wondered if their offspring would have the same freckles as their mother. Would they have his horns?

His mind whirled with possibilities. Their deaths had locked the door to a normal life. Despite it, he couldn't help but imagine it unlocked. He couldn't help but ponder the dangerous, unanswerable question lurking in his mind:

What would their life look like if they had never died?

32

Outside the Lost City of Elathia
The Radiant Sea

The ocean floor outside of the bubble remained lit by the artificial light of the orbs hovering over Elathia and the glow of the three moons beaming through the gentle waves. Cast in teal light, the group worked into the late evening hours.

Kackaroth pressed himself flat against the ocean floor, eyes watching as the group tied casks and vial-filled crates of Parnix's detoxification potion around its elongated neck. The dragon's scaled skin twitched and flexed as they tethered the last barrel. They walked around, testing the braided ropes.

Quistix stroked Kackaroth's massive face lovingly. Its eyes closed, enjoying the gentle touch. "He really is quite docile when he's not on drugs."

"Perhaps it's time we make our ascent before you put the scaly mammoth to sleep," Violet said softly.

Omen climbed onto the dragon, situating himself in one of the makeshift rope harnesses. "I suppose we should surface soon so we can risk our lives distributing this muck."

"If we get fired upon when we get up there, at least you can't die," Quistix said. "The rest of us have to depend on Aurora."

Silence spanned between them all for a beat too long. The esteg stepped forward, her face fraught with worry, her tone apologetic. "No," Aurora said, the word sounding small and strained as it tumbled from her lips.

"What?" Twitch stared at Aurora. The esteg made her way through the water to Parnix's side.

"I'm so sorry." The tremor in Aurora's voice was like an emerald dagger to her heart as her tears flowed freely down her furry cheeks.

Twitch's ears folded back. Quistix's eyes bulged.

Irenas stroked the esteg's mane to soothe her. Then, he looked at Quistix. "I offered to let her stay here, where it's safe. She can further her academics, and I can mentor her. In exchange, she can help aid in my aquatic studies."

"Aurora?"

"I promise you all that she will be well cared for as long as she is here in the dome."

"You cannot be serious," Quistix asked weakly. "We need you, Aurora. We're about to go to war."

"No, you need my horns. And in case you haven't noticed, I don't have much in the way of those right now," Aurora said.

"You saw how much healing Vervaine's face took out of me. Imagine me on the battlefield, Quistix. Imagine me navigating through a sea of outstretched hands, all needing my help. Don't put me in that position."

Quistix looked at the ocean floor, shame washing over her.

"Parnix has offered me an opportunity to author a tome with him about ocean life. I have the chance to document an undocumented *world*. I won't just be reading books. I can help *write* them. I will be the first of my kind. This would be the greatest honor to my kind, to whom knowledge is paramount. *Sacred*."

Twitch stepped forward. "But—"

Quistix laid her hand against the wyl's chest to stop him.

"Twitch, she has no way to defend herself," Violet said quietly into his ear. "At least here you know she's safe."

"I cannot wield a weapon. I wasn't built to fight. I can't watch more bloodshed.

For the majority of my life, I have lived in peace. I am a being of light, healing, and higher learning. You two are my family. If I thought I could end this and spare you both, I would lay down my life. You *know* I would." She walked forward, eyes dancing back and forth between Quistix and Twitch. "Please forgive me."

"There's nothing to forgive." Quistix approached, wrapped her arm around Aurora's neck, and hugged her. "You're right. This... is awful... but it is for your own good."

Irenas smiled. "I promise that I will care for her as if she were my very own. Omen can tell you the truth. One does not have to be my actual kin to be considered my family. It will be an honor to have such a brilliant being down here to help me with my work. And you may come visit her any time."

Unable to stop himself, Twitch snarled. "So that's it then? Years of journeying together and fighting beside one another... it all meant nothing? You are just going to cast us aside in the name of research and some dusty old *books*?"

"Books change lives. Swords *take* them," Parnix's voice boomed. "Do *not* fault her nature, when you find yourself bending to your own. You're a wyl. Have you not stolen? One cannot change their very nature so easily."

"We have fought to the death to keep each other safe." Quistix turned, rubbing her hand along Twitch's raised hackles to calm him. "And I will never stop fighting for *either* of you. *This* is how we protect her, Twitch. We let her go."

Flattening his ears, Twitch growled, shooing Aurora as he turned and walked away.

Quistix turned to stop him, but Violet held up a hand to stop her. "I'll go talk to him. You stay, say your goodbyes. We must leave soon."

Quistix sighed and turned back to Parnix. "Take care of her or I *will* kill you."

Parnix nodded. "I'll guard her with my life."

Quistix swallowed the massive lump in her throat and feigned a smile despite the overwhelming desire to fling the esteg on Kackaroth's back and drag her with them.

"I don't have a lot of people I like, Aurora. I am what most people consider a prickly person."

"*You don't say*," Aurora retorted with a grin.

That made Quistix smile genuinely. "I know it hasn't always been easy to travel at my side. I'll never forget how you saved my life… more than once."

"I'll miss you… both."

Violet followed Twitch out from beneath the shade of one of Kackaroth's wings. Twitch climbed into the harness on the end, and Violet tangled her limbs in the one beside him. Omen patted the gap on the sea dragon's back where more empty harnesses sat.

"Let's go," Omen hollered.

Clenching her teeth to keep the tears at bay, Quistix waved goodbye. Aurora nodded.

"I'll be back shortly," Parnix said with a smile. Then he climbed atop the dragon and helped Quistix in. They settled into the gap and wrapped the ropes around themselves.

"If you've never ridden a water dragon before, it's intense," the wizard said.

"We've ridden one in the sky," Quistix said, remembering Veynan's cobalt-blue scales.

"Are you talking about Veynan? Oh no. This is *way* more violent," he assured her. The old man raised his hands in the air and shouted. "*Ad superficiem*!"

Hearing it, Kackaroth rose onto his feet and launched off the ocean floor with his powerful legs. With a single flap of his gargantuan wings, they hurtled toward the surface.

33

Hope Harbor Pier
Oakenmeadow, Willowdale

Rising from the Radiant Sea with tsunami-like force, the water poured from Kackaroth's scaly head as its eyes emerged. The waves white-capped from the puffs of gentle air shooting out of Kackaroth's nostrils.

Irenas grinned ear-to-ear. "Easy now. We have to get these to that shore in one piece. Watch the rocks."

Kackaroth lurched forward. Quistix, Twitch, Omen, and Violet wheezed and gasped as their gills closed. Quistix clutched them against her neck, trying to ease the involuntary panic she felt every time her body experienced the transition back to air.

Waving his hand, dribbling water from his robe, Parnix spoke softly, "*Spiritus terra.*"

The gills on their necks sealed again, and this time went a step further, returning to solid patches of flesh or fur as if none of it had ever happened.

Parnix grinned and patted Kackaroth on the head. Then, he pointed to a jetty. "Dock over there so these fine folks can be on their way."

Violet shivered, wet and cold. Twitch put an arm around her, offering his warmth. Watching it, Quistix smiled.

Omen cleared his throat as if to warn Twitch that he was watching and didn't approve. But the wyl ignored him. Omen cleared his throat again, louder this time, far more obvious.

Twitch turned his face and glared at the man. "Sounds like you're getting a cold.

Perhaps you should find some licorice or tea once we are on land."

Omen just stared at the snarky creature.

"Hey," Quistix dipped backwards into Omen's line of sight. "Mind your damned business. She's grown."

The dragon glided through the bay, its curved neck resembling the figurehead on a ship.

"Twitch, do you ever tire of being obnoxious? Or is it simply your norm?" Omen asked.

"Do *you*?" the wyl asked.

Omen chuckled and looked at Quistix. "I see you keep him around for his sparkling *wit* and utter originality."

"You learn to tune him out," Quistix said, watching the landmass ahead of them approaching. "Sometimes he's like a fly buzzing around you while you're trying to eat."

"You *would* think that," Twitch grumbled. "You're skilled in the art of tuning out *all* of your comrades. After all, the only person Quistix cares about is Quistix."

Quistix pinched her eyes closed and shook off his words before turning her attention back to Parnix. "Do you think Ceosteol saw our message?"

"I have no doubt." He stated flatly. "If she is as connected as I've heard, then she has no doubt seen, or at the very least, *heard* about it."

"That's what I was afraid of. You're right, though. She's too connected *not* to know. She'll be there." Quistix whispered to no one in particular, "*And we will be ready.*"

"It will please you to know," petting Kackaroth, Irenas smiled, "I called in some reinforcements."

All eyes turned to him. The old man stretched his neck up with pride.

"I assure you, the rest of the magic community wants her gone just as much as you do. Necromancy has always been strictly prohibited. We all want it to stay that way. I was able to call in some favors. Years ago, back when I was still a professor at the institute, I discovered and helped eradicate a rampant illness that was spreading through Apex. It turned out to be a vicious reaction to the poisonous pollen of an invasive weed. My quick thinking kept them from evacuating the whole floating city. So, some mages should be waiting to aid you with your mission to stop that old bird."

"Thank you," Quistix said sincerely. "We need *all* the help we can get."

Omen spoke up, gripping his ropes tighter as the dragon navigated the jutting boulders and rock mounds near the shore. "Maybe one of those mages can come up with a way to capture her. She can open portals and teleport. I've seen it. I've experienced it. She could be clever enough to evade us when we are getting the upper hand."

"The mages of Apex can help with that. Just let them know everything you know about her. Information is critical in defeating someone with her kind of power."

"No one knows her full capabilities," Omen replied. "Maybe we will have sheer numbers on our side between the mages and warrior turnout. I hope it'll be enough."

"And now we don't have Aurora." Twitch glared at Quistix. "One wrong move and we're done. There's no one to heal us now. *Someone* just… let her go."

Quistix flashed him a fiery glance. "And what would you have me do, Twitch? Drag her along on a mission that'll almost certainly claim her life? She can't defend herself. It's one less person to try to protect. But clearly you have something to say, so just say it."

"You didn't even fight for her," Twitch growled. "Where was that infamous temper when your only saving grace on the battlefield just tucked tail and ran from the enemy? You said *nothing*."

"I don't keep anyone around just to use them, Twitch! She's free to do what she wants. People leave. She doesn't owe us anything... much less her life. She's her own being. It was her choice!"

He trembled slightly, and Violet stroked his back in an effort to comfort him. His voice quaked with a flood of emotion and rage. "She was *family*, Quistix."

"Dammit, Twitch..." Before Quistix could say another word, Omen placed a gloved hand on the back of hers and squeezed. "As much as I can't stand the bastard, he did say goodbye to a friend. Abruptly. He's angry. Give him a minute to let it all soak into that *thick* skull of his."

Violet whispered something in Twitch's ear, her words swallowed up by the gentle sound of the ocean waves.

Quistix stared at Omen's hand for a moment, allowing his warmth to radiate through her. She glanced up into his sapphire eyes beneath the flames that perpetually engulfed him.

"We're here," Parnix said, interrupting the tension between them all.

"Thank the Gods," Quistix muttered. She untangled herself and dismounted with haste, helping Parnix off the beast and onto the jetty. Omen watched her curvaceous form as she untied the casks, her body bathed in the somber hues of the trio of full moons above. The tightness in his chest that he experienced when they touched made him feel uneasy.

Parnix snapped him out of his thoughts with a desperate wave. "Come! Everyone! We must get these casks off Kackaroth quickly before anyone lays eyes on him! We've much to do and so little time."

34

The Wilds of Bellaneau
Bellaneau

It's freezing, Werner thought, looking around at the unfamiliar rolling hills the quichyrd's portal led to. Dense forest surrounded them, sunset painting the lush trees in hues of gold and orange. It was a wilderness that seemed unsullied, as if the area itself had rejected civilization.

Where are we?

Bellaneau, she replied.

That's a large province. Care to be more specific?

No, Ceosteol replied curtly.

They approached a clearing a short walk from the hill's peak. Werner felt his breath catch in his throat at the sight of the city far, far below. It was as if the province had bowed before them, lending them a spectacularly unimpeded view.

Pillars of winding smoke drifted up from chimneys miles away, basking in the fading colors of the setting sun.

He wrapped his arms around his chest and shivered, still following Ceosteol closely.

You'll learn to adjust to the weather soon enough. You are colder than normal due to your... condition, she thought.

Werner replied, *I didn't even get a nobleman's death. I died vomiting in the streets like a filthy vagabond. I can't even sleep since you did this to me. Every time I close my eyes, all I see are the eyes of all of those people who watched me die. They simply stared while I floundered in the streets. Watching, doing nothing at all.*

The dreams will pass. You'll feel better once our soul bond strengthens.

Why is that?

Because if I sleep, you feel rested. Our bond is nourishing, she paused, *for both of us. I take care of my children. You'll see.*

Are you dead, too?

No, she snapped, cinching her robe tighter. *That is why I need the Illuminator. Together, I believe she and I can abolish death.*

She scanned the tall grass, finally spotting the thing she'd been hunting for. She walked straight toward it, her excitement visible.

Ceosteol looked at Werner, and her eyes flashed bright green. The landigo lost all control over his body in an instant, his mind blank and tranquil as she willed him to walk in her direction. She forced his claws out and made him kneel by two grave markers like an obedient dog. She forced his head toward the newer one.

Dig, she ordered.

Werner struggled to regain control of his body, trying to shout, trying to reclaim any part of himself, his mind.

But it was no use.

The quichyrd was in control.

Fresh soil flew as he shredded the grass and gouged his powerful claws into the soil like a burrowing filibrat.

Werner dug through sunset, tearing through gnarled roots and soft dirt.

In the light of the three moons, he finally unearthed something swaddled in a layer of green burlap. Disgusted, he watched as his hands, no longer under his control, unwrapped a corner. Beneath were loose tufts of hair, bones the color of eggshells. He felt the urge to vomit, but his body only carried the corpse's remains out of the hole and laid it at Ceosteol's feet in the moonlit grass.

In a flash, she uninhabited his mind and Werner reeled back in horror, nearly falling into the grave from the vertigo caused by the transition. He scuttled away as she unwrapped the small bundle lovingly.

She pulled a pouch from her pocket, uncorked a jar of bizarre liquid, and sprinkled it on the remains. Then, she clawed open her forearm until it bled, and she dribbled some of the fluid on the bones.

Aloud, she chanted on a loop, "*Vita redeat. Corporis mei. Filius meus.*"

The liquids seeped into the porous bones. From the bones, tiny slivers of something pink poked out like a fuzzy mold. It thickened and spread, overlapping in different directions. Muscles, skin, and hair slowly regenerated before Werner's very eyes until all that remained was the body of a young boy in her frail arms.

Werner shrieked when the boy's eyes pried open, blinking away eternal sleep before his irises flashed a bright shade of green.

The panicked boy gasped and immediately began to hyperventilate.

"That's it. Catch your breath. Easy now. Shhhhh," Ceosteol hissed. She caressed the boy's cheek adoringly, her eyes lighting up like she'd just unearthed the most precious buried treasure of all. She smiled and cooed, "Welcome back, darling Danson."

About the Author

Heather Wohl is an award-winning author who also coordinates an oil field laboratory based in Casper, Wyoming. She also writes romance under the pen name Aurora Alba and thrillers under the pen name H. M. Wohl. Heather is a proud supporter of chronic illness support, mental health awareness, and is a Pit Bull advocate.

Creature Glossary

Aestuo Quichyrd: *(Ah-ee-stoo Kwih-chard)* A hybrid of bird and human with armored feathers, these bird-humans are battle-ready. They have talon-like hands and a beak.

Akiah: *(Ahh-kai-uh)* Often mistaken for demons, a once-forbidden species, the akiah people have been responsible for carrying out various atrocities under the rule of Master Tempest. With human body shape and features, their defining trait is their ram horns and crimson eyes.

Azure shifters: *(Ah-zur Shif-turs)* These underwater creatures have the face and upper torso of a human, and a fish-like tail for legs. Its golden horns glitter below the surface, luring its prey to the water's edge so they can attack. White eyes and scaly skin are another hallmark of the shifter. Unable to speak or be reasoned with, this remains one of the most deadly creatures in Destoria.

Baiya: *(Bi-uh)* These are the thick-skinned lizard folk that scarcely populate the isle. With its weather changes, most baiya find the land inhospitable, but a thicker-skinned few call the Destorian Isle home. Covered in small, flexible scales this blend of human/lizard-like features make an undeniably desirable warrior with their damage-resistant flesh.

Barbarian: Larger than humans, barbarians are known for their large stature and muscular build. Ideal fighters and human-like features make these characters a staple.

Black-Eyed Beings: Black-Eyed Beings are creations of Ceosteol. Imbued with her life force, these deceptive beings seem human, though their eyes are wholly black. Such creatures can protract fangs and turn vicious when the mood strikes.

Bramolt Bear: *(Brahm-olt Bear)* Like a polar bear, these massive fur-covered bears fight with their 3-inch long talons and walk upright. Unable to speak the human language, these bears are both lovable and formidable.

Crolt: *(Krohlt)* Two-headed giant. Barely able to fit through doorways, these creatures have two functioning heads that work independently of one another. Their shared body is massive and muscular, making these giants a solid protective force. However, their intelligence is one step above that of a symph.

Dwarf: Dwarves are typically three feet tall with red hair. Both men and women of this species grow beards. They are typically ornery in nature.

Dragon: A massive beast typically no longer found in Destoria or the neighboring isles. Hunted to extinction, the few that exist are adept at sticking to the shadows and hiding in the wilderness until called upon. They typically can speak in their own native tongue, though they can learn and practice any language they hear. With scaled bodies and leathery spikes protruding from their face like a lion's mane, dragons are calm, sensible creatures who tend to bond with one owner, able to fiercely protect them with fire-breathing magic, claws, and a broad tail that can bring down a house in a single swipe. Dragons are not exclusive to the land or sky, however. Underwater dragons also exist, though varying slightly in appearance.

Druid: *(Droo-id)* A race gifted with the ability to shape-shift. This magic class can only temporarily transform into any living being they've interacted with firsthand. Like a muscle, this ability can strengthen with training, lengthening the possible duration of the shift while draining less stamina, though, even skilled druids can completely deplete and lose consciousness. This ability replenishes with rest.

Eaflic: *(Ee-flik)* Hippo-human hybrid. With gray skin and a massive snout, these creatures are docile until threatened. With rounded ears and a flicking tail, these creatures are undeniably lovable.

Elf: Elves have the features of a human, but typically have a yellow tint to their skin and pointed ears. Adept at magic, elves are typically upper class.

Esteg: *(Ess-teg)* Sentient deer. Estegs are voracious readers and intelligent. They can speak and comprehend spoken and written words. Their unusual horns (which both the male and female of the species grow) are neon green with healing powers. They are often poached for their antlers.

Ewanaian: *(You-way-nee-an)* Frog people. These creatures are a blend of humans and frogs. With slick, green skin and a tacky tongue, these creatures walk and talk like human beings. When startled, their response is to faint and pass gas as a biologically-programmed deterrent.

Frumlan: *(From-lin)* Sentient wolf/bird hybrids. Larger versions of symphs. With a wolf-like face and furry feathers along its body and wings, these creatures can walk, talk and fly with ease.

Goblin: *(Gob-lihn)* Beings that are short in stature (averaging about 2.5 feet in height) with large noses. Sly, cunning and often reclusive. Their fondness for gold keeps them from hiding away completely.

Grindylow: *(Grin-dee-low)* They have a long face with rows of muskie-like teeth and eyes similar to an alligator. They have thin human bodies, often pale, with webbed extremities that create swift, fluid movements. They have winding ibex-type head horns and long claws to shred prey. Used to pull ships along on windless days, Grindylows are working creatures that are best never seen.

Half-Elf: Human and elf hybrid with often-blunted ear tips. With lightly yellow-tinged skin, it is truly a flip on a coin as to if they inherit magical abilities from their elvish side.

Human: *(Hue-mon)* With varied skin tones and averaging five feet eight inches in height, humans' greatest gift is their passion and ability to love.

Inelm: *(In-elm)* These woodland creatures live inside of host tree trunks and pry themselves away when danger or disrespect occurs. They are a proud and communicate through a network of roots below ground.

Kleax: *(Clee-ax)* Lion and human hybrids. This creature is known for their long manes, flitting tail and uneven temperament. Fur covers them and long claws make them formidable fighters.

Landigo: *(Lahn-dig-oh)* Leopard-human hybrid. Equipped with a graceful tale, leopard face, and fur-covered forms, these spotted beings are known for their quick temper.

Orc: *(Ork)* With skin in various shades of green, orcs are muscle-bound brutes with a reputation for being strong, fearless warriors. They have thick bottom-row incisors that jut out past the lip.

Pleom: *(Plee-ohm)* Miniature dragonlings. Pleoms are small dragons that live for an average of 8 years. Their scaly skin comes in various colors and their tiny claws are adept at lock-picking, making them an ideal companion for thieves. Pleoms typically prefer to spend their time with estegs who can heal them after their clumsy exploits.

Quichyrd: *(Kwich-urd)* A bird-human hybrid. These creatures have a varied appearance, but always with a beak, feathers, and taloned hands. They walk upright, are typically gifted in magic, and are often despised.

Raakaby: *(Ray-kah-bee)* Rabbit-bird hybrids bred for meat. These adorable, poisonous creatures produce a hallucinogenic saliva that is used in dikeeka. More than one bite is fatal.

Semdrog: *(Sem-drahg)* Lizard-human hybrid. These lizard people have skin flaps on their heads and scales. Their eyes have slit pupils, but otherwise they have human features.

Symph: *(Simf)* A small wolf/bird hybrid. They are colorful creatures with a wolf-like face and snout equipped with wings and paws. They are small enough to land in your hand and howl instead of chirp.

Tailed Infernals: *(Tailed In-fur-nahls)* An abomination created by Ceosteol, these zombified creatures are two wolves crudely stitched together with a snake tail. Dangerous and decaying, they can be taught and controlled through Ceosteol's soul bond (which she shares with all of her undead atrocities).

Tundra Goblins: *(Tun-druh Gob-lihns)* These snow-white creatures are violent, seeking warmth in the merciless cold of Evolt. They kill and burrow in their prey. Their fur is highly sought-after and valuable. With long fangs that stick out past their lower lip, these creatures are the perfect combo of cute-and-deadly.

Undead: Reanimated corpses. Undead species of any creature, humans being extra susceptible. A creation from black magic wielders, which is a strictly forbidden magic, only used by nefarious mages.

Water Dragon: Imposing like their land-dwelling kin, these reptilian creatures reside almost exclusively underwater. With a muscular body, scales, a narrow snout, spine spikes, and a long tail, they glide through large bodies of water at dizzying speeds. Water dragons typically do not harm unless threatened or starving.

Wizard: Practitioners of magic who can control the elements. These ultra-proficient mages usually focus on more experimental magic.

Wyl: *(Wy-uhl)* Often known for thievery, and superior lovemaking skills. While most wyl's spend their time on *Wyl isle*, others lie, cheat and steal their way across the rest of Destoria. They come in a variety of colors. Their hallmark face and pointed ears make them easy to spot.

The Harbingers of Hope
BOOK FOUR OF THE ILLUMINATOR SAGA
Heather Wohl

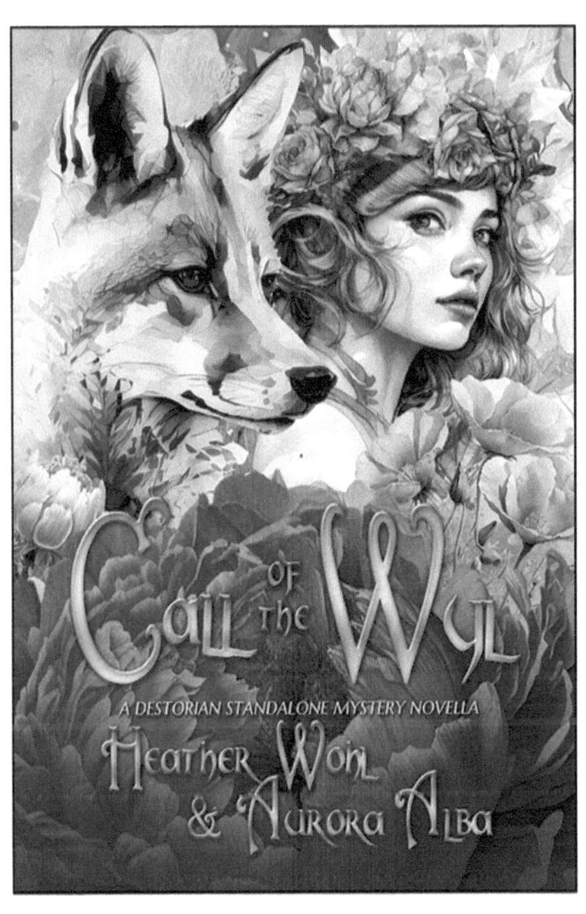
Call of the Wyl
A DESTORIAN STANDALONE MYSTERY NOVELLA
Heather Wohl
& Aurora Alba

AN UMA BLANCHARD COZY MYSTERY
TRIXIE
FAIRDALE
MOURNING
WAFFLES
BOOK ONE

www.ingramcontent.com/pod-product-compliance
Lightning Source LLC
Chambersburg PA
CBHW032138050726
47591CB00001B/16

* 9 7 8 1 9 6 2 8 5 4 5 4 2 *